"Let me know if you need backup...

"The timer is counting down on the whole situation," Cade continued. "Max wasn't bluffing about getting the courts involved if that's what it takes. I don't want to think about what will happen when he wins."

Shelby drew a sharp breath. Did Cade really believe a victory for Max was a forgone conclusion? Cade must have realized how that had sounded and tried again. "Sorry, I meant to say *if* he wins."

Shelby could tell Cade had serious concerns that the town's best efforts were doomed to fail. She didn't want to even consider that a possibility. They both knew if a court ordered the museum to surrender the nugget to Max Volkov, it would likely have side effects that tumbled like dominoes throughout the town.

Although Cade hadn't mentioned it lately, he must still worry that failure to save the nugget could cost him his job.

If he left town, where would that leave the two of them?

Dear Reader,

I am so excited about the release of *The Lawman's Promise*, the first book in the Heroes of Dunbar Mountain, my new series from Harlequin Heartwarming!

Although Dunbar Mountain and the town that shares its name are both fictional, I've set them in one of my favorite areas of Washington State, near one of the passes that crosses the Cascade Mountains. I love the rugged, snowcapped mountains; the glacier-fed streams; and towering forests. So beautiful!

Like my hero, Cade Peters, I grew up in Missouri and loved exploring the Ozarks. But once my husband and I moved to Washington for his job, we knew we'd never want to leave. Cade feels the same way.

I've really loved "building" the town of Dunbar and getting to know all of the new characters. It's been especially fun seeing it through the eyes of both a newcomer like Cade, the new chief of police, as well as someone who has lived there her entire life like Shelby Michaels, the curator of the town's museum.

I hope you enjoy getting to know Cade and Shelby, along with some of their more interesting friends and neighbors.

Alexis

HEARTWARMING

The Lawman's Promise

Alexis Morgan

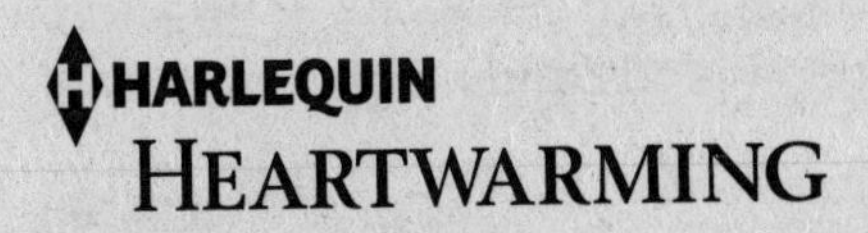

HARLEQUIN®
HEARTWARMING™

Recycling programs for this product may not exist in your area.

ISBN-13: 978-1-335-58499-1

The Lawman's Promise

For questions and comments about the quality of this book, please contact us at CustomerService@Harlequin.com.

Harlequin Enterprises ULC
22 Adelaide St. West, 41st Floor
Toronto, Ontario M5H 4E3, Canada
www.Harlequin.com

Printed in U.S.A.

USA TODAY bestselling author **Alexis Morgan** has always loved reading and now spends her days imagining worlds filled with strong heroes and gutsy heroines. She is the author of over forty-five books, novellas and short stories that span a variety of romance genres. She lives in the Pacific Northwest with her husband and family.

Books by Alexis Morgan

Love Inspired The Protectors

The Reluctant Guardian

This book is dedicated to the furry members of all our families, past and present. They fill our hearts and teach us to be better people.

CHAPTER ONE

"THERE HE GOES."

"There who goes?"

Although Shelby Michaels already knew. The new chief of police was nothing if not predictable. At precisely ten o'clock every morning, he walked down to the coffee shop to pick up a latte and a pastry. She set aside the book she was about to shelve and joined her friend at the window. "We shouldn't stare."

Elizabeth laughed. "Are you serious? There isn't a woman in town who'd miss out on a chance to watch Chief Peters's daily prowl down the street."

That had Shelby leaning in closer to the window to get a better look. "Seriously, you think he prowls?"

Despite being on the near side of menopause, Elizabeth fanned herself and sighed. "Yes, Shelby, he prowls. If I wasn't married…

well, let's just say there's just something about the way that man moves that reminds me of my hubby. Back in the day, Jimmy could really turn heads with the best of them. Still does in the right crowd."

Really? Shelby tried to think past Jimmy Glines's slight paunch and receding hairline to the hot guy he used to be but couldn't quite bring the picture into focus. Still, it was nice that Elizabeth saw her husband in that light. Maybe that was one reason the couple had stayed happily married for over twenty years.

The police chief was out of sight for now, so Shelby went back to shelving the books the library driver had dropped off earlier. Dunbar was too small of a town to merit its own library. Instead, weather permitting, the bookmobile came through every other Thursday morning. It parked in the lot behind city hall so the locals could browse the available selections. At the same time, the driver left any books that someone in town had requested with Shelby. She kept them on a shelf in the post office until that person stopped by to pick them up. There was also a bin there for books people wanted to return the next time the bookmobile came through.

Elizabeth wandered over to watch her work. She leafed through a mystery by a popular author and then handed it back to Shelby. "Speaking of Chief Peters, did you hear that a couple of the ladies in town are organizing an official sign-up sheet to provide meals for him?"

Okay, that was ridiculous. "Why? I'm sure the man can cook for himself."

Shrugging, Elizabeth said, "I don't think they care. The problem is that there have been a couple of unfortunate instances when two or more of them have shown up at the same time, casseroles in hand. The last time it happened, things turned ugly. I won't mention names, but somehow Lady One's elk stew was 'accidentally' knocked off his desk onto the floor. She retaliated by flipping Lady Two's best taco casserole upside down into the wastebasket."

By that point, Elizabeth was laughing. "I really wish I'd been there. Rumor has it that Chief Peters threatened to lock them up for disorderly conduct. Probably would have if he'd had two cells in the jail instead of just the one. It would've been a bloodbath if they'd had to share. Instead, he banned them from his office indefinitely."

She patted Shelby on the shoulder. "I can tell you who has the sign-up sheet posted in her office if you want to get in on the action."

"No thanks. I'm not interested."

That statement earned her an undignified snort from her friend. "You might be able to convince yourself of that, but I'm not buying it. You're a young, healthy woman in the prime of life. There is also a sad lack of available men your age in town, so you'd be a fool not to at least consider testing the waters with him. A man like Cade Peters won't stay single long if the women around here have anything to say about it."

Elizabeth checked the time on the grandfather clock in the corner. "Oops, I've got to finish my errands. Jimmy is scheduled to guide a couple of fly fishermen later this afternoon and needs the truck."

Shelby followed her to the door. "By the way, ask your kids when they want to do another pizza and movie night at my place. It's their turn to choose the toppings, but I get to pick the movie."

Her friend's face lit up. "They've been asking when you'd have them over again. They love spending time with Aunt Shelby."

They weren't actually related by blood, but that didn't matter. Shelby loved Elizabeth's brood. Money was often tight, and offering to entertain the kids gave Elizabeth and her husband an evening to themselves without needing a babysitter.

Elizabeth gave her a quick hug. "Jimmy will be thrilled when I tell him."

With that, she was out the door and gone, leaving Shelby alone to ponder the puzzle that was Cade Peters. She might not admit it to her friend, but she'd definitely noticed the man and more than just the way he moved. It was also the tight fit of his uniform across his broad shoulders and the thick lashes that framed his dark eyes, which she thought best described as the color of bittersweet chocolate. That didn't mean she wanted to join the endless parade of women finding every excuse they could to visit the city jail.

It had been that way since Cade first arrived in Dunbar two months ago to take over as the new chief of police. So far, he was doing a great job, but she had to wonder how long he'd stick around. From what she'd heard, he'd spent a lot of years in the military police. If true, that kind of experience should have qualified him for a job anywhere in law enforcement. Why would he settle for one in a town that was barely a wide spot in the road?

Not that she personally would want to move anywhere else. She'd lived in Dunbar with its population of six hundred hardy souls her entire life. Located on the western slopes of the Cascades in Washington State, the town had originally sprouted up to serve several small mines in the area. Even though the gold had mostly run out ages ago, the town had managed to survive—barely. These days its citizens primarily depended on the tourist trade to eke out a living.

It was hard to believe a man like Chief Peters, who likely had lived all over the world, would be happy for long in Dunbar. If he wasn't going to stay, she wasn't interested in testing those waters Elizabeth had mentioned.

The bell over the door in the museum chimed, drawing Shelby's attention to the other half of her little corner of the world. She managed the entire two-story building that had been subdivided to serve different purposes. The area where she currently stood was both the local post office and the library, such as it was. The other half of the first floor and the entire second floor housed the town's pride and joy—the Dunbar Historical Museum.

A deep voice called out, "Hello? Is the museum open?"

The docent scheduled to work that morning had called earlier to say she would be in after her doctor appointment, which left Shelby to cover for her. "I'll be right there."

She dusted off her hands, locked the post office door and put the sign out that let people know to come to the museum if they needed her. Hurrying through the door that separated the two halves of her domain, she prepared to greet the visitor, who turned out to be a bit of a surprise. Their usual patrons tended to be mostly older tourists taking a break from driving by doing some sightseeing after a meal at the café down the street. This guy was much closer to her own age. He might not be as tall and muscular as Cade Peters, but he was definitely attractive in his own way with curly blond hair and a friendly smile.

It almost made her wish she could quickly sneak into the ladies' room to put on some lipstick. Too late now. She offered him a bright smile and handed him a map of the museum.

"Sorry if I kept you waiting, but welcome to the Dunbar Historical Museum. I'm Shelby Michaels, the curator here. Our displays are self-explanatory, but please feel free to ask me any questions you might have."

He gave the map a quick glance. "Thank you. I'll just wander around for a little while if that's okay. I picked up a flyer about this place at the hotel where I stayed last night and thought I'd come check it out. I love museums of all kinds, and sometimes they provide the most unexpected inspiration."

That was a new one. "May I ask inspiration for what?"

His smile turned shy. "I'm a freelance writer. I mostly do articles for travel and history magazines as well as for newspapers looking for local interest stories."

He fished a business card out of his wallet and held it out to her. "My name is Maxim Volkov."

"Well, it's not every day I get to meet a writer." She studied the card. "I hope you find that the trip was worth your time."

His smile faded a little. "I'm sure it will be."

Then he shoved several bills into the donation box and started slowly making his way around the exhibits. Shelby picked up some paperwork that needed to be filed in the museum office since it was likely he'd be heading upstairs next. She'd barely reached the second floor when she heard the familiar creak of the third step up from the first floor. Mr. Volkov was already on his way up.

She hustled across the room to her desk, wanting to look busy when he finally appeared. Although she couldn't quite put her finger on why, there was something about him that seemed odd. He wasn't giving off any kind of scary vibe, but she'd bet anything that he had an agenda that didn't include looking for inspiration for a story. Otherwise, wouldn't he spend more time studying the displays and maybe taking some notes? As it was, he just barely glanced at most of them before moving on to the next.

Of course, maybe her imagination was running wild, and their museum really had appealed to a writer's innate curiosity. Besides, he wouldn't be the first person who'd driven miles out of his way simply to get a peek at the town's prize possession—the Trillium

Nugget. It wasn't the largest chunk of gold ever found in the state, but it was definitely impressive. Considering the price of gold, it was no wonder the town had ponied up to pay for an expensive security system to protect the nugget and the rest of the museum.

She watched as the writer circled ever closer to the nugget. So far, he hadn't so much as glanced in its direction, but she'd bet her last dime that he was almost painfully aware of it. Finally, after completing a second circuit, he approached the case that held pride of place in the center of the room. He got within touching distance of the glass and froze, staring at the three-lobed piece of gold. It was that shape which had given the nugget its name. Trillium, a plant native to the area, had green leaves and a white flower with three large, pointed petals.

"It's impressive, isn't it?"

Mr. Volkov jumped and glanced back over his shoulder at her, frowning as if he'd forgotten Shelby was even there. "Yes, it is."

Next, he used his phone to snap several pictures in rapid succession. After shoving the phone in his pocket, he took a step back. "Do you know if there's a book about the nugget?"

"Well, a few years back one of the museum's docents wrote a book on the local history of the area that we sell downstairs in the gift shop. It might have something."

"I'll take two copies."

He charged back down the steps, which left her no option but to follow. He was already thumbing through one of the books by the time she joined him at the checkout counter. Besides the second copy of the book, he'd added several postcards and a map of the area that marked places where people could still prospect for gold.

She rang up his purchases and gave him his change. "Thank you again for stopping in, Mr. Volkov."

He took the bag from her and mustered up a smile that wasn't quite as warm as the one he'd offered her when he'd first arrived. She couldn't imagine what she'd said or done that would've offended him in some way, but he definitely wasn't as friendly on his way out as he had been on the way in.

Most of the time visitors came and went without leaving much of an impression, but she wouldn't be forgetting Maxim Volkov anytime soon. Rather than worry about it, she decided to take an early lunch. If anyone needed her, they'd know they could find her at the café down the street. After locking up, she grabbed her purse and hustled out the door.

Titus would run out of her favorite comfort food if she took her usual one o'clock lunch break. After all, like time, chicken and dumplings waited for no one.

CADE PETERS STEPPED through the door of the only café in town. While it would've been nice to have more choice in restaurants, he couldn't complain about the quality of food Titus, the owner-slash-cook, offered to his customers. Thursday was always the busiest day of the week, thanks in no little part to the day's special of chicken and dumplings. Cade was far from the only person who looked forward to gorging on tender chicken, savory vegetables and fluffy dumplings.

Unfortunately, every table was taken. Most folks wouldn't mind Cade joining them if they had a spare seat, but he'd learned to be careful about his choice of companions. Some men might be flattered by so much feminine attention, but he wasn't one of them. He preferred to eat a meal without having to fend off invitations to dinner seasoned with hints about a special dessert for two. He never asked for details and did his best to refuse without offending.

Glancing around the room, he immediately zeroed in on the one woman he wouldn't mind sharing his meal with. Thanks to her dark red hair and quiet beauty, Shelby Michaels would stand out in any crowd. With luck, she wasn't saving the empty chair at her table for anyone else and wouldn't mind sharing it with him. He made his way through the cluttered café toward where she sat near the back wall. His timing was perfect because the waitress was approaching Shelby's table from the other direction. If he hurried a little, he would get there just in time to place his order.

"Hi, Shelby. Do you mind if I join you? I forgot how hard it was to find a place to sit on Thursdays."

Okay, that was a lie, but she'd probably believe him because he hadn't been living in Dunbar all that long. "Of course, Chief Peters."

Cade pulled out the chair and sat down. "I thought we'd agreed that there was no need to be formal. It's Cade, not Chief Peters, especially when we're both about to pig out on Titus's chicken and dumplings."

Her fair skin flushed rosy. "Sorry, I forgot."

The waitress finally arrived. "Shelby, Chief. What can I get you to drink? I'm assuming you'll both be wanting today's special."

Shelby smiled at her. "You would be right about that. I'll have iced tea."

"Make it two." Cade handed back the menus neither of them had needed. With that taken care of, he tried to think of a topic of conversation. He settled on asking about the one thing he knew Shelby was passionate about. "How are things at the museum today?"

She sighed. "Slow. I only had one visitor stop in this morning. A man who said he was a freelance writer looking for inspiration. He claimed to write articles for magazines and local interest pieces for newspapers."

Interesting. Whether or not she realized it, the slight emphasis she put on the word "claimed" spoke volumes. "Do you have any reason to think he was lying about that?"

She looked startled by his question. "No, not really. He seemed nice enough, especially when he first came in. He even gave me his business card. I suppose it could be fake, but I don't really think so."

"But something bothered you."

She toyed with her napkin for several seconds before answering, looking more perplexed than concerned. "Nothing specific I can put my finger on. He said he found out about the museum through a flyer that the town stocks in a lot of the hotels in the area, so he knew about the nugget. He wouldn't be the first person who came to Dunbar just to see it. After taking a few pictures, he bought two copies of a book on our local history and left. I doubt we'll ever see Maxim Volkov again."

Cade saw no reason not to take Shelby at her word about the situation. She had a reputation for being levelheaded and a good judge of character. That said, he felt compelled to offer her one piece of advice. Fancy security system aside, that chunk of gold she babysat every day was worth more than enough to tempt someone into making a grab for it.

"If anybody ever does make you uncomfortable at all, promise you'll call me. Even if it turns out to be a false alarm, it's better to be safe than sorry."

When she didn't immediately say anything, he added, "Promise?"

Finally, she nodded. "Fine, Cade. I promise."

Their waitress was back with two plates heaped high with deliciousness. They ate in silence not for lack of anything to say, but out of respect for Titus's culinary magic.

CHAPTER TWO

THE NEXT DAY, Moira Fraser, one of Cade's recent hires, appeared in his doorway and patiently waited for him to acknowledge her. When he finally looked up, she offered him an apologetic smile. "Chief, there's a man out front wanting to ask some questions. I offered to help him, but he prefers to see you. I told him you were busy, but he insists I won't do."

It was an attitude she had some experience with here in town. Some of the old-timers didn't think a young female police officer could possibly handle the rigors of the job. Moira had also grown up in Dunbar, and they had trouble seeing past their memories of her as a girl in braces to the competent cop she was today. Whether they realized it or not, the town was lucky to have someone with her abilities and experience.

Cade saved the report he'd been working

on and closed his laptop. "Send him on back and then take your lunch."

"I'm going to the café. Want me to bring something back for you?"

Good thought. Considering the amount of paperwork Cade still needed to get through by the end of his shift, eating at his desk made sense. "Do you know what today's specials are?"

He already knew they didn't include chicken and dumplings since Titus only served that one day a week. In fact, Cade planned to invite Shelby Michaels to join him for lunch again when Thursday rolled around next week. He'd already circled the date in red on his calendar.

Moira checked the weekly menu they kept posted on a bulletin board in the hall. "The entrée is elk ragout. The sandwich is a Cuban with a choice of slaw or caprese salad for the side."

"I'll take the sandwich with the caprese salad." He handed her enough money to cover the cost. "Stay and enjoy your lunch, Moira. When I'm done with our guest, I can keep an eye on the counter."

"Okay. I'll send Mr. Volkov on back."

Volkov? The name niggled in the back of his mind. It sounded familiar, but he couldn't remember in what context. While he hadn't been in Dunbar long enough to have met every one of its six hundred or so citizens in person, he had made a point of familiarizing himself with their names. He was pretty darn sure there wasn't a Volkov in the bunch.

Only one way to find out what was going on. He sat back in his chair and waited to see what was so important that a total stranger needed to talk to the chief of police. Volkov was likely a tourist who had gotten a parking ticket and wanted to complain about it. That had happened twice recently. Cade stood up when his unexpected guest walked in. Interesting. Considering the expensive suit the man wore, he'd felt it necessary to dress up for the occasion.

Mr. Volkov's body language was even more intriguing than his wardrobe. If he was aiming for unassuming and friendly, he'd failed miserably. There was a brittle edginess in his smile, and he had a death grip on the pair of file folders in his hand. White knuckles combined with a clenched jaw practically shouted this wasn't about anything as mundane as a disputed parking fine.

"I'm Chief Peters. Come in and have a seat."

Cade considered reaching across his desk to shake the man's hand, but the guy wasn't there to exchange niceties. Once they were both settled in their respective seats, Cade waited to see if Volkov would jump right into making whatever demands he had in mind. When he didn't, Cade gave him a gentle prod. "How can I help you?"

Volkov finally set the file folders on the desk, laying his palm on the top one as if he was afraid that Cade would suddenly leap forward to steal it. After drumming his fingertips on the file a few times, Mr. Volkov pulled a business card from his shirt pocket and slid it across the desk. "My name is Maxim Volkov."

The combination of the card and the full name finally flipped the switch, and Cade now knew where he'd heard the name before. This had to be the same guy who'd made Shelby uncomfortable when he'd visited the museum yesterday. Cade had been right when he told her to trust her instincts.

"This isn't your first visit to Dunbar, Mr. Volkov."

If Volkov was surprised that Cade had heard of him, he didn't say so. "You're right, Chief Peters. I was in town yesterday. I had lunch at the café and checked out several of the shops in town. I also stopped at the museum to look around."

Cade gave the file folders a pointed look. "As excellent as Titus's cooking is, I can't imagine that you drove here from Portland for lunch. And if you wanted to buy something at one of the shops, that's where you'd be right now."

He leaned forward, elbows on the desk to look his guest straight in the eye. "So, why don't you tell me what about the museum brought you back here today?"

Of course, there was only one item in the museum worthy of a trip to Dunbar, and they both knew what it was—the Trillium Nugget. Volkov's interest in the nugget might be something innocent. Like wanting to remove the nugget from its case long enough for a photo shoot. After all, the man claimed to be a freelance writer. If he'd managed to convince some magazine or one of the newspapers in the area to do a spread on the giant chunk of gold, he'd probably want to get a better picture of it than he could get with a cell phone through the glass case.

Despite the opening Cade had given him, Maxim Volkov wasn't in a big hurry to explain. Finally, he picked up the top folder and set it in front of Cade. Then he pulled an old-fashioned photograph out of the second folder. After staring at it for the longest time, he turned it around so Cade could see it. "I apologize if this seems rude, but I'd rather not let you handle this photograph. I can't risk anything happening to it."

Of course Cade was insulted by the insinuation that he'd damage the darn thing. He bit back the urge to tell the guy what he could do with the picture. That wouldn't help the situation.

Forcing a calm he didn't feel, he studied the sepia-toned photo of a man who appeared to be a miner. Based on the style of clothing he wore, Cade's best guess was that it had been taken a century ago, give or take a decade. "Fine. I've looked at it. Now, tell me what all of this is about."

Volkov shoved the picture back in the folder

and then pulled a photocopy of it from the second folder and offered it to Cade. "I wanted you to know that I have the original photo and that this copy is accurate. Nothing has been done to alter it."

Cade didn't touch the photocopy. One look had been enough. It wasn't who was in the picture that was important. No, it was *what* the man was holding that had Cade's pulse picking up speed at an alarming rate. Unless he was mistaken, it was the Trillium Nugget. "Again, fine. I don't have the time or patience to play guessing games, Mr. Volkov. I have better things to do. Start talking."

"Mr. Volkov was my father's name. I'd appreciate it if you called me Maxim or even Max. I'd prefer to keep this on friendly terms."

"Considering I still don't know what *this*—" he gestured toward the folders and the photocopy "—is, Mr. Volkov, I think it's too early to know how friendly we can be."

"Fair enough. I'll come to the point. The man in the picture is my great-grandfather, Lev Volkov. Back in the early 1890s he left Russia for the United States. He ended up here in the Pacific Northwest. From what I've learned, he held a variety of jobs to put food on the table—working on the docks in Seattle and as a deckhand on the fishing boats. He even tried his hand at being a lumberjack."

"Sounds typical for that time period."

Maxim stared at a spot on the wall behind Cade. "True, but none of those jobs are the reason I'm here."

Then he met Cade's gaze head-on. "Grandpa Lev also did some prospecting for gold. As you can see from the picture, he was far more successful at that than he was at anything else."

After dropping that little bombshell, Maxim crossed his arms over his chest as he waited for Cade's response. What did the guy think he would say? Right now most of the words that were fighting to roll off his tongue were ones that shouldn't be used in the commission of his duties as an official representative of the city of Dunbar.

He settled for going on the offensive. "All that picture shows, Mr. Volkov, is that your grandfather may have held the Trillium Nugget at some point in the past."

Not bad for an opening salvo, but they both knew that Maxim had more than a family picture in that folder or else he wouldn't be there. Right now, all Cade could do was wait for the man to finally get to the point. Maxim's next comment blew that hope right out of the water.

"I apologize for springing all of this on you with no warning. Having said that, there's no easy way to break this news. I am well aware that the people here in Dunbar are not going to be happy when they learn about the situation. You'll need time to prepare."

"For what exactly?"

"I would've thought that would be obvious. I'm here to reclaim the gold nugget that my great-grandfather dug out of the ground near here. It belongs to my family, and we want it back."

"That's not happening, Mr. Volkov. Not on the basis of a single photograph."

"If that's all I had, I wouldn't be here. I've copied all of my research for you in that file." He pointed to the one he'd set in front of Cade. "I know you'll want some time to read through it and maybe do some investigating of your own to verify everything in the file. With that in mind, I've made reservations to check into the bed-and-breakfast down the street next Monday afternoon. I have business elsewhere until then, but I'll be around after that whenever you're ready to talk."

The innocent-looking file was a ticking time bomb, and they both knew it. Cade couldn't bring himself to touch it, not with Maxim practically daring him to dive right in while he sat and watched.

"One question, Mr. Volkov. You are obviously aware that the people around here believe that nugget belongs to the town as a whole. Why did you come to me instead of approaching the mayor and city council with your claim?"

That produced the first genuine smile Cade had seen on Volkov's face. "Well, Chief, I've done my due diligence by reading up on all of the major players here in Dunbar. For one thing, you're new to the area, so maybe not as invested in the belief that the nugget belongs in that glass case across the street. I also talked to several of your former comrades-in-arms, and they all said the same things about you—that you're levelheaded and as honest as they come. You won't fudge the facts in order to make your employers happy. Once I've proven my claim, you'll back me."

"What makes you think that?"

"Because according to your friends, your honor won't let you do anything less."

Who had been talking behind Cade's back? Whoever it was, he wished they'd kept their mouths shut or at least given him a heads-up that someone had been asking questions. Maxim Volkov either had friends with clout or he had more charm than he'd shown so far today. Not that it mattered. He wasn't wrong. Cade had a well-earned reputation for playing by the rules.

"I'm not the one who can authorize handing over the nugget."

Max shrugged. "I know eventually I'll have to talk to your mayor and the council. I just wanted to avoid that as long as possible. Nothing I've read about Mayor Klaus and his wife, who is evidently the previous mayor of this fine town, makes me think they'll be reasonable without someone riding herd on the two of them."

Yeah, that was probably true. Cade liked both Otto and his wife, Ilse, but the couple seemingly lived to feud with each other in the most spectacular way possible. If even half the stories were true about when Klaus had decided to run for mayor against Ilse last year, the entire election season had been incredibly entertaining for their constituents. If Klaus got backed into a corner and had to surrender the Trillium Nugget to Maxim, Ilse would have a recall petition circulating before the sun went down.

"I'll read the file. That's all I can promise."

"That's all I ask."

Yeah, right. Maxim wanted the nugget, and he'd probably ask for an armed escort out of town if he succeeded in getting it. Cade really liked this job, but his career in Dunbar would be over and done with if he let that happen. It had been hard enough to get hired in the first place, and not everyone in town had been happy that he'd gotten the job.

"You can see yourself out."

Maxim looked as if he had something more to say. They both knew it was nothing Cade wanted to hear. "Let me know when you're ready to talk."

Then he was gone, file in hand.

Sadly, it was too late to cancel his lunch order. Everything Titus served was delicious. But after the discussion he'd just had with Maxim Volkov, Cade was pretty sure he wouldn't be able to tell the difference between a Cuban sandwich and sawdust.

And if that wasn't a darn shame, he didn't know what was.

TUESDAY MORNING SHELBY just happened to be at the front window at ten o'clock as Chief Peters walked out of his office across the street on his daily coffee run. No, make that Cade. After all, that's what he insisted she call him. When he happened to glance in her direction, she waved and then went back to tidying up the same stack of papers she'd straightened less than ten minutes before. Wouldn't want the man to think she was one of his many admirers who gathered along his route every day hoping for the chance to say hello.

Poor man. He seemed to take all the attention with equanimity, but he was bound to get tired of being stared at constantly. Hopefully, the women would soon find someone else to lavish their attention upon, so Cade could walk down the street without feeling as if he were the newest display in the Dunbar Zoo. Not that they actually had a zoo, but the principle was the same.

Now that the unruly stack of paper was

properly cowed into behaving, she retreated behind the counter to finish sorting the day's mail. It was lighter than usual, which wasn't uncommon for a Tuesday. The mail was usually heaviest on Monday which made her grateful that the museum was closed on that day. Sometimes she needed every minute she could scrape together to get everything sorted and into the boxes before people began showing up to pick up their mail.

After shoving the last few coupon mailers into the appropriate boxes, she decided the room could use a quick polish. The town paid Jane Soule to do the heavy lifting when it came to keeping the museum vacuumed and dusted, but Shelby was responsible for providing the same services in the area that housed the small post office. She was down the hall getting out the vacuum cleaner when the bell over the door signaled the arrival of a customer.

"Shelby, are you still here?"

She froze. Was that who she thought it was or was it just her overactive imagination jumping to hopeful conclusions? When Cade called her name a second time, she shoved the vacuum back in the closet and then checked her appearance in the small mirror on the wall. It was the second time in less than a week that she wished she had her lipstick close at hand. Oh, well, it wasn't as if the man hadn't seen her without it before today.

"Chief Peters, is there something you'd like me to do for you?"

Odd. He seemed to be fighting a smile for some reason. What had she said that he'd found amusing? Oh, right, his name. "Sorry, I meant Cade. Old habits are hard to break. I would've never thought of calling your predecessor by his first name."

By that time, he'd given up all pretense and was sporting a full-on grin. "Actually, I saw you working through the window and thought you might like something from the coffee shop, too."

He held up a cardboard tray containing two tall cups and a paper bag. Her eyes widened when she spotted the grease stains on the paper. "Are those what I think they are?"

Looking rather proud of himself, he nodded. "Yep, two of Bea's apple fritters still warm from the deep fryer. They're almost always gone by the time I get there, but she's running late for some reason today. I thought I'd share my good fortune with you."

"Let's take them to the small break room in back. If any of my friends happened to drop by, they'd demand I share mine with them."

He gave her a look of mock despair. "It would be a shame to lose a friend over a fritter. But then a real friend wouldn't ask you to share, would they?"

She put the sign on the counter to ring the bell if someone needed her. "I like the way you think."

As they made their way down the narrow hall to the break room, she had to wonder what had possessed Cade to buy her coffee and a fritter. She wasn't complaining, but he'd never done anything like this before. Maybe he was wanting to test the waters himself. That was a happy thought despite her misgivings over getting involved with a man who might view his time in Dunbar merely as a stopping off point on the way to somewhere better. Bigger.

"Have a seat, and I'll grab us some napkins."

When she sat down, he checked the names on the coffee cups before handing one to her.

She took a cautious sip. It was perfect and just the way she liked it—with cream and two sugars. "How did you know how I take my coffee?"

"I would point out that I'm a highly trained detective, but I actually cheated and asked Bea."

Oh, no. That wasn't good. He might as well have marched through town with a megaphone announcing what he'd done. Shelby gave it an hour before people started dropping by to find out what was going on between her and the police chief.

He hadn't lied about being observant. After swallowing the bite he'd taken from his fritter, he asked, "Did I do something wrong?"

Should she tell him? Yeah, probably. There was no way to staunch the flow of gossip in a town the size of Dunbar. It was only fair that he know he was going to be featured in the latest broadcast.

"Bea has a tendency to share interesting news with all of her customers."

"Yeah, so…"

"So, even as we sit here, she's telling everyone she sees that the new chief of police just bought coffee for me, not to mention one of her highly prized apple fritters. That might not be a big deal where you come from, but it's a banner headline in these parts."

He took another bite of his fritter as he mulled over that little bombshell. "Will that stop the flow of casseroles into my office? If that's all it would take, I'll buy you a fritter every day."

She laughed. "It might, but it could just as well stoke the fires of competition. My guess is all the ladies will be upping their game."

"Well, that is disappointing." His dark eyes took on a devilish glint. "Why don't we really give them something to talk about? Because I was wondering if you'd like to go for a hike with me tomorrow. I thought I'd ask Titus to put together a picnic basket for our lunch. What do you think?"

She didn't hesitate. "I have to sort the mail before we leave, but I'd love to go."

He wadded up the paper bag and tossed it into the wastebasket as if shooting a basketball. "Then it's a date."

They chatted about this and that while they finished their coffee, and then she walked with him back to the front of the building.

Pausing on his way out, he said, “I’ll pick you up at eleven if that works for you.”

“I’ll be ready.”

Then he was gone, leaving her staring at those broad shoulders as he cut across the street back to his office. Turning away from the window, she did a little happy dance. She and the handsome chief of police were going on a date.

Life was good.

CHAPTER THREE

MAXIM VOLKOV DEBATED eating another of the small egg muffins his hostess had provided for breakfast even though he'd already had several. As far as he knew, no other guests had checked into the bed-and-breakfast last night, so what the heck. He had nothing at all on his agenda today and could always walk off the calories strolling through Dunbar, Washington.

Sadly, this was his third visit to the town, and there weren't many sights he hadn't already seen. The first time, he'd wandered through some of the shops. After that, he'd enjoyed a surprisingly delicious meal at the only café in town before finally arriving at his real destination—the Dunbar Historical Museum.

It would be nice to go back again and spend more time studying the various displays. He could barely remember anything he'd looked at on his first visit. At the time, he'd wondered if the curator had somehow sensed there was something off about his behavior. Shelby Michaels had maintained a professional demeanor, but there had been a chilly edge to her smile by the time he'd finally left. Despite that, he'd been tempted to invite her to join him for a cup of coffee at the bakery down the street.

Under the circumstances, however, there had been no point in even trying. She was going to hate him if he succeeded in his mission. It would make things so much worse if she thought he'd only pretended to befriend her in order to help advance his cause. After all, there was a good chance her beloved little museum would end up closing its doors once the centerpiece of its collection left town.

The people of Dunbar might never believe it, but he did have a conscience. He felt bad about the potential ripple of negative effects on the town and its economy once the chief of police did his job and handed over the Trillium Nugget to Max. However, his first loyalty was to his family's legacy.

The sound of footsteps interrupted Max's train of thought. That was okay. All of the pieces were now in play, and he could only wait and watch to see how the game turned out. A few seconds later, a young boy appeared in the doorway of the dining room. He froze as soon as he spotted Max, staring at him as if unsure of his welcome.

Max offered him a small smile. "Hi, there. Why don't you come on in?"

The boy frowned and shuffled his feet as he considered the invitation. "I'm not supposed to bother the guests."

After making a show of looking around for other people, Max motioned for him to come forward. "You wouldn't be bothering anyone but me, and I could use some company. My name is Maxim, but my friends sometimes call me Max."

Edging a little farther into the room, Max's young visitor introduced himself. "My name is Carter. I live here."

"Nice to meet you, Carter. Can I fix you a plate?"

The lure of food worked. Carter chose to sit in the chair across from Max. "My mother said I could have one of the egg muffins if there were any left. I like the bacon cheese ones."

Max winked at him. "Those are good, but I like the ones with spinach the best."

Carter wrinkled his nose in disgust. "Spinach is gross, but it's okay if you like them."

"Thank you for that." Max headed over to the table and picked up a clean plate. "So one bacon cheese muffin. Anything else?"

"Some blueberries and a piece of the banana nut bread."

"Excellent choices, young man."

When Max set the plate on the table, Carter grinned at him. "Thank you, Mr. Max."

"You're quite welcome."

They both dug into their meals. Carter was just finishing his muffin when his mother joined the party, and she wasn't looking particularly happy. "Carter, what is the rule about bothering the guests?"

The boy looked across at Max, his eyes wide with panic. Rather than let his young companion take the heat, Max answered for him. "I'm sorry, Ms. Bruce, this is all my fault. Carter told me about the rule, but I invited him to join me."

Carter quickly nodded. "Mr. Max said he wanted company."

His hostess looked marginally happier.

"Since you invited him, Mr. Volkov, I suppose it's all right this time."

"Thank you. I didn't mean to cause the young man any problems."

Carter preened and puffed out his chest a little at being described as a young man. "We both like your egg muffins, Mom, and Mr. Max even likes those icky spinach ones."

It was hard not to laugh at the way the boy had managed to both compliment and insult his mother's cooking in the same sentence. Luckily, she didn't seem to take offense. Ruffling his hair, she told him, "Finish up, kiddo. You've got chores to do."

Heaving a much put-upon sigh, Carter pushed his empty plate away. "Thanks, Mr. Max. Now I have to go pick up my toys and take my dirty clothes to the laundry room."

That was accompanied by a huge eye roll that said without words there wasn't much a kid could do about a mother's rules and regulations. By that point, even his mom was struggling not to laugh. Instead, she directed her next comment to Max. "Is there anything else I can do for you, Mr. Volkov?"

He settled back in his chair, feeling pleasantly full. "For starters, you can call me Max, or Maxim if you insist on being formal."

She subjected him to the same disapproving look she'd given Carter when she first walked into the room. Despite her petite size, that look was actually pretty intimidating. He doubted she would appreciate knowing that he thought it was cute. She reverted to hostess mode. "Would you like some fresh coffee?"

"No, I'm good. " He picked up Carter's plate and his own and then carried them over to the plastic tub in the corner.

"You're my guest, Mr. Volkov. It's not your job to clear the table."

"I don't mind."

Turning back to face her, he considered what he wanted to say next. There was something else he needed to tell her, and he was pretty sure she wasn't going to like it. "I've already made my bed and straightened up the room. I prefer to do those things for myself."

It wasn't that he didn't trust his temporary landlady, but he'd rather no one found out his real purpose for being in Dunbar until he heard back from Cade Peters. Granted, if the man did his duty, Max might have to pack up and leave town before the bad stuff hit the fan. But if Rikki Bruce proved to be the least bit nosey, she would likely toss him and his baggage out in the street. Considering her B and B was the only one in town, it would be highly inconvenient if he was forced to vacate the premises one minute before he was ready to go.

Looking rather insulted, Rikki stared at him with her hands on her hips. "Fine, but don't expect a discounted rate for the room."

He could hardly blame her for being concerned about her bottom line, especially when she had young Carter to worry about. "I wouldn't think of it, Ms. Bruce. I'm sure you've run into other guests who have idiosyncrasies. Surely wanting to make my own bed is a pretty harmless one."

She gave him a long look from top to toe that somehow conveyed the sense that she didn't see anything harmless about him at all. Finally, she let out a slow breath. "Let me know when you need clean towels or linens."

"Will do. For now, I think I'll go for a walk."

She followed him toward the front door, stopping at the desk long enough to pick up a brochure. Flashing him a practiced smile, the same one she'd probably offered to every guest who had crossed her threshold, she said, "You might want to take this with you. The front shows all the shops in town and what hours they're open as well as any restaurants within easy driving distance."

"Thank you." He folded the paper and stuck it in his pocket without even giving it a glance.

Rikki Bruce's smile faded slightly and she gave him a curious look as she opened the front door for him. "You've never mentioned what brought you to Dunbar, Mr. Volkov."

"You're right. I haven't."

Then he stepped through the door and pulled it closed behind him.

"HERE'S YOUR LUNCH."

"I'll return the basket later today if that's okay."

"That's fine. If something comes up for you, tomorrow would be okay, too."

Cade pulled out his wallet and handed his debit card over to Titus Kondrat, who seemed more relaxed than usual. It was really quiet in the café, probably because it was after the breakfast rush and too early for the lunch crowd to start pouring in the door. For sure, the man was never still when things were really hopping during peak hours.

After processing the payment, Titus leaned against the counter behind him and crossed his arms over his chest. The man sported an interesting array of tattoos on his forearms, which Cade suspected were just the tip of the iceberg. Some folks were convinced Titus had gotten most of his ink while in prison and that was also where he learned to cook. While it could be true about the tattoos, Cade thought that last part was hilarious. Did they really think that prison kitchens served up caprese salads, Cuban sandwiches and rustic fruit tarts? Still, considering how closemouthed the guy was about his past, there was no way to know for sure.

Titus glanced at the basket and then back at Cade. "Nice day for a picnic."

Cade was pretty sure those were the most words Titus had ever strung together while talking to him. "It is."

There was a hint of humor in Titus's dark eyes. "Rumor has it you're taking Shelby Michaels on a hike."

Well, rats. Cade had really hoped to keep

their outing secret. Someone must have caught wind of their plans and decided to spread the news. He shrugged. “The joys of living in a small town.”

“True enough. But just so you know, there are more than a few disgruntled ladies here in Dunbar. Seems they think it’s unfair that you would ask Shelby out when she never brought you a single casserole.”

Now Cade knew for sure that Titus was laughing at him. “Is this going to cause Shelby problems?”

That was the last thing he wanted. And it wasn’t just that he was going to need her help to deal with the mammoth problem Maxim Volkov had dumped in his lap. He liked Shelby too much to want to cause her any kind of trouble.

Titus straightened up. “No, but I’m guessing you’re either going to have to start cooking for yourself or eat more of your meals here.”

Considering his freezer was still full of casseroles, Cade wouldn’t have to do either for a while yet. “Thanks for the warning.”

“Here’s one more.” Titus’s expression took on a harder edge. “Don’t mess with Shelby. She’s a nice woman.”

"It's just a hike."

That declaration earned him a sneer. "You may see it that way, but give a thought to how she feels about it. You've also bought her coffee and an apple fritter at Bea's. From what I've been told, that's pretty much a declaration of serious intent around here."

Cade wanted to kick himself for not having thought this whole thing through better. Instead, he mirrored Titus's stance by crossing his arms over his chest and staring right back at him. "It would be helpful if the city council provided a handbook for newcomers that included the social significance of deep-fried pastries."

Titus's answering chuckle sounded rusty as if he hadn't actually laughed in a long time. "Where's the fun in that?"

"I wasn't aware that entertaining the locals was part of the police chief's duties."

Titus finally gave in and grinned at him. "Check the fine print in your contract. I'm betting they slipped in some sneaky wording along the lines of 'and other duties as assigned.'"

The man wasn't wrong, not that Cade was

going to admit it. "I'm out of here. Thanks for doing the basket for me."

He started for the door but decided to ask one more question while Titus was in a chatty mood. "Do you also get stared at when you walk down the street?"

That earned him another rough laugh. Titus pointed to the tats on his arms. "Yeah, but not for the same reasons. Sadly, I've never gotten a single casserole delivered to my door."

Then he disappeared into his kitchen, leaving Cade staring at his back. The man was sure enough an enigma. That was something to ponder at another time. He needed to check in at the office and then meet up with a certain redhead.

SHELBY WISHED THE clock on the wall would speed up. She'd finished sorting the mail an hour ago. There weren't any library books left to shelve, and Helen Nagy had shown up on time to take charge of the museum. Pacing the floor might have helped take the edge off her nerves, but Helen was bound to notice. Considering she was Bea's mother, anything she learned would provide more fodder for her daughter's gossip mill.

The whole town already knew that Cade had asked Shelby to join him for a hike today. She hadn't meant to share that information, but Elizabeth had found it very curious that Shelby was taking a weekday afternoon off work for no particular reason. Before she could come up with a believable excuse, Elizabeth had mentioned oh-so-casually that she also found it odd that Cade Peters had ordered one of Titus's picnic baskets for the exact same day that Shelby was going to disappear for an afternoon.

Surrendering to the inevitable, Shelby had finally admitted that he'd invited her to join him on a hike. While she might have been able to convince Elizabeth to keep it to herself, the same couldn't be said for old Mr. Marley, who'd been next door in the museum. Before they could stop him, he was off and running...well, at least walking faster than his usual snail's pace...to share the news at the bakery shop down the street.

At least the old coot had later apologized to Shelby for gossiping about her. He looked more than a little embarrassed that he hadn't been able to resist lording it over Bea that he knew something that she didn't. He also pointed out that was a rarity in Dunbar, and such moments were meant to be savored. At least he'd bought Shelby a slice of apple strudel to make amends.

Even if he hadn't confessed, Shelby would've known something was up. Several of the police chief's casserole brigade had either shot her dirty looks through the front window as they walked by or else snubbed her completely when their paths crossed out in public. She loved living in Dunbar, but even an unintentional falling-out could make life awkward for a while.

Telling herself that it was their problem, not hers, didn't exactly help solve the situation.

She checked the clock again. Finally! She had just enough time to make one last trip down the hall to the bathroom and then lock the door that separated the two sides of the building. Normally, she left it open in case her assistance was needed in the museum. Almost everyone had come in early to pick up their mail since she'd put a notice in each box that she'd be unavailable after eleven o'clock. The remaining few had said they'd wait until the next day to get theirs.

There was a knock at the front door just

as the clock chimed the eleventh hour. She turned off the lights, and made sure the sign in the front window said "closed" before opening the door. It seemed odd to see Cade out of uniform during his normal business hours. Instead, he had on jeans with a plaid flannel shirt. His sleeves were rolled up several turns, revealing the white thermal T-shirt he wore underneath for extra warmth. His hiking boots looked well broken in and comfortable. She found it amusing that the only difference between their outfits was that her flannel shirt was dark green instead of red. It might be summer, but it could still be chilly near the mountains.

He greeted her with a big smile. "I'm really looking forward to this. One of the reasons I took this job was the opportunity to spend more time outdoors. It hasn't actually turned out that way so far, but I'm hoping that will change now that I've finally filled the two vacancies in the police department."

She slung the strap of her backpack over her shoulder. "I'm really glad that you hired Moira. We grew up together, and it's nice having her back in town."

"We're lucky to have her. It's hard to find

people with her kind of experience who would willingly settle for a job on a small-town police force." He grimaced as he looked at her. "Sorry, that came out wrong. We need quality people, but the opportunity for advancement is pretty limited."

He led her over to his SUV and opened the passenger door for her. "I thought we'd do a short stretch of trail up near Dunbar Mountain. I hope that's okay with you."

"Sounds lovely."

After he shut her door, Cade circled around to his side of the vehicle. Shelby couldn't help but wonder if he was aware of the attention they were getting from up and down the street. Her good friend Elizabeth just happened to be seated by the front window in the bakery. It was no accident that Bea was personally delivering Elizabeth's order at that exact moment despite the fact that she never waited tables. People were expected to pick up their orders at the counter.

Shelby cringed when she spotted three of the most persistent members of the casserole squad standing just down the block watching as Cade closed his door and started the engine. Pulling away from the curb, he gave her a quick look. "Should we wave as we go by? Maybe I should've bought some Mardi Gras beads to toss out the windows as we drive through town."

That had her laughing. "And some penny candy for the kids and all of your most ardent admirers."

If she wasn't mistaken, Cade's cheeks had just flushed red. "Not funny, Ms. Michaels. I'll have you know that Titus Kondrat went out of his way to warn me that I'll probably have to start cooking for myself now. It's that or eat all of my meals at his place."

Fighting back a big grin, she placed her hand on her chest and gasped in mock horror. "Please don't tell me that the flood of casseroles is already tapering off. I heard they'd only recently gotten themselves organized with a sign-up sheet and everything. Whatever will you do?"

"Very funny. Just so you know, I can cook. I just haven't had to in recent memory." He turned onto the highway that led out of town. "At last count I still have at least a two-week supply of casseroles in my freezer."

Shelby wasn't sure why she found that so funny, but she did. "So I've been wondering what you do with all the containers when they're empty. I can't imagine that everyone used those disposable aluminum ones."

"Yeah, that was a problem." He stopped talking while he passed the slow-moving truck ahead of them. "I seriously thought about dropping them off at the thrift shop in town, but Officer Lovell warned me the owners wouldn't appreciate having to buy their stuff back. Instead, I just left them on a table in the front of the office and let the owners sort them out. I did post a thank-you sign above the table to be polite."

It was cute how proud he looked of his effort to show good manners. "And did that work?"

"So far. Even the aluminum ones disappeared pretty quickly. I can only hope that everything got back to where it belonged. If there have been any complaints, no one has told me."

Then he frowned. "Wait a minute. Did you say they actually had a sign-up sheet posted somewhere?"

"That's what I heard from a reliable source. She offered to tell me where it was in case I felt like marching in the Feed Chief Peters

Parade. They posted it after you almost had to throw two of them in the slammer for disorderly conduct. I never heard who had to clean up the mess they made."

"I did. I should've made them do it themselves, but I'd run out of patience at that point. I kicked them out of the office and told them to stay gone unless they wanted to end up behind bars."

"Would you have really done that?"

"Guess we'll never know."

They rode in silence for a few minutes, but it felt comfortable rather than awkward. Rather than let it drag on too long, she tried to come up with another topic of conversation. Finally she settled for bringing up his previous career. "I've heard that you were in the military police."

"I was. I enlisted at eighteen and retired after fifteen years. Saw a lot of the world, but now I want to see how I like staying in one place for a while."

She winced. That was her one hesitation about getting involved with Cade on any level. If he meant that his stint as the chief of police in Dunbar might only be temporary, she couldn't risk becoming emotionally involved with him. There was no use in opening herself up to that kind of hurt. Not again. This was her home, and she had no desire to live anywhere else. With that unhappy thought, the sunshine outside of the SUV's windows was no longer quite as bright.

CHAPTER FOUR

CADE'S COMPANION HAD gone suspiciously quiet. Had something he'd said upset Shelby? Thinking back over their brief conversation, he couldn't think of anything that was particularly offensive. Yeah, he'd made fun of the ladies and their casseroles, but Shelby had made a few pointed comments on that particular subject herself. She'd been fine right up until she'd asked about his time in the military.

Did it bother her that he'd left the service solely because he'd grown tired of bouncing around the globe? He heard through the grapevine that she'd happily spent her entire life in Dunbar. He would've thought she'd understand why he wanted to find a place to call home. Somewhere he could put down some roots, and maybe even start a family if given the chance.

He'd never given much thought to what

kind of woman would make the perfect wife. But if he had, Shelby Michaels would check off most of the boxes on his personal list. She had a warm personality, was easy to talk to and said she enjoyed spending time outdoors. Without exception, the people in Dunbar spoke of her in the highest of terms. Then there was the fact that he'd always been a sucker for a redhead, especially one with great legs.

But he was getting ahead of himself. As much as he'd been looking forward to spending time with Shelby away from the ever-curious eyes in town, that wasn't the only purpose behind their outing. He dreaded having to confess his ulterior motives for asking her to accompany him on the hike.

Without a doubt, she was going to be upset with Maxim Volkov and his claim about the nugget and Cade himself for taking the threat seriously. She wouldn't be happy that someone from outside of Dunbar had called into doubt the town's ownership of the Trillium Nugget. While Cade sympathized with her and the town, he couldn't simply ignore the evidence Maxim had gathered to support his family's claim.

It could very possibly end up being a matter for the courts to decide. If a judge came down on Maxim's side, Cade would likely be the one to turn the nugget over to its rightful owner. There were a few hotheads in town who might relish the thought of running both him and Volkov out of town before that could happen. He glanced at his companion. Considering she was the curator of the museum, would she understand the position he was in?

He'd find out soon enough. For now, he wanted to enjoy as much of his time with Shelby as he could. Aiming for what he hoped was a noncontroversial topic, he turned the conversation to the lunch he'd brought for them. "I hope you like Titus's fried chicken. I also ordered double the usual desserts. I confess to having a bit of a sweet tooth."

Shelby perked right up. "Me, too. What kind of desserts? Because he makes some really good ones."

They'd just passed a sign that said the entrance to the trailhead was only a mile ahead. "I think I'll let our desserts stay a surprise. It will give you something interesting to ponder as we trudge up the trail."

The twinkle in her eyes belied the outrage

in her voice. "I'm quite shocked to find out that you might have something of a mean streak, Chief Peters. Do the mayor and the city council know about that?"

Cade chuckled at her question. "Considering Mayor Klaus ran against his own wife in the last election, he doesn't have any room to talk."

"True enough. People were stunned when he threw his hat in the ring. Rumor had it Ilse refused to talk to him other than during their debates until after his victory was declared official. Even then, her concession speech was less than gracious."

She laughed and shook her head. "I heard she made their grandson teach them how to text so they could still communicate with each other at home."

"You're not serious."

"Yep, I am."

Cade shook his head. "I'm surprised she didn't whack him upside the head with a skillet at some point for daring to run against her."

Shelby looked at him in mock horror. "Oh, Ilse would never do that. She was a hippie back in the day and still believes in flower power and nonviolence. In Otto's defense, he and Ilse were on opposite sides on a particularly hot issue. Taking her place as mayor was the only way he could ensure she couldn't carry out her plans."

Having spent some time with the couple, Cade could easily picture Otto going to such extreme measures to thwart his wife. "So what was the hot issue? I figured there had to be some reason why Otto wanted to oust her from office, but no one has ever mentioned what it was."

Shelby giggled. "The city council had allotted money in the budget to give that van the town owns some badly needed mechanical upgrades. While they were at it, Ilse convinced the rest of the council to have it painted. She thought the official town vehicle having multiple rust spots and dings in the fenders made a poor impression on visitors."

"Why would Otto object to that if the town can afford to have the work done?"

"Oh, he was fine with getting the van all fixed up, which would be cheaper than buying a newer one. It's that Ilse wanted them to paint big flowers all over the van to brighten things up. She even brought in pictures of the VW van she and Otto owned in their hippie days to show everyone what she had in mind."

They'd reached the small parking lot by the trailhead. Cade parked the SUV as he tried to picture Ilse's plan for the van. "So you're saying Ilse wanted to turn the town's official vehicle into a hippie hut?"

"Pretty much."

He drummed his fingers on the steering wheel as he tried to get his head around that concept. "Am I the only one here who's having trouble picturing Otto and Ilse with long hair and love beads?"

Shelby was back to laughing. "Don't forget bandanas, tied-dyed shirts and fringed jackets."

Try as he might, Cade couldn't imagine the bald potbellied mayor wearing 1960s hippie attire. "No way."

"Yes, way." Shelby held up her hand as if swearing an oath. "I've seen the pictures. Besides, they both dress up like that every year at the town's Halloween party."

It was hard not to shudder at the thought. "Well, I guess I have something to look forward to when October rolls around."

Time to move on. Turning off the engine, he smiled at Shelby. "Are you ready?"

"Yes, I've been looking forward to this ever since you asked me. I really enjoy hiking. But even if I didn't, just knowing my efforts will be rewarded with some of Titus's fabulous food would be inspiration enough."

After they both got out, Cade unfolded a map on the hood of the SUV and followed the trail with the tip of his finger. "There's supposed to be a good place to stop and have lunch about two miles up from here. After we've had a chance to catch our breath, we can decide if we want to go farther or call it good and head back to the car from there."

Shelby studied the map for a few seconds. "If that's the place I'm thinking of, it's a perfect spot for a picnic. There's a great view of Dunbar Mountain."

"Sounds good."

He stuffed the map back in the side pocket of his pack. "If you've got everything you need, I'm ready."

Considering they didn't know each other very well, he'd been worried that it might be hard to think of things to talk about, but that didn't turn out to be the case. Shelby had shaken off whatever had caused her to go quiet earlier in the SUV. She seemed especially interested in hearing about the various places around the world where he'd served over the years. He'd downplayed his combat tours, focusing instead on his time in Germany and Japan. He'd also been stationed at the joint bases over near Tacoma for a year, which is why he knew he'd wanted to return to the Pacific Northwest after he retired.

In return, she talked about growing up in such a small town and offered up amusing stories about some of what she called the more "interesting" citizens in town. He liked that none of her tales were in the least bit mean-spirited, but instead revealed her deep affection for everyone in Dunbar.

The weather was perfect for their outing, and he loved the occasional glimpse of the mountains whenever there was a break in the trees. It was nice that most of the trail was wide enough for them to walk side by side. He wanted to enjoy every minute of Shelby's company while he could.

Something told him that the mood on the trip back down to the SUV might not be nearly as cordial, which had him wanting to kick himself. What had he been thinking? Yes, he needed to discuss the matter about the nugget with Shelby, but he should never have misled her about the reason he'd asked her to spend the afternoon with him. He couldn't remember the last time he'd enjoyed a woman's company as much as he did Shelby's. If her bright smile was any indication, she was having fun, too.

Telling her about the threat to the Trillium Nugget was sure to put a damper on her good mood. He could always delay telling her until after they were back in town, but he really wanted to get it over with. Besides, maybe they could come up with a plan of attack before he had to inform the mayor and city council. Only time would tell.

SHELBY LEANED AGAINST a handy tree trunk and stretched her legs out in front of her. She'd probably eaten more than was wise considering Cade had yet to break out the desserts he'd promised her. The hike up to this point had taken more energy than she expected. If they were going to make a habit of doing things like this, she needed to put more serious effort into her exercise routine.

Cade finished putting away the leftover chicken and salads, but she was far more interested in the items he'd just taken out of his pack. He carefully carried four small containers over to where she was sitting and sank down on the ground beside her.

"Okay, Ms. Michaels, before I pass out the desserts, I have some questions for you."

Her interest piqued, she sat up straighter. "Okay, ask away, Chief Peters."

"Do you prefer fruit pies or cream pies?"

That was easy to answer. "I like both, so it depends on which flavors we're talking about. Peach is the best fruit pie, but coconut cream pie trumps everything else."

He picked up each container in turn and peeked under the lid. Once he determined what was inside, he either set it down next to her or back out of her reach. After handing her a fork and a napkin, he shifted to lean against a large rock, taking his share of the bounty with him. "Go ahead and dig in."

She popped the lid off her first dessert and sighed happily. "So did Titus tell you I love his peach pie or was it a lucky guess on your part?"

"I didn't have any say in it. Thanks to the

gossip mill, Titus already knew you would be sharing the picnic basket with me. That's why the other fruit pie is Dutch apple. I order it whenever it's available."

After savoring a big bite of the fresh peaches seasoned with just the right amount of nutmeg, Shelby hazarded a guess as to what was waiting for her in the other container. "So that one is probably coconut cream. If he didn't have that, it's chocolate."

"Right on both counts. He said he was experimenting with a new recipe and wanted your opinion. It's chocolate coconut cream."

If she weren't so comfortable sitting where she was, Shelby might have gotten up to do a full-on happy dance. "Chocolate and coconut together is the best of both worlds. Sometimes, I could just hug that man. Well, I would if I wasn't afraid Titus would growl at me. He doesn't exactly project a cuddly nature, does he?"

No, he didn't, and that was fine with Cade. The last thing he wanted was to see Shelby with her arms wrapped around Titus Kondrat. Rather than comment on that subject, he reached for his own second dessert. "He gave me sweet potato pie."

"That doesn't count as a dessert." Shelby wrinkled her nose. "It's more of a vegetable side dish."

Cade shot her a smug look. "Not according to my grandmother. She made the best sweet potato pie I've ever had, although Titus's is a close second. I think of her every time I eat some."

Shelby gave up the argument. "In that case, I'll accept that it can be considered a dessert under limited circumstances."

"Gee, that's big of you." He scooped up more of his pie, clearly savoring every bite.

She finished off her peach pie and set the container aside. "I love that Titus dishes up these smaller portions. Big enough to satisfy, but also small enough that I don't have to feel too guilty for eating more than one."

When she didn't immediately reach for her second container, Cade gave it a hungry look and asked, "Aren't you going to eat that?"

Seeing his hand was already inching toward her chocolate coconut cream pie, she snatched it out of his reach. "Back off, buddy. It's not my fault that you've already finished off your share of the goodies."

"It was worth a try." He relaxed again and

took a long drink of water. "We couldn't have asked for a nicer day or a better view. I love living so close to the Cascades."

"Did you grow up near mountains?"

Cade shook his head. "Not exactly. My family lived south of St. Louis. We weren't all that far from the Ozarks, but they aren't anything like the Cascades. They're beautiful in their own way, but there's just something so powerful about snowcapped mountains."

"I love them, too, but then living here by them is all I've ever known."

Cade stared off into the distance, his expression more somber than it had been only seconds before. What was he thinking about? He hadn't mentioned when he needed to get back to town. While he was entitled to some time off, she suspected he wouldn't feel comfortable being out of contact for much longer.

As soon as she finished the pie, she sighed happily. "I'm definitely giving that a five-star rating."

"Titus will be happy to hear that."

After tucking the last bit of their trash into the basket. he returned to where he'd been sitting. "There's something I need to talk to you about, Shelby. Let me start by apologizing for bringing you up here on what might sound like false pretenses. Don't get me wrong. I really wanted to ask you to join me on a hike. I've had a great time and hope you have as well."

The worried expression on Cade's face had her regretting eating that second piece of pie. It now felt like a solid lump of tension in the pit of her stomach. "I've enjoyed myself, too, Cade, but I don't understand what you're trying to tell me. What kind of false pretenses?"

"I figure you won't be happy about what's happened." He took off his baseball cap and ran his fingers through his dark hair, obviously frustrated. "I've come at the problem from every direction I can think of, and there's just no easy answer."

"Just tell me what's wrong, Cade. It can't be all that bad."

"I really wish I could say that was true." He lurched up to his feet and paced back and forth across the small clearing before speaking again. "Okay, here's the thing. Remember Maxim Volkov?"

It only took her a second to place him. "You mean the guy who came into the museum last Thursday? That writer I told you about?"

When Cade nodded, she asked, "What about him? Did he complain about me for some reason?"

He waved that off. "No, but it turns out you were right about there being something off about his behavior that day in the museum. He came back the next day to see me."

"Why?"

As soon as she asked the question, Cade came to an abrupt stop and sat down on a nearby boulder, his hands clenched tight in his lap. "Because he needed to show me a file of his research into the Trillium Nugget."

"Is he going to write an article about it? If so, that could provide some good PR for the town and the museum."

As soon as she said it, she knew she was way off base. If Mr. Volkov wanted permission to write about the nugget, he would've either come back to her as the curator of the museum or perhaps approached the mayor and city council directly. All of them would jump at a chance to share the town's prized possession with a broader audience.

Cade muttered something under his breath and sighed. "That's just it, Shelby. He's not writing an article. He plans to prove that the nugget doesn't actually belong to the town. He insists it belongs to his family, and he wants it back."

That was ridiculous. She started to laugh, hoping Cade would join in. This had to be a joke, even if it was in poor taste and absolutely not funny. But Cade didn't laugh. He didn't speak. He just stared at her as still and silent as the boulder he was sitting on.

"That awful man is lying. I don't care what kind of so-called proof he has." She refused to believe that Volkov had any kind of claim on the nugget, not for an instant.

As mad as she was at Volkov for stirring up trouble, she wasn't all that happy with Cade either. While she wasn't exactly angry, her feelings were hurt. He could've just as easily told her about Maxim Volkov's plan yesterday over coffee and a fritter. "Did you really drag me halfway up this mountain just so you could drop this little bombshell on me away from everyone else in town?"

Even though he nodded, she still couldn't believe it. "You said it was a date when you asked me."

He flinched as if she'd actually slapped him. "I did, and I meant it."

"Maybe this is how things are done where you're from, Chief Peters. But for future reference, when a handsome man asks me out, it shouldn't just be so he can break the news that some outsider is trying to steal something from the town."

She picked up her pack and turned her back to him. "Thank you for lunch, Chief Peters, but it's time to go home."

Then she stalked off, not much caring if he came with her or not.

CHAPTER FIVE

CADE KICKED A rock and sent it bouncing down the slope. It was bad enough that he'd lied to Shelby in the first place, but he'd also managed to hurt her. That was the last thing he'd meant to do. Fool that he was, he'd thought a simple apology would suffice.

He'd be lucky if she wasn't waiting down the trail with a tree limb to teach him some manners. All things considered, he'd probably let her. Of course, if Titus caught wind of what he'd done, things could really get ugly. Cade doubted the man had spent time in prison, but he'd never question his ability to fight. He'd put Titus's age somewhere in his early thirties, but some of those years had been hard ones. Whatever he'd seen, whatever he'd done, it had definitely left a mark on the man's soul. Cade recognized the look because he saw it in his own eyes every time he glanced in a mirror.

He'd face off with Titus if he had to, but right now he needed to catch up with Shelby. He set off down the trail at a faster pace than was actually safe considering the terrain. At least she was showing slightly more sense, so it didn't take him all that long to catch sight of her in the distance. He picked up speed and caught up with her just before the next bend in the trail.

She had to have heard him approaching, but she simply ignored him and hurried on her steady march. "Shelby, slow down. We're coming up on that rocky stretch. Don't risk taking a bad fall because you're upset."

When she didn't respond, he did an end run through the trees to block her way. As soon as she came to a stop in front of him, he pulled a bottle of water out of his pack and held it out to her. "I won't touch you, but you need to slow down and take a drink of water. Please, Shelby. It's okay to be upset with me, but I can't stand the thought of you getting hurt because I mishandled the situation."

Maybe his concern got through to her because she stayed right where she was until she caught her breath and begrudgingly held out her hand for the water. "Fine, but don't talk to me right now. I need to think things through."

"You have my word."

That earned him a huge eye roll, saying without words how little that meant to her right now. After taking several sips of water, she screwed the top back on and tossed the bottle back to him. Then she brushed past him and continued on down the trail. At least she took more care as she maneuvered around the rocks and roots that jutted up in the path. He maintained a small distance between them, not wanting to crowd her.

As they walked, he tried to figure out how to make peace between them before returning to Dunbar. All too soon, they reached the parking lot where they'd left the SUV. When he pushed the button on his key fob to unlock all the doors, she silently tossed her pack in the back before climbing into the front passenger seat and buckling herself in.

He stuck the key into the ignition but didn't immediately start the engine. She'd probably prefer if he remained silent, but it would be better for everyone if they could put their personal problems aside long enough to discuss the issue at hand. "I know I've handled this whole situation badly. I'd apologize again, but I figure you aren't ready to hear it."

Nothing but silence.

Well, she wasn't the only one who was upset. Unfortunately, he couldn't take his own frustrations out on her. "Be that as it may, it doesn't change the fact that Maxim Volkov has every intention of pursuing his claim. I wanted to give you a heads-up because you're in charge of the museum. I could've taken the problem to Mayor Klaus, but I can't trust him to respond in a rational manner."

Shelby didn't say anything, but at least she was listening. He stared out toward the horizon as he continued. "I've read and reread the file that Maxim gave me hoping to find he was full of smoke."

She twisted around to look at him directly for the first time since they'd gotten into the car. Icebergs were warmer than the expression on her pretty face at that point. "So you two are chummy enough to be on a first-name basis now?"

"Absolutely not. I've talked to the man exactly once, and that was when he dropped this mess on my desk. He left the file with me and said he'd be back in touch after I'd had time to read it. He said he was checking into Rikki Bruce's bed-and-breakfast, but I haven't seen or heard from him since."

"Why didn't you just tell him to take his pack of lies and leave town?"

His own temper started to fray. "You think that isn't exactly what I wanted to do? If he's right about his claims, this will hurt the whole town. He knows that and doesn't care. He honestly believes that someone along the line stole that nugget from his family. We'd all be happier if he'd never come to town, but at least he's giving us a chance to prove him wrong. He could've just as easily filed a lawsuit demanding it be handed over."

Her eyes flashed wide. "The courts would allow that?"

He prayed for patience. "Yes, Shelby, they would if they decide his case has merit. Even if they ruled against him, it could cost the town a small fortune to defend the case."

He leaned back against the headrest and let his eyes drift shut. "I'm well aware of the effect that losing the nugget could have on the town. It's been the center of Dunbar's self-image for decades, not to mention it's the reason that a lot of tourists come to town. And in case it hasn't occurred to you, if he does win the case, I'm likely to be the one responsible for handing the nugget over to him and making sure he gets out of town in one piece."

Then he opened his eyes and looked into her worried eyes. "I know it's self-centered of me to be concerned about this next part, but how long do you think I'd still have a job if I have to do that?"

That apparently shocked her. "This isn't your fault."

No, it wasn't, but he knew a few people who would love to use it against him anyway. "No, but not everyone was happy when I got the job as chief of police. This might just give them the excuse they need to correct the situation."

"What do they have against you?"

He shrugged. "I'm trying to modernize the police department. The old chief was a good man by all reports, but he'd let things slide. The town is growing, and we needed more staff. It was already an uphill battle to convince the council to hire two more officers and upgrade the computer system. Eventually, we'll need to expand even more."

Cade lapsed into silence for a few seconds.

"But that's a problem for another day. This nugget thing can't wait."

She didn't even try to dispute the truth of his assessment of the situation. "What kind of proof could he possibly have to support his claim?"

"Well, for starters, he has a picture of his great-grandfather holding the nugget. It looks like the photo was taken outside of the mine where he found it."

That silenced the rest of her objections, at least for the moment. He had no doubt she was already marshalling further arguments. For now, she simply said, "Take me home."

He started the engine and asked a question he wasn't really sure he wanted her to answer. "What are you going to do when you get there?"

"I haven't decided. But even if I had, I'm not sure I would tell you."

WHEN CADE STARTED to get out to escort Shelby to her front door, she told him not to bother. He ignored her command and followed her as far as the porch and then walked away without even saying goodbye. She had good reason to be upset with him, but his silence still hurt. After all, the first half of their "date" had been so much fun, the most she'd had in a long time.

The smart thing to do would be to go inside and lock the rest of the world out—especially Cade Peters. But somehow she found herself watching him walk away, hoping…well, she wasn't sure for what exactly. But anything would be better than this awful loneliness that left her feeling bereft. She gave up and started to unlock the door when the sound of footsteps charging in her direction had her spinning back around.

The man could really move, because he covered the distance from the driveway to where she stood in a matter of seconds. A smarter woman might've hustled inside and locked the door after seeing the determined expression on Cade Peters's face. Evidently Shelby wasn't that woman. Despite him lying about the reason for their date and her worry about the nugget, her curiosity about what was going on in his head right then overrode her common sense.

When he crowded closer, she stood her ground and refused to retreat even a single step. "Did you forget something, Chief Peters?"

Her attempt to put some emotional distance between them by using his title didn't go over well. "I want to make one thing clear, Shelby. Right now, I'm not acting as the chief of police."

"Then who are you?"

"I'm the man who's been thinking about kissing you from the first time I saw you. I might never have the chance again after today's fiasco, but darned if I'm going to spend the rest of my time here in Dunbar wondering what I'd missed."

Before Shelby could do much more than sputter, he planted his hands on the door on either side of her head, effectively trapping her between his arms. His dark eyes gleamed with heat as he leaned in until his breath brushed against her skin. Just when she thought he was finally going to make good on his threat—or maybe it was a promise—he spoke, "Tell me to stop if you don't want this."

Darn him for being so honorable. She wanted to get swept away, to be able to blame this bit of foolishness on him, but she was made of sterner stuff than that.

"Don't think I'm not still mad at you, Cade Peters."

Then she yanked his head down to her level and kissed him.

FOUR HOURS LATER, Cade sat on the front porch of the log cabin house he rented through a local property management company. He had no idea who actually owned the place and hadn't really cared when he first moved in. All he'd been looking for was a place to sleep until he got a feel for the town that was going to be his new home. Thanks to his years spent in the army, he'd learned to never get too attached to anything, including the roof over his head.

But even after such a short time, he found himself looking around the place more and more often and wondering if the owner would consider selling. Good thing he hadn't acted on that impulse. Depending on the outcome of Maxim Volkov's efforts, Cade's time in Dunbar could come to an abrupt halt in a matter of days, weeks at the most.

Located on the outskirts of town, the house sat along the edge of a small clearing surrounded by enormous Douglas firs and cedars. While he liked most of the locals he'd met, he also valued both his privacy and his downtime. That's why he went on the alert when a vehicle turned into his driveway. He'd wondered how long it would take for Shelby to sound the alarm in town about the threat to their most prized possession. It seemed unlikely that his unexpected visitor was running point for a lynch mob headed in his direction, but he didn't entirely discount the possibility.

He relaxed, at least a little, as soon as a battered pickup rolled to a stop and the driver got out. But when he remembered what Titus had said about treating Shelby right, he tensed up again. It wasn't as if he and the man were good buddies. The only question was if he should stay seated or prepare to defend himself.

Titus settled the question himself after he strolled up onto the porch with a six-pack in hand and took the chair next to Cade's. He didn't speak until after he put his feet up on the railing and popped the top off a longneck. "You look just as grim now as you did when you returned my basket. It's definitely not the look of a man who spent the day with a beautiful woman. What went wrong?"

Cade kept his gaze focused on the trees rather than turning to face his uninvited guest. "So you can decide if you need to teach me some better manners?"

That earned him an exasperated sigh. "No, so I can hear your side of the story."

That was unexpected. It wasn't as if Titus had ever indicated he was interested in getting together to share their trials and tribulations. "Let's just say that I screwed up big-time and leave it at that."

Titus handed him one of the beers. "Been there. Done that. The real question is how are you going to fix it."

"What would you suggest?"

Titus's rusty laugh rang out over the clearing. "Do I look like I run an advice column? I don't know where you went off the rails with Shelby. You're the only one who can decide whether you want to fix things or take the easy road and write the whole thing off as an unfortunate mistake."

He took another long pull off his drink. "Although if you don't make at least some effort to iron things out, it could cause you other problems. You'll have a hard time avoiding her in a place the size of Dunbar, and most people in town are likely to take her side."

They both lapsed into silence as they sipped their drinks and watched a group of black-tailed deer cautiously step out of the trees to stare at Titus and Cade. The three does must have decided that the two humans posed no threat, because a few seconds later they started grazing. It wasn't the first time they'd kept Cade company as dusk settled in around his home.

Keeping his voice pitched low, hoping not to scare them off, he finally answered Titus's question. "First of all, what happens next isn't just up to me. No matter what I want, Shelby might never be interested in a do-over. There are some outside considerations that could put the two of us on opposite sides of a potential problem."

Titus sat up taller and put his feet back down on the porch, his heavy biker boots hitting the wooden boards with a clunk. "Could this mysterious problem have something to do with the guy who is renting a room from Rikki Bruce?"

Cade tried but didn't quite hide his shock at Titus's question. "What makes you ask that?"

"He's been spending a lot of time in my café. It's the only eatery in town, but it's not the kind of place where people normally hang out with their laptops for hours at a time. I don't even offer free Wi-Fi because I don't want people playing on their computers while other folks need a place to sit."

That made sense. "So he sticks out in the crowd."

"He does." Titus went back to staring at the deer. "I've heard that he's a writer of some kind, which probably explains why he is such a people watcher. Even if that's true, there's just something off about him. Those deer are less jumpy than he is."

How much should Cade share? What the heck, the whole story was going to come out sooner rather than later. "This isn't Maxim Volkov's first time visiting Dunbar. He came through twice last week. The first time, he visited a few stores and the museum. He also mentioned having a surprisingly good meal at your café."

If Titus appreciated Maxim's assessment of his cooking, he gave no indication of it. "So what did he see at the museum that brought him back?"

Cade had already decided to never underestimate Titus's intelligence. He also had a talent for connecting a bunch of random dots to make a cohesive whole. "The nugget, what else?"

"I assume he wasn't casing the joint, hoping the town didn't have adequate measures in place to keep the nugget safe from sticky fingers."

"No, but then he might not need to break any laws to get his hands on it. And without going into details, let's just say the information he gave me makes for a convincing case."

Titus let out a low whistle. Then his eyes narrowed in suspicion as he turned toward Cade. "Don't tell me you invited Shelby to go on a hike so you could break the news about Volkov's plans with no one else around."

"Okay, I won't tell you."

"So you lied to her about why you were asking her out? And on top of that, the real reason could tear apart the town she loves."

Cade cringed. He knew he'd messed up big-time, but Titus was looking at him as if he'd just crawled out from under a rock. "I might've misled her more than I should have."

A flash of anger sparked in his companion's

eyes. "Don't play games with me or yourself. Just admit you lied to one of the nicest people in town."

Cade wanted to hit something. Or maybe someone. Titus might be a handy target for his frustration, but Cade was mad at himself, not the man next to him. "Fine, I lied. I already confessed my sins to her and asked for forgiveness even though I don't deserve it. Happy now?"

"No. I don't get my jollies watching people screw up their lives. God knows I've messed up my own bad enough. I wouldn't wish that on anyone."

He didn't offer up any details, and Cade didn't ask. "Like I said, she knows what I did and why. The ball is in her court now. If she wants to give me another chance, I'll be eternally grateful. If she doesn't, well, maybe I deserve that."

Titus stood up, startling the deer into bolting back to the safety of the trees. "You asked for my advice, so here it is. Don't give up on Shelby or yourself so easily. Believe me, forever is a long time to live with those kinds of regrets. Keep the beer. You need it more than I do."

Then he got in his truck and left.

CHAPTER SIX

SHELBY FINISHED ARRANGING the refreshments on the buffet in her dining room for the guests who were due to arrive in just over an hour, around eight o'clock. All in all, she was rather proud of how well everything had come together on such short notice. The executive board for the museum wasn't scheduled for their next meeting for another month, but the problem Cade had dumped in her lap yesterday meant they couldn't wait that long. She'd called all of the members the previous evening to announce an early morning emergency meeting at her house. Rather than explain the situation half a dozen times, she'd insisted on waiting until everyone was there before answering any questions.

Considering her lack of sleep, she started the coffee early. Hopefully, a major infusion of caffeine would help clear out enough of the cobwebs to enable her to offer the board a coherent explanation of what was going on. She could always make a fresh pot before her guests arrived.

It was hard to guess which of yesterday's events had left her too frazzled to sleep much less come up with a counterattack to the threat posed to the museum and the town as a whole. Her anger at Maxim Volkov alone might have allowed her some clarity of thought. However, it had gotten all tangled up with a whole different set of emotions that had nothing to do with the Trillium Nugget and everything to do with Cade Peters. As a result, she'd lain awake for hours after going to bed with a single memory of her so-called date with Cade Peters spinning through her mind.

That unexpected kiss.

Even now, just thinking about it had her lips tingling and her breath catching in her chest, which was simply ridiculous. There had been other men in her life, other kisses. Admittedly, she'd been going through a bit of a dating drought lately, but that was no reason for a simple kiss to knock her sideways. She had far more important things to worry about.

Way before the crack of dawn, she'd given up on sleep altogether and started baking. She hadn't stopped until she'd run short on key ingredients. To be honest, she was shocked by the wide array of goodies her late night baking spree had produced. By the time she'd stopped, the counter had been covered from end to end with cookies, brownies, mini tarts and nut breads. Considering the board only had seven members, the meeting would need to last for two days before they'd make a dent in that amount of food.

All things considered, she might have gone a little overboard this time with her baking therapy. There had to be someone who would appreciate a surprise platter of cookies. When Cade's name popped into her head as a likely candidate, she rejected the idea. Delivering food to his office would be skating a little too close to her signing up for the casserole brigade. Of course, he wasn't the only one who worked at the police station. There was Moira, Officer Lovell, and the new guy Cade had just hired.

The front doorbell saved her from any further thoughts on the subject. Whoever had rung it immediately followed up by knocking on the door. Boy, somebody was awfully impatient this morning. To forestall another summons, Shelby called out, "I'm coming."

Why would one of the board members show up so early? Probably someone who thought Shelby would share the news before the others arrived. Fat chance. She'd said she wanted to only explain things once, and she'd meant it. But when she opened the door, it was her friend Elizabeth who had her fist poised to start pounding again. She pushed past Shelby to get inside before spinning back to face her. "I came as soon as I heard. Are you okay?"

What had her friend so worked up? "Heard what?"

Elizabeth put her hands on her hips and gave Shelby an exasperated look. "Don't play coy with me, missy. I heard that your date with Cade didn't end well. Rumor has it that the two of you had a big blowup over something or that he tried something you didn't like. I'm not sure which. Regardless, I know for a fact you're no longer speaking to each other. Tell me what he did so I can go give him a piece of my mind."

"Sit down and catch your breath." She urged Elizabeth toward the closest chair. Once she got her settled, she asked, "Who on earth started that rumor?"

"Well, I heard it from Bea when I stopped to pick up doughnuts for the staff room at the school. It's one of those teacher training day things. I really hope they like the selection I chose. You never know if people prefer cake doughnuts or maple bars."

Normally, Shelby didn't mind her friend's tendency to wander off on unexpected tangents, but right now she needed her to focus. "The teachers will be thrilled with whatever you bought for them. I'm more worried about the rumor you heard."

"Oh, that. Well, Bea heard it through the grapevine that Cade came back from your date in a foul mood. From what Officer Lovell told Bea, Chief Peters picked up his messages, made a couple of calls and then marched back out without saying a word. Everybody at the station is hoping he'll be in a better mood today. You know how hard it is to work when the person in charge is all surly and short-tempered."

Shelby's issues with Cade were exactly that—hers. Well, and his, of course. She certainly did not appreciate their outing being gossiped about in such a fashion. However, if she confronted Bea, it would only stoke the flames. Instead she did what she could to calm her friend. "Maybe he was just tired after the hike. I know I went to bed early last night."

Not that she'd actually slept more than a couple of hours.

Elizabeth looked as if she was about to say something, but then she stopped to sniff the air. "Hey, have you been baking?"

Then she spotted the food on the buffet and that the dining room table was set for seven. "Are you having a party?"

"No, it's my turn to host the meeting for the museum's executive committee."

"Didn't you just meet a week or so ago?"

It wasn't worth trying to lie. Elizabeth was like a dog with a bone once she got an idea in her head. "Something came up that can't wait until the next meeting. I can't say more than that."

Well, she could, but she needed to do damage control until the committee had a chance to figure out what to do about the threat Maxim Volkov presented to the museum.

"Would you like to take something home? I made extras."

Without waiting for a response, Shelby headed into the kitchen and started loading goodies into a bag for her friend. "I made both chocolate chip and oatmeal raisin cookies. How about a loaf of the pumpkin nut bread? Isn't that's one of Jimmy's favorites?"

Elizabeth took the bag away from Shelby as she eyed the available choices. "It is, but don't think offering me baked goods is going to make me forget that you haven't answered my question. Something went wrong on your hike with Cade. Don't bother trying to deny it. We both know you only go nuts baking like this when you're upset about something."

It was time to raise the white flag. "You've got to promise me that what I tell you won't go any further. I mean it. I do not want to have my words repeated back to me by anyone in town."

If anything, Elizabeth looked even more concerned. "Fine, I promise."

"Cade and I enjoyed a very pleasant drive to the trailhead, and we both had a great time on the way up the trail. He bought one of Titus's fried chicken picnic lunches and even sprang for four of those cute little mini pies Titus makes. I had the peach and his new chocolate coconut cream. Cade had Dutch apple and sweet potato pie."

Elizabeth shared Shelby's views on that last one. "I hope you pointed out that sweet potato pie should be classified as a vegetable side dish."

Shelby grinned. "I did, but Cade's grandmother used to bake him sweet potato pies, so I had to give him a pass on the subject."

"Yeah, you can't argue with a man's grandmother. After all, Jimmy's grandma used to make him mince meat pies. I've been known to make him one now and then, and you know how I feel about those. So gross."

Realizing they were heading off into weird tangent land again, Shelby picked up the narrative where she'd left off. "Anyway, after we finished our lunch, he admitted he'd actually asked me to go on the hike for two reasons. One was that he wanted to spend some time with me. The other was that he had something he needed to tell me. He wanted to make sure we could talk about it away from everyone else."

Her friend looked horrified. "So it wasn't a real date?"

"Yes, it was. At least it started off that way. In Cade's defense, he realized he'd mishandled the situation and apologized. At first, I was...well, disappointed, of course. We were on better terms by the time he left."."

Sort of, anyway. There was just something about that kiss that had taken the edge off her bad mood. Not that she was going to share any of that with Elizabeth or anyone else.

"So what did he want to talk to you about?"

It was too much to hope that Elizabeth wouldn't ask that. "I'm sorry, but I can't really say right now. I swear I'll fill you in as soon as I can."

Elizabeth didn't even try to hide her disappointment. "Fine, but I'm going to hold you to that promise."

Then she looked at the food on the buffet and the place settings on the table. "Whatever it was, it has to do with the museum or you wouldn't have called an emergency meeting."

While it might be all right if Shelby didn't tell Elizabeth everything, it wasn't okay to lie to her. "Yes, but that's all I can say right now."

Her friend studied her for several seconds.

"Okay, I understand. Sort of, anyway. I probably should get out of your way, at least for now. If you need me, I'll be at home the rest of the day."

She gave Shelby a quick hug and headed for the living room with her bag of goodies in hand. As she opened the door, she grinned back at Shelby. "Let me know if you want my help in giving Cade Peters his comeuppance for treating you so shabbily."

Shelby started to laugh but stopped mid-chuckle when she realized they were no longer alone. "Why, Chief Peters, what a pleasant surprise."

"I'm not so sure about that." He glanced from her toward Elizabeth, who blanched.

She slowly turned to face Shelby's unexpected guest. "Chief Peters, I was just leaving."

He stood back to facilitate her escape, by that point looking more amused than insulted by what he'd overheard. He waited until Elizabeth had put a little distance between them before calling after her. "For the record, Mrs. Glines, I don't normally condone violence against police officers. But in this case, I probably deserve whatever punishment you and Shelby think is appropriate."

Then the rascal winked at her.

Looking even more flustered, Elizabeth got into her truck and drove away without once glancing back.

"Nicely played, Cade. It's not easy to rattle Elizabeth."

Shelby leaned her shoulder against the door frame, trying to look far more relaxed than she actually was. Cade was back in uniform, all spit and polish, but she suspected he hadn't gotten much more sleep than she had. His dark eyes lacked their usual spark, and the lines around them seemed to have more to do with worry than laughter.

He took off his hat, fiddling with it as if not sure about his welcome. "I didn't mean to rattle her. When you talk to her again, tell her I meant what I said. I also should have called ahead, but I was in the neighborhood and wanted to see how you were doing."

"I've been better, but I'm hanging in there."

Just then, a neighbor from down the street drove by, slowing down to a crawl as he tried to see what was going on. He immediately sped back up when Cade gave him a narrow-eyed look. While Shelby didn't like being stared at either, it would've been better to just ignore the man's curiosity. Too late now. She could only imagine what story would be making the rounds in town as soon as Mr. Barker told someone the chief of police himself had been on Shelby's doorstep so bright and early.

She also found it interesting to see the normally self-assured chief of police looking so ill at ease. "Look, would you like to come in?"

"If you're sure."

That was debatable. Inviting him inside wouldn't protect them from further gossip considering his cruiser was parked in front of her house. At least they wouldn't be stared at in her kitchen. "I just made coffee. Would you like a cup?"

"Bless you, woman. I'd love some."

"Let's sit in the kitchen."

She was aware of him slowing down to study her house as they walked down the short hall. "I like your place."

"Thanks. It used to belong to my parents, but I bought it from them when they moved to Arizona after my father retired. He likes to be able to play golf year-round."

Which was more than Cade really needed to know, but at least it was a safe topic of conversation. She motioned for him to take a seat at the small drop leaf kitchen table. When she noticed him sniffing the air with interest, she had to smile. He hadn't been lying about that sweet tooth.

She poured them each a huge mug of coffee, figuring they both could use a jolt of caffeine. "I bake when I'm upset. I've got cookies, nut bread and mini tarts. Name your poison."

When his eyes flared wide, she realized that hadn't been the smartest thing to say, all things considered. "Okay, let me rephrase that. I'd never poison you…or anyone else. I did a lot of baking and not a lot of sleeping, so I'm kind of a mess this morning."

"You're not the only one." From where he was sitting, he could see into the dining room. "And I'm guessing you've already called in the troops."

There was no use in denying it. "Yes, I did. They'll be here in less than an hour. I told them there was a problem, but nothing else. I didn't want to have to repeat the same information six times and then again at the meeting. It will be hard enough to explain about Maxim Volkov even once."

His dark eyes were sympathetic. "Do you want me to tell them?"

The offer came as a surprise, but his determined expression made it clear that he'd willingly take the heat for her. "I appreciate the offer, but let me think about it for a minute."

While she mulled over the idea, she put several cookies, a couple of the mini tarts and three thick slices of nut bread on a plate. After setting it in the center of the small table, she grabbed some napkins and sat down across from Cade. He dug right in and finished off one of the mini tarts in two bites. She couldn't help but smile as he did the same with a second one.

"I have plenty more where those came from. Remind me to pack some up for you to take with you. I can also give you a loaf of the nut bread and a dozen of the cookies."

His happy expression quickly faded into something much sadder. "I'm sorry what I did yesterday was so upsetting for you."

"I'm mostly upset with Maxim Volkov. He was the main reason I couldn't sleep last night." She dredged up a small smile. "But you'd be doing me a favor to get some of this stuff out of my house. I don't need all that temptation within such easy reach. You can share it with the other officers or not. I won't tattle if you decide to keep it all to yourself."

He studied his options. "How about you wrap up some tarts for me? I promise I'll share the rest of the bounty with my co-workers."

"Fair enough. I'll get it all boxed up." As she got up to do that, she came to a decision about his offer to stay for the meeting. "First, I want to apologize for getting so upset yesterday. My anger was mostly aimed at Max Volkov, and I shouldn't have taken all of it out on you. Regardless, I'll tell the board what's going on myself. You shouldn't have to take all the heat for something that isn't your fault."

He set down his mug with a decided thump. "It's not your fault either, and I'd rather they be mad at me."

"I'm the curator of the museum, Cade. It's my job to deal with any problems that arise. That includes preventing someone from stealing the nugget."

If they'd somehow made peace after yesterday's events, it was short-lived. Cade sat up taller, his expression no longer as friendly or relaxed. "Regardless of how you feel about Maxim's claim on the nugget, this could easily end up being a legal matter. If the courts were to decide in his favor, the museum and the town will have no choice but to hand the nugget over."

That might be true, but not until they'd exhausted every possible remedy. She'd fight long and hard to protect the town's legacy. Either way, there was no use in arguing about it now.

"My guests will be arriving soon, and I need to finish getting ready for the meeting."

"Maybe I should stay."

Why was he being so insistent? "I can handle this, Cade."

"I never said you couldn't. I just want to make sure they understand that this problem can't just be swept under the rug or ignored. They're going to be angry. Better they aim it me and not you."

She prayed for patience. "I am perfectly capable of explaining the situation. They'll handle it better coming from me."

The aggravating man clearly wanted to

argue the point some more, but she wasn't having it. "Cade, please go before they start arriving."

As tired as she was, her control over her temper wasn't all that great. For a brief second, she was tempted to send him on his way empty-handed, but that wouldn't be fair to Moira and his other officers. They were the ones who were going to have to deal with his bad mood for the rest of the day. She packed up four of the tarts in one container and everything else in a larger one. After practically shoving them into his hands, she offered him a brittle smile. "Thank you for stopping by to check on me."

She followed him back to the entryway. He shifted the containers to one hand and opened the door, but still he hesitated. "I seem to spend a lot of time apologizing to you, but I am sorry that I have no choice but to follow the law. It's not just my job. It's also who I am. That doesn't mean I'm not furious that one man could do this to Dunbar. I care about the town."

His expression softening just slightly, he reached out and gently pushed a lock of her hair back behind her ear and traced the curve of her cheek with his fingertip. "I care about you, Shelby. Never doubt that."

Then he walked out, closing the door behind him.

CHAPTER SEVEN

SHELBY CHUGGED DOWN another cup of coffee after Cade left. An extra spoonful of sugar did little to mitigate the bitter taste left behind by their discussion. Once again, the man had managed to leave her with a tangled-up mess of emotions. She understood that Cade had to follow the law as well as the dictates of his own conscience. It was what made him both a good man and good at his job.

However, her first loyalty belonged to the town and the museum. While she wouldn't break the law, she might not hesitate to bend it a little if that meant the town's heritage remained intact. It was bad enough that Maxim Volkov could walk away with the nugget in his pocket. But if he could prove the nugget had been stolen from its rightful owner, Dunbar's founders would go down in local history as thieves. That simply wasn't acceptable.

A glance at the clock reminded her that

she had guests who would be arriving soon. She stopped in the bathroom to check her appearance in the mirror and was glad she had. At some point, she must have run her fingers through her hair, leaving it a disheveled mess, which meant she'd looked like she'd spent time in a wind tunnel when Cade had arrived. Maybe that's why he'd felt compelled to push a strand of her hair back behind her ear.

She brushed her hair back into a ponytail. That helped her look more in control but did nothing for the raccoon circles under her eyes. She normally didn't bother with makeup at home, but she'd make an exception today. After putting some concealer to good use, she added just a hint of blush and some mascara. A bit of lipstick was the finishing touch to make her look presentable without going overboard.

Now that she didn't look like a zombie, she also needed to change into something more presentable. Hustling down the hall to her bedroom, she changed into a clean pair of jeans and a dark green Henley shirt that brought out the color of her eyes.

After checking her appearance one last

time, she returned to the kitchen to put the kettle on and to start a new pot of coffee. It had just finished brewing when the doorbell rang. Two deep breaths did little to calm a new surge of jitters, but it was the best she could do. Pasting a smile on her face, Shelby greeted the first of her guests. As usual, Helen Nagy had picked up three of the other docents on her way, and Earl Marley was just pulling into the driveway. He had Ilse Kraus with him, so that accounted for everyone.

"Come on in, everybody. I apologize for the short notice, but I'll give you a little time to get settled before we start. Help yourself to refreshments. The coffee is ready, but I also have tea if anyone would prefer that."

Helen eyed the array of goodies on the buffet and frowned. "Considering the size of this spread, the problem you mentioned on the phone must be a dandy."

Her assessment of the situation cast an immediate pall on the rest of the committee members. They silently filled their plates before taking their seats at the table and only spoke to give her their drink orders. "I'll be right back with the coffee and tea."

Her elderly friends finally started talking

in low murmurs while she poured coffee into four cups and added hot water and tea bags to three more. Ilse joined her in the kitchen on the pretense of helping to deliver the hot drinks. The older woman gave Shelby a long look and then pulled her close for a brief hug.

Shelby had known the other woman her entire life, but she could only recall a handful of times where Ilse had actually hugged her. It made her wonder what had compelled her to do so now. As if sensing Shelby's confusion, Ilse smiled at her. "The others might not notice, but you're definitely looking sort of stressed right now. I also know you wouldn't have called for an emergency meeting for anything less than a dire situation. Whatever it is, don't think you have to bear the full burden of responsibility all by yourself. We might be old, but we're feisty."

Then she carried the small tray holding the tea into the dining room. Her thoughtfulness went a long way toward soothing Shelby's nerves. Ilse was right—the weight of the problem currently rested squarely on Shelby's shoulders. Logic said it wasn't her fault for having let Maxim Volkov into the museum in the first place, but it still felt that way. Drawing one more deep breath, she picked up the coffee tray and headed into battle.

The room went silent again when she finally sat down at the head of the table. "Did you all get everything you needed?"

When everyone nodded, she passed out the short agenda she'd put together earlier while the pumpkin bread was baking. There was really only one topic to discuss, but she wished she'd written herself some notes. It might've made it easier to keep everyone focused, but somehow she doubted even the most detailed plans wouldn't prevent this meeting from turning chaotic as soon as she explained what had happened.

"I hereby call this meeting to order. I'm sure there will be a lot of questions and comments. I would ask that you hold them until after I have a chance to explain the situation that came to my attention yesterday."

Oscar Lovell immediately blurted out, "I knew something bad happened yesterday when you and Chief Peters went on your date. I was on duty when he came back to headquarters looking like someone had kicked his dog. Well, if he had a dog."

Ilse snapped, "Oscar, didn't you hear what

Shelby said about holding your comments until the end?"

While Oscar might not fear Shelby, only a fool would cross Ilse Klaus. "Sorry, Shelby. I'll be quiet now."

Shelby acknowledged his apology and started talking again. "Actually, the problem started last week when a man named Maxim Volkov visited the museum. I was covering for the docent that morning, so I was the one to welcome him to the museum. He introduced himself and explained that he was a writer. According to what he told me, he primarily writes travel pieces for magazines and the occasional local interest story for newspapers."

She stopped for a few seconds, replaying the events of that morning in her head like a movie. "He was friendly and seemed interested in our local history. I couldn't help but think if he liked the town and the museum, he might be inspired to write about his experience. If so, both the town and the museum would get some valuable publicity."

Several people nodded. They all knew how hard it was to draw tourists to a small town that was a bit off the beaten path. Finding new ways to advertise not just the museum, but also the shops and other businesses in town that catered to tourists was a major challenge for everybody concerned. Social media helped, and the seven of them took turns posting on the various sites on a regular basis.

"Anyway, he seemed to prefer to investigate the displays on his own. I told him that I would be around if he had any questions and went upstairs to do some filing. Since the star of the show is on the second floor, I knew he'd make his way up there sooner rather than later."

Tension and talking had left her throat dry. A sip of coffee helped. At least she was able to continue. "Looking back, I think I sensed then that there was something off about his behavior."

"How so?" Ilse prodded when once again Shelby quit talking.

Good question. "It was as if he were looking at every display but without actually *seeing* them. Like he was only pretending to be a tourist. He claimed he'd read about the Trillium Nugget in a brochure he'd picked up at the hotel where he'd stayed the night before. I believed him. We often get visitors that way who otherwise wouldn't have heard of Dunbar or the nugget."

That set off another round of nods as she continued. "Although Mr. Volkov browsed the displays along the perimeter of the second floor, he spent far more time studying the nugget. After taking several pictures of it, he asked if I knew of any books that might mention the nugget. When I told him about the one on local history in the gift shop, he bought two copies along with some postcards and a map showing where people mined gold in this area. He left right after that."

She set aside her copy of the agenda. "I should've known something was wrong later that afternoon when I discovered that he'd stuffed four fifty dollar bills in our donation box. I just thought he was being extra generous. That doesn't happen often, but some people like to support small museums like ours."

Once again, Ilse gave her a verbal nudge to get on with it. "So what has he done that has you so upset?"

"He came back the next day, but not to visit the museum. Instead, Mr. Volkov insisted on meeting with Chief Peters. On the day of his first visit, I happened to share a table at the café with Cade. He asked how things were going at the museum, and so I told him Mr. Volkov had been our only visitor that morning, and that something about him had bothered me. He told me to trust my instincts and that if any of us ever had a visitor that we were unsure of not to hesitate to call him."

Earl Marley sat back and crossed his arms over his chest. "Good to know. I admit I worry some about you ladies being alone in the museum with total strangers."

Ilse shot him a disapproving look, no doubt irritated that he'd think she couldn't take care of herself. At least Ilse didn't launch into one of her long diatribes on what she thought were his antiquated views on so many subjects.

Shelby hastened to get everyone back on topic. "Evidently I mentioned Mr. Volkov's name at the time, because Chief Peters quickly realized that Volkov and the man who had made me uneasy were one and the same. As it turns out, Mr. Volkov already knew about the nugget before he came to town, but not because of our pamphlet. He has a picture of his great-grandfather, a man named Lev Volkov, holding the nugget in his hands. The photo was allegedly taken right after Lev discovered the nugget. Maxim claims the nugget actually belongs to his family."

Shelby had expected everyone to explode in fury. Instead, a chilly silence settled in the room as the six committee members stared at her as if waiting for the punchline to a joke that would never be funny. It was no surprise that it was Ilse who finally spoke up. "What does the mayor have to say about this?"

Shelby didn't know how to respond to that question. After all, Ilse lived with her husband, the mayor. Surely if he knew anything, he would've already shared it with her. Or maybe not, considering how contentious things got between the pair when it came to politics and the business of running the town government.

"As far as I know, the only people who know about this are Chief Peters, me and now all of you. Well, besides Maxim Volkov, of course."

"Why did the chief tell you first?"

That question came from Oscar Lovell. Did he think he should have been informed first because he worked for Cade? Feeling a little defensive, she struggled to keep a hint of anger from leaking into her voice. "Because as curator I'm responsible for the museum and its collection."

Earl asked, "Can we safely assume that Chief Peters ran the man out of town?"

If only that were true. "No, he couldn't do that."

Helen Nagy looked outraged by that answer. "Why not? It's what we pay him for. His job is to protect the town from scoundrels like this Volkov person."

Praying for patience, Shelby tried to calm the waters. She understood why everyone was upset, but their anger shouldn't be directed at Cade. "He can't ignore evidence, Helen. It's his job to investigate allegations like this."

"So you're okay with this man waltzing into town and stealing the nugget?"

This time Shelby didn't even try to be polite. "I find that insulting, Helen. Of course I'm not okay with the situation, and I certainly did not ask all of you here to say this is a done deal and that the nugget is no longer ours. I called the meeting so that we can discuss options."

Ilse rejoined the conversation. "Options for what? To come up with something of equal value and equal interest to tourists? Because

I don't see that happening. We can't very well make a plaster mold of the Trillium Nugget, paint it gold, and pass it off as the real thing."

Oh, for Pete's sake. That was ridiculous, even for Ilse. "No, we can't. For now, Cade is studying the information that Mr. Volkov provided him to see if his claim sounds legitimate."

Helen mumbled, "Which it isn't."

Shelby looked around the table and made eye contact with each member of the committee. "We can only hope that is true. Once Cade has finished reviewing the material, I'm sure he'll discuss the matter with the mayor and the city council. I know he will appreciate all of you keeping this matter confidential until we and the town council can come up with a plan."

With that, Shelby stood up, signaling an end to the meeting. "In the meantime, I'll be searching through the museum's records for any kind of documents that explain how the nugget came to be in the museum."

She frowned. "I don't know why it never occurred to me to ask about that or why the information wasn't included when the display was first set up. Have any of you ever seen any files like that?"

One by one, the board members silently shook their heads. Ilse finally spoke up. "I'm afraid that a lot of the paperwork has gone missing. Your predecessors didn't have your organizational skills, and then there was that broken pipe that flooded the basement. We saved what we could, but a lot of stuff was lost."

That had happened long before Shelby took over the museum. "Well, I'll see what I can find. I suggest we meet again in a week's time. Hopefully by then, I will have a better feel for where we go from here."

Her guests remained seated, clearly not ready to leave. She suspected Oscar spoke for them all when he said, "We already know where we go from here. We hunt down this Volkov fellow and tell him to stay the heck away from Dunbar. It's our nugget."

Then for emphasis, he pounded his fist on the table and repeated, "The Trillium Nugget is our heritage. Always has been and always will be, no matter what it takes."

That earned him a round of applause and more pounding of fists on her table. Unfortunately, Helen missed the surface of the table and caught the edge of her plate instead, which sent it flipping over on the floor. Luckily the carpet cushioned the landing so it didn't shatter. Everyone gasped as Shelby quickly rescued the plate and set it out of reach.

Helen apologized. "I'm sorry, Shelby. I'm just overwrought by the knowledge that this… this stranger thinks he can steal the town's most precious possession like this."

Feeling somewhat overwrought herself, Shelby patted Helen on the shoulder. "No damage done, Helen. We're all upset. It's only to be expected. Now, I'll see all of you out. If you'd like to take any of the leftover snacks with you, I'll pack them up for you."

The promise of free goodies got everyone up and moving. It was another twenty minutes before Shelby waved goodbye to the last of her guests. She locked the door, relieved to have its solid presence between her and the rest of the world. She didn't regret informing the board of the situation, but she couldn't help but wonder what kind of trouble she'd just unleashed.

Right now her energy level was running on empty, but she needed to make one phone call. She dialed Cade's direct number. It was a relief when it went to voice mail, but she had to at least leave him a message. Keeping it short and sweet, she said, "Cade, it's Shelby. I just told the board about Maxim Volkov and his evil designs on our nugget. Watch your back."

Having given the man fair warning, she picked up her purse and headed off to work.

CHAPTER EIGHT

AFTER LISTENING TO Shelby's message three times, Cade finally decided she hadn't meant that last part as a threat but more as a warning that other people weren't taking the news about the nugget very well. As a result, he deliberately delayed taking his lunch break until the worst of the rush would be over at Titus's café. He wasn't sure how quickly the news would spread about the potential threat to the nugget, and it would be nice to eat in peace. If necessary, he'd get his meal to go and lock himself in his office while he ate. He supposed he could also go home and scrounge something there, but that held little appeal.

He'd been about to leave when Oscar Lovell showed up to work his afternoon shift. Rather than immediately heading out on patrol, the older officer presented himself at Cade's door.

"Is there something you need, Officer Lovell?"

Oscar inched a little further into the room, looking ill at ease yet determined. "Yes, sir. I want to know what our department is going to do to protect the Trillium Nugget from being abducted by that outsider. We need to take the threat seriously."

Cade leaned back in his chair, not happy to have one of his own employees all but accuse him of being slipshod about his duties. "Two questions, Oscar. First, how did you learn about the problem?"

"I attended the emergency meeting of the museum's executive board at Shelby Michaels's house."

It figured. Worse yet, Cade knew this was only the first salvo. "Second, just what would you have us do? The security system at the museum is top quality, so the nugget is just as safe over there today as it was yesterday and the day before. Short of parking an officer there around the clock, it's about as secure as we can make it."

"There has to be something more, Chief. Have you bothered to investigate this Volkov fellow? Maybe he's a scam artist."

Enough was enough. Hunger and frustration never made for a good combination. He also knew Oscar meant well and was merely concerned about the situation. "I have already checked his record, and it's clean. His credentials as a writer are also valid. I've talked to several people who have published his work, and he has a reputation for getting his research right and being fair when he does a travel review."

He stood up. "Now, if you'll excuse me, I'm going to stretch my legs and then get some lunch. Call if you need me."

Recognizing a dismissal when he heard one, Oscar had already started to back out of the doorway when Cade stopped him. There were two more things he wanted to know, only one of which he could actually ask about. "Out of curiosity, how did the board meeting go?"

"Everyone is upset. No one can understand why anyone in their right mind would take that man's claim seriously. After all, if this guy's family had a legitimate claim, they would've come forward long before now." Oscar's faded blue eyes shifted to the side and looked everywhere but at Cade, meaning he was the anyone they were talking about. "Anyway, we plan to meet again soon. Shelby said you'd be presenting the information to the mayor and the city council next. She asked us to keep it to ourselves until you've had a chance to do that."

That was nice of her, but he bet the story leaked out sooner than that. He wondered what Ilse Klaus would do with the information. He could see her wanting to lord it over her husband that she knew about the crisis before he did. If so, Cade would no doubt have the mayor on his doorstep by late afternoon. It was almost as likely she would keep the information to herself just so she could steal her husband's thunder when he got home with the news.

He also wondered if Shelby had let it slip that Maxim Volkov was staying at the bed-and-breakfast. Hopefully she'd kept that little tidbit to herself. "You can let the board know that I'm scheduled to speak to the mayor and council members tomorrow. I tried to get in to see them today, but Otto had a prior commitment he couldn't change. Until then, I would really appreciate everyone's discretion. It would be better if we can get a handle on the situation before it goes public."

Although after reading through Maxim's

notes yet again, he had no idea what they should be doing next. "Like I said, I'm going to do a foot patrol and then have lunch."

Oscar nodded and disappeared back down the hall. Cade gave him a two-minute head start before following to ensure Oscar couldn't resume their conversation. Stepping out onto the sidewalk, he paused to look up and down the street, finally zeroing in on the building where Shelby worked. He couldn't see her, but she could be in the break room or in the museum.

Regardless, she'd probably had enough of his company for the day. He did need to tell her about his upcoming appointment with the mayor tomorrow morning, but he could easily convey the information in a text message. But just in case he happened to run into her while he was out and about, he'd hold off doing that until he got back to the office.

Following his usual route toward the café, he waved back at the people who waved at him. How much longer would he be greeted with smiles as he walked through town? The constant supply of casseroles and baked goods had ended as soon as it got out that he'd invited Shelby to go hiking with him. It was doubtful things would start up again, especially when the news about the nugget became common knowledge. It was far more likely people would be tossing rotten tomatoes at him just because he couldn't run Maxim out of town.

A few might even be asking for his resignation. From the start of the interview process, it was clear that at least a couple members of the city council viewed him as an outsider who didn't understand how things were done in Dunbar. Given half a chance, they might use this as an opportunity to prove they were right. As disappointing as that would be, he'd have no choice but to comply. It had taken him months to find a job that met all of his criteria. After leaving the army, he'd decided to settle in the Pacific Northwest permanently. He also wanted to stay in law enforcement, but at a slower pace than working in Seattle or one of the other larger cities in the area.

If things went badly with the nugget, he'd have to start the hunt all over again. Only this time, he'd be carrying the baggage of having been asked to resign from his job. Who knew how adversely that would affect his chances of getting a comparable position somewhere else?

"Did you forget something, Chief Peters?"

Cade hadn't realized that he'd coasted to a stop right in front of Bea's bakery. She was watering the two whiskey barrel planters full of petunias that flanked the door to her shop. "No, I just got lost in thought. How are you doing today?"

"I'm fine. Things were busy early this morning, but I'm glad to say they've slowed down. Sometimes a body needs time to think, not to mention to order supplies. Flour and sugar and such don't just magically appear on the shelf. Then there's the paperwork."

Cade sympathized. "I know what you mean. I spend a good part of my time filling out reports myself. In fact, considering the stack of work on my desk, I'd better get a move on. Nice talking to you."

It was never easy to get away from Bea. He suspected that she didn't like to let anyone leave before they told her something she could share with the next person who happened by. "Where are you headed?"

"I was working on some of those reports I mentioned and lost track of time, so I'm taking a late lunch today."

She offered him a knowing smile. "I guess

you got behind on account of taking yesterday afternoon off to go hiking."

Did she think he was slacking off on his job? "Actually I'm covering for one of the other officers this weekend, so I took some time off during the week instead. Have a nice afternoon."

After touching the brim of his hat as a polite goodbye, he hustled on down the street before she could think of another nosy question to ask him. It was a relief to step inside the café and find all of the tables were empty. None of the servers were in sight, so he picked up a menu and headed for the last stool at the counter.

He'd barely sat down when Titus appeared with a carafe of coffee in his hand. "I'm out of the special, but I've got one serving of the meatloaf with all the fixings left. Otherwise, you can have a burger and fries. I can also probably scrounge a piece of pie if you're extra hungry."

"Meatloaf will hit the spot. I'll take the pie to go."

"Won't take but a minute." Titus filled Cade's coffee cup. "Move over to the table in the corner. I was about to take a break myself, and there's no use in either of us sitting alone."

Before heading for his assigned seat, Cade put the menu back where he'd found it. He didn't know why he had bothered to take one in the first place when Titus was making all of his decisions for him. He'd barely moved his coffee over to the table when Titus brought out two plates heaped high with food. He immediately headed back into the kitchen only to reappear a few seconds later with two stainless steel bowls that he set on the floor. One was filled with water and the other held a huge helping of dog kibble.

After Titus settled on his chair, he gave a sharp whistle. Cade was only mildly surprised when a beast of a dog trotted out of the kitchen and headed their way. From its coloring, the mutt looked to be mostly German shepherd with some golden retriever thrown in for good measure. He probably weighed in at around eighty pounds. "That your dog?"

Titus studied the critter in question for a few seconds before answering. "Actually, I'm not sure, but no one else has claimed him. He shows up every day to get fed, but he won't come inside my house to sleep at night. He does defend my yard as his territory, though, so he's giving off some mixed signals."

Cade swallowed a bite of meatloaf, which was as delicious as any of Titus's other entrees. "So what does the health inspector have to say about you bringing a dog into the café?"

"The subject hasn't exactly come up. The dog makes himself scarce when anyone like that comes around. Not sure how he recognizes them as being a threat."

He frowned. "Are you going to report him or me?"

Cade laughed. "What kind of fool do you take me for? I wouldn't do anything to jeopardize my only source for sweet potato pie. As long as the dog behaves himself, you won't get any grief from me. If you run into problems, let me know."

The dog took a break from his meal to lay his head on Cade's thigh. He risked giving him a soft pat on the head and stroked his back several times. "Like I told your friend here, dog, we're good as long as I don't get any justifiable complaints about your behavior. But if you ever need a place to hide out, I've got an empty corner in my office."

The dog gave Cade's hand a quick lick to

seal the deal and then returned to wolfing down his lunch. Titus shook his head as he patted the dog's back end. "Seems like he's taken to you, Chief, which is a mighty big compliment coming from him. He mostly ignores everyone else. That includes me a good part of the time."

"Does he have a name?"

"Not that he's told me. I took him to the vet to get shots and a physical. They also checked to see if he'd been chipped, but no dice. After that, I've tried calling him by several different names, but he doesn't seem taken with any of them. Do you have any good ideas?"

Cade watched the dog finish off the last of his meal. "He doesn't seem like the kind of dog who'd want to be called something too fussy. How about Ned?"

Upon hearing Cade's suggestion, the dog sat down, his ears pricked forward and his tail doing a slow sweep across the floor. "Hey, I think he likes it."

Titus gave the dog a thorough scratching. "So, what do you say, boy? Do you want to be called Ned?"

He answered with another tail wag. "Okay, Ned it is."

When the door of the café opened, the newly christened dog immediately disappeared into the other room. Titus scooped up Ned's bowls and carried them into the kitchen before returning for his and Cade's empty dishes. "I'll get that piece of pie you wanted and be right back."

Then he turned to greet whoever had just come in. His voice was a whole lot less friendly than it had been a few seconds ago when he'd been talking to the dog. "Mr. Volkov, have a seat anywhere."

Cade had been reaching for his wallet to settle the bill, but he froze when he realized who had just walked in. Maxim had been about to sit down at a table at the opposite end of the café, but now he was headed straight for Cade.

The last thing he wanted to do was get embroiled in a conversation with Maxim right now. It wasn't as if he had any answers for him and probably wouldn't even after he spoke with the mayor tomorrow. That didn't mean he'd go out of his way to be rude. There was no use in making things any more complicated than they already were.

"Chief Peters, may I join you?"

Hoping he looked sincerely regretful, Cade shook his head. "Sorry, but I was about to leave. I'm just waiting for my check."

Maxim looked doubtful, but then Titus reappeared with both the bill and Cade's pie boxed up and ready to go. "Mr. Volkov, I'll be over to take your order as soon as I get Chief Peters taken care of."

"Okay, no rush."

Cade followed Titus over to the register while Maxim returned to the table that had been his first choice. After handing Titus enough cash to cover the bill as well as the tip, Cade started for the door, hoping to make good on his escape without any further interaction with the man who might end up costing him his job.

He almost made it, too. Unfortunately, he already knew how determined Maxim could be. Just as he was about to open the door, he heard footsteps headed his way. Surrendering to the inevitable, he turned to face his nemesis. "Was there something you wanted, Mr. Volkov?"

"I want my nugget, and I expected to hear back from you by now. Are you ignoring me in the hope that I'll simply give up and go away? Because that's not going to happen."

Cade was well aware that the two of them were not alone. Titus was nearby, leaning against the counter and listening to every word. At least he seemed content to remain silent. If he had questions, he would no doubt track Cade down later and demand a few answers.

"No, Mr. Volkov, I didn't think you would simply disappear, but these things take time. I should know more about what the town's response will be tomorrow or the day after."

Come to think of it, this was the second time in one day that someone had hinted that Cade was failing in his duty. He moved closer to Maxim and rather enjoyed that his single step forward had the man backpedaling in a hurry. Injecting some ice into his next words, he said, "For future reference, I do not take kindly to any suggestions that I'm not doing my job. You'll hear from me when I have something to tell you and not a minute before. Got that?"

Maxim's face flushed red. "Yes."

Cade deliberately turned his back to him, saying without words that Maxim presented no threat to a man with Cade's training. "Thanks again for the meal and conversation, Titus. I'll see you again soon. In fact, I'll pick up a six-pack and a pizza for tonight if you're interested."

Titus arched an eyebrow as he glanced in Maxim's direction and then back to Cade before nodding. "I'm interested. Say about seven thirty?"

Cade wasn't sure if Titus was interested in the pizza and beer or the conversation he'd just witnessed. Either way, Cade would welcome his company. "Sounds good."

Then he stepped out into the sunshine and started the long walk back to the office.

CHAPTER NINE

"HOW COULD YOU let something like this happen?"

Cade fought for patience as he tried to come up with an answer to Mayor Klaus's question that wouldn't get him fired. Otto had already asked the same thing three times in the last thirty minutes. Adding in the variations on the same theme from the other members of the city council, Cade had already explained the situation a dozen times. He leaned back in his chair and fought to remain calm. Someone had to be the grownup in the room.

"As I said, Mr. Mayor, Maxim Volkov showed up in my office with no advance warning. That was the first I learned of his claims about the Trillium Nugget. I read through the file of information he gave me and made some calls before taking any other action in case he was a crackpot." He paused for emphasis. "Sadly, he isn't."

Eileen Southworth sputtered in indignation. "Of course he is, Chief Peters! No one in his right mind would think he could waltz into our town and steal the nugget. We shouldn't encourage such foolishness by dignifying his demands with any kind of response. That will only encourage him."

A silver-haired woman somewhere in her seventies, Eileen was the newest member of the council. From the beginning, she'd taken an inexplicable dislike to him. He didn't care about that, but she was shaping up to be a major problem in dealing with this situation. Like Otto, she didn't seem to comprehend that the town couldn't simply ignore Max Volkov and hope he would go away. He tried one more time to explain why that was.

"I'm sorry, but I respectfully disagree, Mrs. Southworth. As I said before, I am not the one who will determine the validity of Mr. Volkov's claims. If we're not careful, he's very likely to get attorneys and the courts involved. None of us wants that to happen."

Herb Crisp, who had remained silent up until this point, leaned forward with his elbows on the table. "You mean he might sue the town?"

"He hasn't mentioned that possibility, but it wouldn't surprise me." He turned to Julius Hayes, the town's treasurer. "Can we afford to defend a long court battle?"

"Nope."

His one word answer landed hard. None of the other members seemed to know how to respond, and Cade was perfectly content to wait them out. Finally, Otto sighed. "Chief Peters, what do you suggest we do next?"

"For starters, I'm sure Ms. Michaels will be researching the provenance of the nugget. While she's doing that, you all should read Mr. Volkov's file for yourselves. After that, I would see if there's room in the town's budget to pay an attorney to review the case and give you a professional opinion on the matter. Once you've done those two things, you'll be better situated to make a reasonable decision on how to proceed."

Otto looked marginally happier now that someone had given him a path to follow. "Fine, I suggest we table this matter until our next regular meeting and discuss those options then."

Really, that's what he'd gotten from the discussion? Was Cade the only one feeling this sense of urgency and impending doom? Granted, this was a matter for the council to handle, but he had to try to get them to see reason. "I'm sorry, Mr. Mayor, but I'm thinking waiting that long wouldn't be wise."

"Why not? That's how these things are done. We put items that need discussing on the agenda for the next meeting. You said yourself that we should read over Mr. Volkov's preposterous claims for ourselves. We need time to do that."

"And when is the next meeting?"

Herb checked the calendar. "Three weeks from next Thursday."

Should Cade just give up or try one more time?

He glanced around the table. "This matter is now firmly in your court, but be aware that anything that looks like a delay tactic might seriously compromise the town's chances of negotiating a positive outcome with Mr. Volkov."

He held up his hand to stave off the flurry of protests coming at him from all directions. "I do not claim to know the man well at all, but I have spoken with people who have had dealings with him. They respect his integrity and his determination to get the job done right. He has a reputation for doing his research and verifying the facts. That's why you need to read the information he has provided and see how it might look to outsiders."

"And why would we care what outsiders might think? This is our town, not theirs."

Right now, Cade figured Eileen Southworth was including him in that group considering she all but sneered at him. Rather than retaliate in kind, he kept his voice low and level. "It all depends on who those outsiders are, Councilwoman. If they are outside law enforcement agencies or the courts, you should care very much. Now, unless you have any more questions for me, I should get back to the office. Let me know how you choose to proceed. I'll need to update Mr. Volkov on the situation very soon."

He was almost to the door when the mayor stopped him. "Fine, Chief Peters, you've made your point. We'll all read the file and meet again in a couple of days. We'll want you to attend. I will also ask Shelby Michaels to update us on her efforts and see if she can offer some insight into the history of the nugget. Meanwhile, Julius, check the town budget and see how we can pay an attorney to give us an opinion."

At least Cade had finally convinced them that inaction wasn't the answer. "I'll be here, Mayor."

Herb finally asked the one question that Cade was really hoping wouldn't come up. "How much time do we have, Chief Peters? When is this Volkov character supposed to come back to see what we've decided?"

Bracing himself for another explosion of outrage, Cade didn't even try to break the news gently. "Well, actually, he's never left."

The mayor lurched to his feet. "What do you mean he's never left? Have you been talking with him all this time?"

If Otto's face got any redder, Cade was worried they'd have to call for the paramedics. The man's blood pressure had to be hitting the danger zone.

"He's been staying at Rikki Bruce's bed-and-breakfast since shortly after he delivered the file to my office. I've only spoken to him once since that first day when I happened to run into him at the café. He asked me for a status report, and I told him I'd be meeting with you today."

"Has he been spying on us? I don't like the idea of him lurking here in Dunbar trying to pick up information he can use against us."

That came from Herb Crisp. Paranoid much?

"From what I've heard, Mr. Volkov spends most of his time in his room at the bed-and-breakfast and takes his meals at the café. I've seen him out walking around, but I haven't heard that he's making a pest of himself."

"Why is that Bruce woman even letting him stay there? We cannot allow that to continue. The man is a threat to the town. The chief here should tell her to evict him immediately."

To Cade's surprise, it was Otto who contradicted Eileen's outrageous demand. "He can't do that without probable cause, Eileen. If Mr. Volkov pays his bill and doesn't cause her any problems, Rikki can't just throw him out. It would be different if her rooms were otherwise booked, but we all know that isn't likely to be the case. It's hard enough for our small businesses to make a profit. We cannot ask her to turn away a paying customer just because we don't like why he's here."

Cade agreed with Otto's assessment of

the situation. If he hadn't spoken up, Cade would have. It was better coming from Otto, though, considering the woman's ongoing antipathy toward Cade. Given the current circumstances, he tried not to take it personally. They were all understandably upset, he was a handy target for their anger.

Still, he hesitated to leave quite yet. Getting them to this point had been like herding the proverbial kittens, and he was afraid they'd scatter again the minute his back was turned. He waited until they were packing up their papers to make his escape.

It was tempting to seek the sanctuary of his office, but someone should tell Shelby there would be the city council meeting in a couple of days. The mayor's office would likely reach out to her, but that didn't mean Cade couldn't give her a heads-up himself. He hadn't seen her except from a distance since they'd last spoken at her house, and he was worried about her.

As he stepped out of city hall, he thought back to the previous evening. As promised, Titus had come over to Cade's place for dinner. Once again they'd sat out on his front porch and watched the deer grazing in the clearing. It wasn't until they'd demolished the pizza that Titus finally brought up Maxim's name. Even though Cade hadn't yet met with the town council, he felt pretty safe in telling Titus about what was going on. There was something about him that made Cade think the man had a lot of experience in keeping secrets.

Telling the story from start to finish had helped Cade organize his thoughts. Titus had very little to say on the subject, but it wasn't as if Cade had expected him to offer any advice. Well, other than to repeat what he'd said before—that living with regrets never got any easier.

Which brought Cade right back to the current minute. He'd been heading for his office, but now he was having second thoughts. If he and Shelby appeared to be the only ones taking Max's claim seriously, maybe the best way to solve the problem was for the two of them to put their heads together and come up with a plan.

With that in mind, he crossed the street and headed for the museum rather than his office.

Hoping to catch her alone, he approached the building slowly to see if she was in her usual spot sorting the mail and library books. However, the office was empty. It seemed unlikely that Shelby would've taken more time off work, so maybe she was working next door.

The lights were off on the museum side of the building. What was going on? He tried the door only to find it locked. That was definitely odd. Cade's cop Spidey senses were going off big time.

THE MAIL HAD been especially light and hadn't taken Shelby long to get it all sorted. For once, she wished she had more to do, preferably something that would keep her mind off Cade and his meeting at city hall. She'd briefly considered locking up and going with him but rejected the idea. Better to let Cade break the news. She suspected he'd do a better job guiding the mayor and the city council into a reasonable plan of action without an audience.

Having run out of busy work on that side of the building, she decided now would be a good time to start looking through the museum's files for anything that could be used to counter Max Volkov's narrative about the Trillium Nugget.

As soon as she walked into the museum, she stopped to look around. Why weren't the lights on? It was well past time for one of the docents to be there. The hours the museum was open to the public varied, but the docent on duty for the day was supposed to be there by ten o'clock unless he or she let Shelby know ahead of time. She'd have to check the schedule to see who was supposed to be there and call to find out what was going on. If necessary, she'd contact another one of the docents to cover today's shift.

She left the lights off downstairs but flipped on the ones over the staircase knowing they would cast enough light for her to take a quick look around on the second floor. On her way up, she noticed something else odd. Earlier, she'd set a small package on the steps to take the rest of the way up later when she was done working in the post office. It was gone, which meant someone else had been in the museum at some point.

Her footsteps slowed as she paused to listen. Nothing but silence. Whoever had been there was gone now. Picking up speed again, she reached the top of the steps where she paused to look around. Nothing seemed out of place, and the package she'd been concerned about was sitting on the corner of her desk. No unauthorized intruder would have known that's where it went. That meant the docent on duty today must have come through while Shelby was busy next door.

She checked the schedule and saw that Helen Nagy was supposed to be there today. Maybe the elderly woman had come in early to get ready for the day and then left to get a cup of coffee and a treat from her daughter's bakery down the street. If so, why hadn't Helen stopped to ask if Shelby might like something? That's what she normally did. All in all, Shelby's instincts were insisting that something was definitely out of whack, but what? To find out, she started at the first display on the right and then slowly continued around the room. Nothing appeared to be disturbed, at least along the perimeter.

That left one last place to check. By that point, her pulse was pumping a heavy dose of adrenaline through her veins. It took every bit of willpower she could muster to approach the display case that housed the museum's most prized possession—or at least used to. Feeling sick and scared, she stared at the empty custom-made stand.

"This is bad. This is so bad."

The words quickly became her mantra. Mumbling them over and over again did nothing to resolve the problem, but she couldn't seem to stop herself. Actually, the situation wasn't simply bad; it was catastrophic. Or it would be as soon as the news got out.

With that in mind, she immediately hustled back downstairs to lock the doors. It might disappoint random tourists, but her desperate measures wouldn't keep the locals out for long. Meanwhile, she would call Helen and ask if she knew what had happened to the nugget, or better yet, *if* she'd actually been the one who took it. It wasn't like Shelby had proof that Helen was involved one way or the other. All of the docents had keys to the building and access to the security codes that would have allowed them to remove the nugget without setting off the alarm.

Regardless of who was behind the theft... no, she couldn't call it that. None of the docents would actually steal the nugget. More likely one or more of them decided that it needed to be squirreled away someplace they deemed safe until the threat presented by Max Volkov was eliminated. Didn't they know that Cade would have a very different take on the situation? As the curator of the museum, her duty was to inform him immediately of the situation. But before she'd gone two steps toward the phone to do exactly that, an image of Helen, Earl or even Ilse being locked up in the town's single jail cell popped into her head.

She shuddered. There was no way she could let that happen. She believed right down to her bones that the intentions of whoever had taken the nugget had been misguided, not criminal. That made it imperative she find out who had taken the nugget and demand its return before anyone else noticed it was gone.

But before that, she needed to come up with a believable excuse for the museum being closed for the day. As she headed back down to the first floor, she turned off the lights again. That got her to thinking. Everyone knew the wiring in the building was old. Maybe claiming there was some kind of malfunction would buy her some time. She hurried over to the box and switched off two of the circuit breakers. The lie wouldn't hold for long but might buy her enough time to make some calls.

That was what she was contemplating when a knock at the front door scared the wits out of her. When she saw who was waiting out on the sidewalk, she froze. What was Cade doing there? Had he somehow figured out what had happened? She immediately rejected that idea. The man was good at his job, but that didn't mean he could somehow magically sense when a crime had been committed. At least she hoped that was true. If it wasn't, she was in big trouble.

They all were.

CHAPTER TEN

CADE WAITED IMPATIENTLY for Shelby to respond to his summons. She shook her head at him, maybe hoping he'd assume she was busy and didn't have time to talk. She should've known better. Seeing her hovering in the back corner of the room and looking guilty was bound to set off all kinds alarms for him.

When she still refused to come near the door, he scribbled a note that said if she didn't open the door, he would break the glass and let himself in. When he held it against the window, she crept close enough to read it. She shot him a narrow-eyed look that made it clear that she didn't appreciate the threat, but at least she unlocked the door before retreating back into the shadows near the staircase.

What on earth had her so spooked? Not wanting to draw any attention from people out on the street, he slipped inside and locked the door again. As soon as he got a good look at her face, he took her by the arm and led her to the other side of the building and down the hall to the break room.

"Sit down before you fall down."

At least she gave in to his demand without protest. After making sure she'd stay put, he began rummaging in the cabinets. Pulling out a granola bar, he shoved it toward her. "Eat that."

Her chin came up in protest. "Stop bossing me around, Cade Peters."

"I will stop issuing orders as soon as you aren't looking like death warmed over. Eat."

She took several small bites. Meanwhile, he turned the other chair around and straddled it, leaning his arms on the back and keeping a wary eye on her. Oddly enough, something about his actions caused her to smile.

He tilted his head to one side and frowned at her. "What's so funny?"

"I was just trying to decide if you're watching me like a hawk or more like a mother hen."

Cute. He pushed his hat back further on his head and relaxed. "Let's just assume it's a bit of both."

Her smile turned brittle. "So, what brings

you to my neck of the woods today, Chief Peters?"

"We'll get to that in a minute. Right now, I want to know what's happened that has you so spooked?"

She'd been about to take another bite of the granola bar, but she dropped it back down on the table and threaded her fingers together in a futile attempt to hide the fact her hands were shaking. "Well, Cade, we… I…the town might have a little problem."

He sat up straighter, his hands latching onto the back of the chair with a white-knuckled grip. "And what's that?"

Her eyes glistened with tears as she whispered her answer. "The nugget."

"What about it?"

"It's gone."

As soon as the words left her mouth, Cade had no choice but to transform from a concerned friend into his alter ego, the cop.

"Run that by me again."

"The Trillium Nugget is gone."

"Since when?"

Right now she was looking everywhere but at him. "I don't know, Cade. I noticed no one had turned on the lights in the museum and went over to take a look around. I had set a package on the steps earlier and noticed it was missing. I went upstairs to see if someone had taken up there without me hearing, and that's when I realized it was missing. The nugget, not the package."

In an effort to control his temper, he spoke slowly, carefully enunciating each word. "When were you going to call me? Because that's what people normally do when they discover something has been stolen."

Her eyes flared wide at that last word. "I only found out a few minutes ago. Besides, I never said it was stolen."

"So you didn't mean what you said about the nugget being gone?" Then he pointed toward the ceiling. "If I go upstairs right now, will I find it safely inside that glass cabinet with the security alarms turned on?"

"Well, no. Not right now. Maybe later, though."

He sighed. "Shelby, I don't have the time or energy to play word games. Did you or did you not just tell me the Trillian Nugget has gone missing?"

She dropped her gaze back down to the

table, her shoulders slumping in defeat. "Yes, I did say that."

"Then explain what happened."

"When I went upstairs, I noticed the case was empty."

He whipped out his notebook and started writing. "To your knowledge, has the security alarm gone off since the last time you saw the nugget in the case?"

"No."

Now they were getting somewhere. If some outsider had broken into the museum, the alarm should have gone off. "Was there any sign that someone broke into the museum? I didn't notice any damage at either of the front doors into this building, but I don't remember how many exits there are."

"Two in front. One in back."

"Okay, I think we can pretty much rule out the front doors. Have you checked the other one?

"Not yet."

He rubbed his forehead and prayed for patience. Couldn't she just tell him what he needed to know without him having to pry it out of her word by word? "And how about windows?"

"None of the front ones have been tampered with. There aren't any windows on the side walls." She pointed toward the small window over the sink in the break room. "That's the only one on the back wall on this level."

The she frowned. "Although I'm not sure it's big enough for an adult to squeeze through. What do you think?"

He gave the window a dismissive glance. "I think it doesn't matter since it isn't damaged. Besides, it has bars on the outside."

"Oh, right. Anyway, there are a couple on both the front and back walls upstairs. They were all closed as far as I can remember, but I didn't check to see if they were locked."

"Okay, we'll do that in a minute."

She angled her head as if trying to read his notes. "What are you writing down?"

He didn't bother to look up. "Information for my official report about the theft."

She stood up almost knocking her chair over in the process. "What report? No one has called the police to investigate anything."

"Then isn't it handy that I just happened to stop by? It saved you having to call. Can't say Dunbar's finest doesn't give prompt service."

"Very funny."

His eyes snapped up to stare into hers. "Do you really think I find any of this amusing? If the nugget has been stolen, the whole town is in trouble."

"That's just it. I don't think it's been stolen. Not really, anyway."

He tossed his pen down on the table hard enough to send it bouncing off the edge onto the floor. "Then please tell me what's going on."

She followed the progress of the pen rolling across the tile and then looked back at him. "I was trying to figure that out when you forced me to let you into the building. I'm sure there's a reasonable explanation for what's happened, but having you sitting here glaring at me isn't helping the situation one bit."

Cade snarled right back at her. "Well, excuse me for being upset about a valuable artifact going missing from the museum. Do you think it's a coincidence that it happened right about the time I informed the mayor and the city council about Maxim Volkov's claim on that very same artifact? How do you think that's going to look to him?"

"Honestly, I don't really care what he thinks."

Cade retrieved his pen and stuck his notebook back into his pocket. "Let's go upstairs."

"Fine, but there's nothing for you to see." She started toward the door, but then turned back. "Quite literally, actually, so there's no reason to go up there. The case is empty, but the door is closed and the alarm is on."

"We still need to check. Then I'm going to need a list of everyone who knows the alarm codes. I have the contact information for the security company on file in my office. I'll be calling them as soon as we get done here. For now, I want to look around upstairs."

SHELBY SURRENDERED TO the inevitable and followed him down the hall. This was so bad and getting worse. Having Cade show up was like dropping a pebble in a quiet pool of water, sending an ever-spreading series of ripples flowing outward. Didn't he realize that the more he poked and prodded at the situation, the worse it was going to get? Not just for her, but the museum and the town.

Even knowing he wouldn't back down, she had to try to convince him to give her a chance to fix things. "Cade, please, I understand why you're acting this way. You're a cop, and you think a crime has been committed.

He cut her off. "And you don't?"

"Let's just say that I'm really hoping that's not the case."

He rolled his eyes. "Then you're either complicit or naive."

"I'm neither one. I just think there's another explanation."

"Such as?"

"Someone took the nugget to protect it."

"And who would that be?"

She wasn't going to accuse Helen Nagy without more solid evidence than just seeing her name on the schedule. "I don't know."

"But you have suspicions."

She nodded before she could stop herself. "But that's all they are. I don't have any proof."

"And you don't trust me enough to let me do my job."

She hated that he was so disappointed in her. There wasn't much she could do about it right now. It was too much to hope that he would go back to his office and let her handle the problem. She scurried to catch up with him, because he was already on his way up to the second floor. Rather than let him stumble around in the darkness, she restored the circuit breakers and turned on the lights before charging up after him.

By the time she reached the top of the steps, she was out of breath and too late to throw herself between him and the empty case. Not that it would've accomplished anything. Nothing changed the fact that the nugget had gone missing sometime between yesterday and today.

As he slowly walked around the display case, Cade asked, "How many people know the security codes? Is it just the people who actually work here at the museum or would former board members know them?"

Visions of him dragging in all of the docents and grilling them for hours filled her head. "We change the codes whenever someone leaves the board or someone new comes on."

"So how many people are on the current board?"

"Counting me?"

He didn't so much as glance in her direction. "Yes, Shelby, counting you."

"Seven."

Out came the notebook. "I need their names and when they work."

Shelby would have no choice but to give him a copy of the schedule at some point. She just wished he'd give her a chance to talk to them first. "Why?"

By that point, Cade had knelt in front of the cabinet to snap several pictures of the lock with his phone. "Don't play innocent with me, Shelby. If no one set off the alarm, then logic dictates that whoever opened the case knew the codes. That gives me a pretty limited pool of suspects."

He finally gave her a quick look. "Unless you know of anyone else who could have the code."

"Well, I don't know if the actual security code is on file in your office or if you only have the password to get the security company to override the alarm."

"How about the county sheriff's department?"

She shook her head. "No, we've never seen the need to include them since the museum is within the Dunbar city limits. That makes it your jurisdiction."

"Okay, I'll check on that when I get back to my office. Now, give me those names."

She just couldn't do it even if refusing only

delayed the inevitable. He could always get them from Oscar. Bracing herself for the worst, she threw her shoulders back and crossed her fingers that she wasn't about to do the silliest thing imaginable. "There's no need to bother any of them, Chief Peters. I'm responsible for the nugget's disappearance."

"Shelby, I don't believe for one minute that you took it. I need you to explain what happened."

When she mimed zipping her lips shut, he growled, "Fine. You want me to play hardball, I will. Shelby Michaels, I'm arresting you for impeding a police investigation."

"That's ridiculous, Cade. You don't want to do this."

He stepped closer, tension pouring off him in waves. "You're right, Shelby. I don't. But I already warned you that I'm a cop first and foremost. There's a price to be paid for interfering with my ability to do my job."

He pointed at the empty case. "Someone stole the nugget. Now, I get that you might not know what actually happened. However, I'm guessing you figure someone you know, someone you like, is responsible for the theft.

You're trying to protect them from the consequences of their actions, aren't you?"

She found herself nodding even when she hadn't meant to. As much as she wanted to move toward Cade, to have him wrap her in his arms and tell her everything was going to be okay, she knew that wasn't his role in this disaster.

He was back to lecturing her. "Shelby, in cases like this, good intentions don't matter. Whether it was one person or the entire board, they don't have the authority to take the nugget. That makes it theft. And based on the amount of money that hunk of gold is worth, it's a felony, not a misdemeanor."

She gasped. "That means someone could end up really going to prison, Cade. You can't let that happen."

"That's the law. That means whoever committed the theft, regardless of the reason, belongs behind bars, Shelby. They should've thought about that before they did something so ill-advised."

Not only were most of the board members getting up there in years, at least one or two had health issues that didn't bode well for them surviving the experience. There was only one thing she could do right now. "Like I said, I hold myself responsible for the loss of the nugget, Cade. Make of that what you will."

He flexed his hands as if fighting the urge to shake some sense into her. "Shelby, there is no way you stole that nugget, and there's nothing you can tell me that will convince me you did. One last time, who are you protecting?"

Looking back, she should've known that someone would panic and do something foolish in an effort to prevent the town's heritage from being stolen. The news of the threat had obviously thrown one or more of the committee members into a complete dither. At this point, all she could do was hope that they'd come to their senses soon and return the nugget to its rightful place. In order to buy them the time they needed to do exactly that, it looked like she'd have to take one for the team.

Taking a leap of faith that her friends wouldn't let her suffer for their sins, at least not for long, she looked at Cade and held out her wrists. "It doesn't matter if you believe me or not, Chief Peters."

"Shelby, you're incredibly brave or totally nuts. I hope whoever you're protecting appreciates what you're doing for them. And just so you know, I don't appreciate it one bit."

Turning away, he started for the steps. "Let's go."

She felt rather foolish standing there holding her arms out like one of those scary creatures in a zombie movie. Dropping them back down to her sides, she asked, "Aren't you going to cuff me?"

His answering laugh was too dark to indicate any kind of humor. "Don't push me, Shelby. Don't forget to lock the doors and grab your purse if you have one."

At least he trusted her enough to allow her the dignity of turning herself in. "I promise I won't be long. I'll head over to your office in a few minutes."

That irritating laugh was back. "Sorry, Shelby, but the police department doesn't operate on the honor system. When we arrest someone, we provide personal escort service. We're nice about stuff like that."

She didn't appreciate his sarcasm, but she strongly suspected Cade was hanging on to his temper by the thinnest of threads right now. Regardless, he gave her time to check all of the doors to make sure they were locked even if he did roll his eyes when she set the alarm on their way out. Both of them knew the town only paid for the security service in order to protect the nugget, and it was a bit too late for that.

Outside, he checked for traffic before marching her across the street. When she stumbled, he took her arm and gently supported her the rest of the way. Moira was at her desk when they finally made it through the front door of the police department.

Moira started to smile, but it quickly faded once she got a better look at the two of them. "Hey, Shelby, Chief. What's up?"

"Ms. Michaels is going to be our guest for a while. How long that will be is up to her."

Still holding on to her arm, he took her purse and handed it to Moira. "Secure her valuables."

It was a good thing Cade had answered Moira's question. Right then Shelby couldn't have strung two words together. Instead, she let her captor lead her around the front desk and down the hall to her new accommoda-tions. She hadn't ventured this far into the police department since grade school when her entire class was given a tour of the place by Cade's predecessor. Looking around, she thought maybe they might have painted the walls at some point, but otherwise it was pretty much the same as it had been back then.

It was mortifying when Cade finally came to a stop in front of the town's only jail cell. He pulled out a ring of keys and used one to unlock the door. Then he offered her a slight bow and swept his hand in the direction of the cell. "Your room awaits."

When Shelby found the strength to walk inside, Moira cleared her throat and asked, "Chief, you don't really mean to do this, do you? What are the charges?"

"Not now, Officer Fraser."

The anger in his voice had the other woman in full retreat. Maybe realizing he was taking his temper out on the wrong person, he softened his next words. "She's here for interfering in a police investigation. And if anyone else has questions, I gave her every chance to avoid this. Ask her if you don't believe me."

Shelby could manage that much. "He did."

With that, Moira disappeared back down

the hall. At a loss as to what to do next, Shelby sat on the narrow cot on the far wall. Cade stared at her in stony silence for several seconds before speaking. "Let's see how long your stubbornness holds up after this cell door slams shut."

Then he swung it closed with a bang. After giving her one more disgusted look, he disappeared into his office and slammed that door, too.

CHAPTER ELEVEN

EVERY MAN HAD REGRETS. Some were harder to live with than others, and those were the ones that sat squarely on Cade's conscience and kept him awake nights, leaving him with a mammoth headache the next morning. Right now, he rubbed his temples and debated whether it was too soon to take a second dose of aspirin. Even if it wasn't, he wondered if the people staging a protest out in the street weren't right, and that he deserved to suffer.

After all, he was the one who had locked the Saint of Dunbar in jail.

His office was in the back of the department, but he could still hear the chanting. He couldn't make out the actual words, but the anger echoed through the building just fine. The entire town was up in arms about his unfair treatment of Shelby Michaels. As it turned out, even his own staff wasn't above making a few acerbic comments under their breath when they passed by.

Cade had finally sent Oscar out on patrol even though it was his day to man the front desk. Although, to be honest, he ought to put the man on administrative leave since Oscar's name was on Cade's short list of suspects along with the rest of the museum's executive board. Eventually, he'd have to ask his officer a few pointed questions, but he kept hoping the culprit or culprits would voluntarily step forward to confess their sins.

It wasn't a surprise that news of Shelby's arrest had spread like wildfire through town yesterday afternoon. Less than an hour after he'd slammed the cell door shut, a delegation of concerned citizens showed up to demand her release. When he'd refused, they'd marched down the street to seek an audience at city hall.

Apparently, the mayor had somehow caught wind that trouble was brewing in town. By the time the delegation reached Mayor Klaus's doorstep, the man had taken off for parts unknown for an overnight fishing trip. A rather gleeful Mrs. Klaus let it be known she planned to use this act of pure cowardice against Otto when she ran for mayor again in the next election. Cade had already made a note to make a donation to her campaign.

TJ Shaw, Cade's most recent hire, appeared in his doorway. "Chief, Titus Kondrat called. He wants to come in the back door. He has Ms. Michaels's lunch and doesn't want to have to wade through that bunch out front."

Cade sighed. "I'll go let him in."

Five minutes later, Cade opened the back door so Titus could slip inside. "Any trouble getting here?"

"Nothing I couldn't handle. A couple of people demanded to know what I was up to. As soon as I explained that I was bringing a meal to the prisoner, they let me pass."

He held up the smaller of two baskets. "This one is for Shelby."

Crossing his fingers, Cade asked, "And that other one?"

Titus's mouth quirked up with the barest hint of a smile as he handed it over. "I figure even a condemned man deserves a decent meal."

"Very funny." Titus's answering chuckle made Cade want to punch him, but he knew better. "But thanks. I appreciate it."

"You're welcome. There should be enough for you and a couple of your officers."

Cade reached for his wallet. "How much do I owe you?"

"It's on the house." Titus leaned against the wall and studied Cade for a second. "Bea from the coffee shop told me all about your dastardly deeds. Of course, I acted suitably horrified until she departed to continue her town crier duties. But after that, well, let's just say I can't remember the last time I've laughed that hard. I feel bad about it because I know you're between a nugget and a hard place right now. The bottom line is that I'll keep you and Shelby both fed as long as she's your guest in this fine establishment."

"Jerk." Cade didn't put any heat in the word. If their positions were reversed, he probably would've laughed, too. Besides, Titus was taking a risk just by being there. No one would fault him for feeding Shelby, but things might not go well if the people in town got it in their heads that he was siding with the enemy. "Let's head into my office. You can keep me company while I eat. I could use some conversation, and apparently you're the only one in town willing to talk to me right now."

After the two of them filed into his office, Cade considered what to do with the second basket. Finally, he sighed. "Change of plans. There's a small conference room down the hall that we can use. I'll see if Shelby would like to eat with the two of us. Better yet, Moira is out front this morning. The two of them are friends, so I'll ask her to join us since you brought enough to feed her as well."

Titus took the baskets and headed for the other room, leaving Cade to face Shelby on his own. It was probably better that way. Neither of them had gotten much sleep last night, and he doubted her mood was any better than his. He'd camped out on the folding cot they kept around for the rare occasion when their sole cell was occupied overnight. He'd tried without success to sleep, because all he could hear was Shelby pacing the floor until all hours.

Did he feel guilty? Yes. He was also really irritated that she hadn't trusted him enough to help her deal with the situation. Now everyone in town was on his case. Didn't they realize he had to do his job? Why couldn't anyone understand that? Sure, people wanted the police to be at their beck and call when it came to arresting criminals. They just never envisioned those same officers having to make the hard call when it came to arresting someone they liked and respected.

He stopped to make a quick call. "Moira, I'd like you to take your lunch break now. Meet me in the conference room. I'm bringing Shelby, and I thought she'd like having you there."

Coward that he was, he hung up before Moira could say a word. Unsure of his welcome, he sidled up to the door of the cell. Shelby was sitting on her cot, back to the wall, knees drawn up on the paper-thin mattress. She looked up long enough to give him a stony look and then went back to staring at the water stains on the ceiling as if they were the most fascinating thing she'd ever seen. Cute.

"Lunch is ready."

She dragged her gaze down to his empty hands. "Not interested."

Time to play his ace. "Titus put together a picnic basket just for you, so I'm betting there's a piece of pie in there. But if you're not hungry, I'm pretty sure I can choke down some coconut cream this one time."

Just that quickly, Shelby was up on her feet and glaring at him through the bars. "Don't you dare. It's mine. Bring it to me."

It was nice to see she hadn't lost her fiery spirit. "We're going to eat in the conference room."

"We?"

"Yep, we. As in you, me, Moira and Titus, so you won't be alone with me." He inched closer. "Well, unless you want to be. I can always send Moira out to do crowd control and tell Titus to get lost."

"Let me out."

He put the key in the lock. Before turning it, though, maybe he should make it clear there were limits to her freedom. "We'll have lunch and some friendly conversation. After that, one of two things will happen."

"Which are?"

"Either you'll tell me who you think took the nugget or you'll be right back here where you started. Understand?"

When she jerked her head in a quick nod, he guided her down the hall to the conference room. Moira was there waiting for them, but there was no sign of Titus. Where had he gone? Then he spotted a note on the table.

After reading it, he wadded the paper up and tossed it in the trashcan. "Evidently Titus got an urgent call that he was needed back at the café."

"That's too bad. I would've liked to thank him for bringing me lunch."

Cade handed Shelby the basket that held her lunch. "You can tell him the next time you see him. He said he'd keep feeding you as long as you remain a guest here at the station."

Moira peeked into the other basket. Her eyes widened in surprise. "Wow, if this is how we feed prisoners, I'm surprised more people aren't acting up just to get a free meal."

Shelby took offense at that comment. "Hey, I'm not in here because I was acting up."

Moira winced. "Sorry, Shelby. I know that. I've just never seen jail food that looked anything like this."

Cade didn't want to discuss why Shelby was there while they ate lunch. "Let's just eat. Titus said there was enough for several people. When we're done, let TJ and Oscar know they can help themselves."

He let Moira take her choice of the sandwiches and side salads first. That didn't mean he was foolish enough to let anyone else put their grubby mitts on the one piece of Dutch apple pie Titus had packed. Luckily, Moira didn't seem to mind having to settle for the blueberry.

Shelby was still pulling items out of her basket. Titus had really gone to town for her. There was a huge slice of quiche, two sandwiches, and three side orders. She looked at him in confusion. "Seriously, how big of an appetite does that man think I have? Not that I'm complaining."

When she finally reached her desserts, she was smiling like Cade hadn't seen her do in far too long. "Coconut cream pie, cheesecake and bread pudding all for me! Titus is a saint."

Moira frowned as she stared at the huge array of food Shelby had pulled out of her basket. "I suspect Mr. Kondrat is a lot of things, but a saint wouldn't be one of them. I'd bet anything that he hasn't always been a short-order cook. I don't actually know him, but from a distance he looks like the kind of guys I used to arrest."

Cade didn't exactly disagree with Moira's assessment of the man. Titus definitely had secrets, and along the way something had marked him in ways that had nothing to do with his tattoos. Even so, Cade wasn't convinced Titus had lived on the wrong side of the law. Maybe he would eventually trust Cade enough to share a few details.

The two women were busy unwrapping their food. Moira had taken the chair at one end of the table while Shelby sat along the side next to her. They would probably both prefer if he parked himself as far away as possible, but that wasn't happening. He deliberately sat down directly across from Shelby. "This is really going to hit the spot."

Neither woman responded, but he didn't expect them to. They were navigating uncharted territory, and it would be all too easy to end up on the rocks. It was too much to hope that a good meal and some time with Moira would convince Shelby to confide in him. He suspected she would continue to protect whoever had taken the nugget no matter what he had to say on the matter.

He could only hope that her friends wouldn't let her take the fall for their misdeeds. Either way, he was going to cut Shelby loose even if they didn't come forward soon. She deserved better than to be used as a pawn in this chess game between him and whoever had taken the nugget. They might think they were protecting the town's heritage, but they were doing so at the risk of ruining their own lives. The nugget was valuable, but it wasn't worth spending their waning years in prison.

But that was a problem for later. Right now, he wasn't going to disrespect Titus's thoughtful gift by bringing up tough subjects while the three of them ate lunch. There would be plenty of time for those difficult discussions after he finished his pie.

IF SHELBY HAD been thinking Cade took pleasure in locking her up, a close look at him would've dissuaded her. Even though he'd chosen to sit across from her, he hadn't given her so much as a glance, providing her the opportunity to study him. He'd insisted on being the one to spend the night at the jail, which probably accounted for why he hadn't shaved. She'd deny it to her dying day, but she liked the hint of scruff and how it emphasized his rugged good looks.

He'd also brought her a few basic necessities like a toothbrush, toothpaste and even a scrunchie so she could braid her hair. She wasn't sure about the ins and outs of jailhouse etiquette, but simple good manners dictated that she should thank him for his thoughtfulness. But not now while they had an audience. Oddly enough, she suspected he wouldn't want to be caught being kind. The same might be true of Titus since he'd bailed rather than stick around to have lunch with them.

After finishing her quiche, she reached for her pie. Before eating it, she separated the rest of her bounty into two piles. On one side, she stacked her remaining two desserts, a sandwich and a salad. The rest she set next to the larger basket that Titus had brought for Cade and his officers to share.

"This is enough for later. Everything else is up for grabs."

Cade had been about to eat his apple pie. "Are you sure? Titus said he'd keep feeding you, so I took that to mean he'd be dropping off dinner later."

"I shouldn't take advantage of his generosity. Well, unless it's Thursday, and we're talking about chicken and dumplings. Then all bets are off."

He gave her an interesting look. Was he thinking about the afternoon the two of them had had lunch together? She'd been hoping they'd cross paths at the cafe again soon, if not for more dumplings, then for whatever special happened to be on the menu. But after everything that had happened, she had to wonder if there was any kind of future left for the two of them that wouldn't be forever tarnished.

It was amazing how much that thought hurt, especially considering they'd only shared one lunch and one semidisastrous hike.

She realized both Cade and Moira were staring at her. How long had she been lost in thought?

Long enough for Moira to find it funny. "Maybe you should try to get some rest this afternoon if your brain is that fried. Didn't you sleep last night?"

No, she hadn't. Not much anyway. The cot in her cell had been miserably uncomfortable. On second thought, it wasn't her cell. It was Cade's or at least he was in charge of it. It was his fault she spent the night tossing and turning, and not just because of the thin, lumpy mattress. Too many strange noises made it difficult to relax. And not for a single second did she forget about the man who'd spent the night right down the hall.

It had been tempting to scream at him for putting her through all of this, but they both knew it wasn't really his fault. The blame belonged to whoever had taken the nugget in the first place. Why hadn't the person come forward when they learned she'd been arrested like she'd thought they would?

She closed the lid on her slice of pie and set her fork aside. "Actually, I am tired. I'm going to take my pie back to the cell and eat it later."

Cade studied her for several seconds and then glanced at Moira. Evidently she could read his silences better than Shelby could, because she immediately shoved all of the remaining food back into the baskets. "I should get back to work. I'll put this stuff in the fridge and let TJ and Oscar know they can help themselves."

She was out the door before Shelby could even say goodbye. "Boy, that was impressive."

Her sole remaining companion leaned back in his chair looking puzzled. "What was?"

"How you managed to send a highly trained

police officer scampering out of the room with just a look. Does that require special training or were you born with that superpower?"

To her surprise, he laughed. "No, just years of practice. I try not to use it too often, but sometimes it saves having to explain myself. She rightly understood that we needed to talk without an audience."

He was right about that, but that didn't mean she appreciated him making the decision without consulting her. "She's a friend, Cade."

"She's also a police officer, Shelby. I assumed that you wouldn't want to put her in a position where she had to choose between your friendship and her duties."

And there he went being right again. "So, what supersecret thing do you want to talk about?"

He shifted to lean in closer, elbows on the table, his dark eyes looking more resigned than hopeful. "Give me a reason not to put you back in that cell."

"I don't know who removed the nugget, Cade."

He nodded as if that confirmed something he'd already suspected. "So even though you said you were responsible for its disappearance, you didn't actually steal it yourself."

It was time to raise the white flag. She'd foolishly thought whichever board member had decided to hide the nugget would come forward when it got out that she had been arrested. Well, more or less. Come to think of it, no one had taken her mug shot or read her any rights. What kind of game was Cade playing here? "No one stole it, Cade. I'm quite sure the nugget is tucked away someplace safe."

"Safer than across the street with the extremely expensive alarm system the town has been paying for?" He shook his head. "Not that it actually prevented someone from waltzing out with the nugget and making a clean getaway. I guess no one ever expected an inside job."

"It's not a theft, Cade. Not exactly, anyway. I should've guessed that someone on the board would panic at the thought of some stranger trying to abscond with the nugget." She sighed in frustration. "I really thought they'd come to their senses by now."

He drummed his fingers on the table. "That would've been nice. I know I lost my temper yesterday, but I can't just ignore the situation.

I have to investigate. It didn't help that you kept claiming responsibility. Why would you do that when you knew you weren't guilty?"

"Think about it, Cade. I'm the only one on the board who is under seventy. Most are in their eighties. I couldn't stand the thought of you having to put one of them in that cell and slamming the door shut. We both know that's what your job would have demanded."

She'd never seen Cade look more confused than he was right now. "Huh? You were worried about me? Not just your friends?"

"Of course I was worried about you. This situation is complicated, and you're caught in the middle. No matter how this turns out, it could be rough going for you. The last thing you needed was to start locking up geriatric citizens."

He huffed a small laugh. "I wish you would have just talked to me, Shelby."

"I would've if you'd—"

Suddenly he held up a hand to cut her off. "Hush for a second."

He stared at the door, leaning forward as if listening to something. Finally, she heard it too. If she had to guess, some kind of ruckus had erupted in the front lobby and was now headed their way. Cade was up and moving for the door. “Stay where you are until I find out what’s going on out there.”

It was tempting to follow him, but for now she did as ordered. There was no use getting caught up in what now sounded like a small riot. Moira’s voice rang out over the noise, but it was hard to decipher what she was saying. Shelby put her ear against the door to see if she could figure out what was going on. As it turned out, it wasn’t necessary. Cade must have been standing right on the other side of the door when he bellowed, “Everybody, shut up!”

The resulting silence lasted but a few seconds before the babbling started up again as one person after another tried to get their point across by hollering over everyone else. Smiling, Shelby gave it another ten seconds before Cade went ballistic. One, two, three… That’s as far as she got before he blew.

“I’ll give all of you one minute to get out of here. After that, we’ll start making arrests.”

“Like you did poor Shelby? Just know we’ll be filing suit if you’ve mistreated her.”

Shelby was pretty sure that threat came from Bea O’Malley. Then Moira joined the conversation. "No one is abusing anyone. I just had lunch with Shelby. She's fine."

Another party joined the fray. "She didn't deserve to get arrested. Everyone knows she'd never make off with the Trillium Nugget. Chief Peters, why haven't you arrested that out-of-towner? He's the only one with a real motive. His claim is bogus and he knows it."

Shelby would've recognized that snooty voice anywhere. While she made a genuine effort to see the good in everyone, she'd been less than successful when it came to Eileen Southworth. The woman had a real knack for sounding as if she were talking down to lesser beings no matter what the subject was.

Shelby opened the door just a sliver to get a peek at what was going on out there. Cade had his hands on his hips as he glared at the crowd that had yet to disperse. He directed his comments to the councilwoman. "Mrs. Southworth, we've already had this discussion. I cannot and will not arrest a man who has done nothing illegal simply because you don't like why he's in town. However, I *will* arrest people for creating a disturbance. We might have only one cell, but I'm sure you won't mind sharing it with your fellow conspirators."

It was hard not to laugh at the outraged gasp that echoed down the hall. Poor Cade, he didn't deserve this. Maybe it was time to set a few people straight on the facts of the situation. She stepped out into the hallway to stand next to him. He shot her a look that made it clear he didn't appreciate her ignoring his orders.

At least her appearance ended the shouting. She took a deep breath and let it out slowly as she considered what she should say. She was saved from having to speak when the back door of the building crashed open and Oscar Lovell rushed in. Upon seeing the mob gathered in the hall, he came to an abrupt halt and desperately looked around for a port in the storm. A second later, he headed for Cade.

"Good news, Chief. The nugget is back!"

CHAPTER TWELVE

OSCAR'S ANNOUNCEMENT SILENCED the crowd for all of five seconds before the shouting started up again. Ignoring the babbling fools, Cade grabbed Shelby's arm with one hand and Oscar's with the other and headed right back for the conference room. As soon as they cleared the threshold, he released his hold on them to close the door and lock it. He'd apologize to Moira later for leaving her to deal with the riffraff, but right now he had better things to do than crowd control.

When the door did little to muffle the noise, he changed his mind. "Stay here. I'll be right back."

Out in the hall, he marched toward the front of the station, forcing Eileen Southworth and her cronies into a slow but steady retreat. "Everyone, go home or back to work or wherever else you should be right now."

"But what was that about the nugget?"

That came from the back of the group, but he was pretty sure it was another of the town council members asking the question. "I will inform the mayor and the council of my findings as soon as possible. Right now I know as much as you do. The longer you keep yammering at me, the longer you'll have to wait for answers to your questions. For now, Officer Fraser will see all of you out."

When Moira nodded that she'd heard him, he added, "Now, everybody."

Then he crossed his arms over his chest and waited for them to disperse. When a few dug in their heels, he upped the ante. "Anyone who continues interfering with my staff's ability to do their jobs will be escorted into the cell down the hall to make sure you don't get in the way. One, two..."

It was hard not to snicker as the remaining lurkers scattered like cockroaches. As much as he regretted putting Shelby in that cell, at least there was one positive outcome—people now knew that Cade didn't bluff.

"Moira, we're in the conference room if you need anything. I'm hoping it won't take long to figure out what's going on."

"Got it, Chief." Then she grinned at him.

"Nicely played, by the way. I bet that's the fastest some of those folks have moved in years."

He laughed and rejoined Oscar and Shelby. The pair had been chatting about something but went silent as soon as he opened the door. Maybe they'd been talking about the weather, but the guilty look on Shelby's face made it clear that hadn't been the case.

Which meant he was going to have to have a talk with Oscar, one that the older man probably wouldn't enjoy. However, that could wait. This conversation was about the nugget and where it had been since it had disappeared from the museum. "No more secrets, Shelby. That's what got us into this mess in the first place. I want the truth. All of it."

Oscar blanched. "Shelby, we can't..."

Cade wasn't having it. "Yes, Oscar, you can and will. For Pete's sake, you're a cop and should know better. There are penalties for withholding evidence in an ongoing investigation."

He half expected Shelby to leap to Oscar's defense, but she didn't. Instead, she motioned for everyone to sit down. When they were settled into chairs, Cade got out his notebook and prepared to take notes.

When he clicked his pen several times to hurry her along, she rolled her eyes. “Fine, Oscar was just telling me that one of the board members thought the Trillium Nugget was looking a bit…dull, isn’t that what you said, Oscar?”

He nodded like a bobblehead doll. “Yes, that’s it exactly. In fact, I’d noticed it myself. I suppose that’s to be expected since the cleaning lady can only clean the outside of the display case.”

It was obvious where they were heading with this. Did they really think Cade would believe such a ridiculous explanation? Evidently they did since Shelby plowed on ahead. “Anyway, this member of the board took the nugget home to give it a good scrubbing and polish.”

Cade set his pen aside and leaned back in his chair. “That’s odd. I wasn’t actually aware that gold could get tarnished.”

Shelby wrinkled her nose. “I think it’s more that it got dusty.”

Right. “Inside a glass cabinet?”

To keep her from only digging herself in

deeper, he redirected the conversation. "And this person didn't think to notify you as the curator of the museum of his or her decision to take an extremely valuable artifact out for a bath?"

Shelby threaded her fingers together as she set her hands on the table. She shot Oscar a quelling look when it appeared as if he was going to interject something into the conversation. "Well, no. She…or he…didn't think to call me or even leave a note. Rest assured I'll be addressing this issue at our next board meeting to ensure that the same thing doesn't happen again in the future. We have procedures in place that should be followed when any artifact in the museum, regardless of its monetary value, needs to be removed from the premises for repair or refurbishing."

She turned a rather tight smile in Cade's direction. "Chief Peters, I hope you will accept my apology on behalf of our entire board for the kerfuffle this has caused."

What was he supposed to do now? She was lying through her teeth about the situation, and all three of them knew it. Again, her apparent lack of trust in him was irritating. Maybe she'd see fit to be more honest with him if they didn't have an audience, especially one that neither of them could trust to keep his mouth shut.

He glanced in Oscar's direction. "Officer Lovell, you may return to your normal duties."

Oscar scurried toward the exit in a heartbeat. Cade waited until he reached the door before adding, "I will expect you in my office at 8:30 tomorrow morning. We will discuss your handling of this entire situation at that time."

Swallowing hard, Oscar nodded. "I'll be there, Chief. And I'm really sorry, Shelby."

That was interesting. What exactly was he apologizing for? That he was abandoning Shelby to face Cade alone? Or that she'd been the one to pay the price for someone else's criminal, if well-intentioned, act? Not that it mattered. At least with him gone, Cade could finally relax. "So, Ms. Michaels, is that the story we're supposed to go with? That just by coincidence when the ownership of the nugget has been called into question, someone decided it couldn't go another day without a good polish?"

At least Shelby seemed to be giving the

matter some thought. "Well, unless you can come up with a better idea. You know, something that doesn't end up with anyone else in that cell. I know good intentions don't mean much when it comes to the law, Cade. But the town will never forgive either of us if you arrest an elderly woman…or man…or both… you know, just for example, and then charge them with a felony."

Her green eyes had a suspicious sheen when she added, "The nugget is back where it belongs, and that's all that matters."

They'd circle back around to that last bit once Cade knew exactly what had happened. "Did Oscar happen to say how he found out the nugget had magically reappeared?"

From the way Shelby fidgeted in her seat, this next part was bound to be another creative explanation. "Helen Nagy went in early to work on the monthly newsletter. When she turned on the lights, she couldn't help but notice the nugget was back in place. She called Oscar since he's both on the board and a police officer. And, well, you might not know this, but he's also her cousin."

Cade pinched the bridge of his nose, hoping

to ease the headache that was making a bad day just that much worse. "Do me a favor."

"Anything you need, Cade."

Several interesting possibilities flashed through his mind, most of which were not at all appropriate under the circumstances. He had to stay on topic. "When you review procedures at your meeting, make sure that every member of the board knows that I'm to be notified whenever there's a matter of serious concern at the museum. Having said that, I will certainly understand if they designate you as the one to reach out to me on behalf of the board. You know, since you're the curator and all."

Then he gave her a smile that held more than a little heat. "In fact, I would prefer that."

She blinked and then blushed. "I'll make a note of it."

"Good. Now, I will notify the mayor and the city council of the extenuating circumstances regarding the temporary disappearance of the nugget. I trust there will be no more unscheduled cleanings."

He let that statement sink in before he continued. While he didn't want to play hardball with Shelby, he had no other choice. "If I pick up even a whiff of someone deciding to remove the nugget from the museum before the legitimacy of Mr. Volkov's claim is resolved, I will personally see that the nugget is taken into custody for safekeeping. Is that clear?"

Her chin came up in a stubborn tilt. "His claim is not legitimate."

"I hope you're right, Shelby, but I don't have the luxury of making that assumption. Regardless, I need to know that you understand what I'm saying. If anyone tries to abscond with the nugget again, I won't let it slide no matter who is responsible."

She flinched as if his words hurt her. "You've made yourself perfectly clear, Chief Peters. Now, may I go home?"

"Of course." He softened his tone, signaling this current crisis had passed. "I'll retrieve your purse from the safe and then drive you there. I'll also retrieve your picnic basket to save you from having to cook tonight."

Looking every bit as tired as he felt, she made no move to stand up. "You know I can walk home. It's not far. I could use the exercise, but also because we seem to keep ending up on opposite sides of this mess. As much as I enjoy your company, it could be seen as a conflict of interest."

Cade walked around the table to offer her his hand. "That might be a problem for everyone else, Shelby. Don't let it be a problem for us. Please let me drive you. At the very least, let's call a truce for today."

He took it as a good sign that she didn't even hesitate. "Okay, that sounds good."

When she stood up, he couldn't help take advantage of their close proximity. He released her hand and instead wrapped his arms around her. She leaned in close, resting her head against his shoulder. "I hate this, Cade. Why did that awful man have to come to Dunbar and stir up trouble?"

How could he make her understand that Maxim wasn't actually a villain?

"From everything I've learned about you, empathy is one of your strongest gifts. Try seeing it from his side for a second. What if your family legend spoke of a gold nugget that your great-grandfather had dug out of the earth with his bare hands? Not only that, you even have a photograph of him holding it. Wouldn't you want to know the truth?"

She sighed and stepped back. "Yes, but that

still doesn't mean he's right. Even if his great-grandfather did find the nugget, there has to be some reason that it remained here in Dunbar. If someone here stole it, there should be some kind of official record of Mr. Volkov's relative trying to get it back. Was there anything like that in the file he gave you?"

In no hurry to see her leave, he perched on the edge of the table. "No, which is one of the points that may play in the town's favor. I told the mayor you would search the museum's records for any documents that would explain the situation."

"I plan to, but I haven't had a chance to get started yet with everything that's happened." She grimaced. "I also hate to admit past boards at the museum didn't keep very good records. I also know a pipe broke in the basement some years ago and damaged a lot of the stuff that was stored down there. I'm not looking forward to going through whatever was salvaged.

Cade didn't blame her. "For what it's worth, I also strongly suggested that the mayor and town council ask a reputable attorney to review the material and give them an opinion on how strong of a case Maxim has made."

He shook his head. "I stayed at the meeting until everyone was leaving for fear they would talk themselves out of even trying if I wasn't there to force the issue. I'm sure that it will not shock you to learn that some members of the council seem to think that they can either ignore the problem or simply have me order Mr. Volkov to leave town."

Shelby looked puzzled. "You know, I'm actually surprised that he's still hanging around. He can't be enjoying his stay here in Dunbar, especially if people have started to figure out who he is."

Cade thought that was probably true. "I won't pretend to understand how his mind works. I've only spoken to him one time after he first showed up in my office."

"So we just have to wait and see how all of this plays out."

He really wished he had better news for her. "Pretty much. Should we head out for your place now?"

"On second thought, I really should head over to my office and check on things."

"That's probably a good idea. I'll walk you over to the museum now to make sure you don't get ambushed by anyone. I'd suggest keeping the doors locked and only let people in one or two at a time. Call me when you're ready to go home, and I'll come pick you up."

"Sounds good."

Before letting her walk out the front of the station, he decided to check the situation. The last thing Shelby needed right then was to be mobbed. On the way out, he ran into a woman armed with a foil-covered casserole. He thought the brunette's name was Carli. She smiled and held out the dish. "Chief Peters, I was just coming to see you. I thought you might appreciate a hot meal, what with all the trouble that Shelby has caused you."

Cade wasn't sure how to respond. Would it be rude to refuse the casserole? Before he could decide, he groaned as the woman in question joined them out on the sidewalk. All he could say was that he hoped Shelby never smiled at him like she was smiling at Carli right now. She looped her arm through his and leaned her head against his shoulder. "Isn't that nice, Cade? She brought us dinner."

Then she sighed and shook her head. "Sadly, we already have other plans. Don't worry, though. I'm sure you can freeze whatever that is and have it another day."

The other woman looked like she wanted

to protest, but Shelby's scary smile was back in full force. While Cade rather liked that she was staking her claim on him, it was time to move on before things turned ugly. Unfortunately, Shelby had more to say to Carli. "We'd love to stay and chat, but Cade was about to walk me over to my office. I have a few things to catch up on before the two of us head home for the evening. As I said, we have plans."

Carli took a step back, looking at Shelby as if she'd suddenly turned feral. Without saying another word, she turned and walked away.

As the two of them started across the street, Shelby called back over her shoulder. "Oh, and one more thing, Carli. If someone has posted the casserole signup sheet again, make sure they get delivered to someone else from now on."

She continued to hold on to Cade as they hustled over to her office but let go as soon as they stepped inside. After setting her purse down on the counter, she gave him a guilty look. "Should I apologize for how I acted out there?"

Cade prowled closer, trapping her next to the counter. "No apologies necessary. In fact, I want to thank you for heading off a new onslaught of casseroles. There's only one person I want showing up with meals for me."

He paused for effect and then leaned in to whisper one word near her ear. "Titus."

When she started to sputter in indignation, he kissed her. She quit struggling, giving in to the moment. He took his time, letting her know without words that nothing that had happened in the past two days had changed anything between them, at least as far as he was concerned. He hoped she felt the same way.

But right now, they had more pressing issues they needed to deal with. He reluctantly eased back on the kiss. "We should check on things upstairs."

She traced his lower lip with her fingertip, smiling when he nipped at it. "Yes, we should."

He took Shelby's hand and headed straight up to the second floor to see for himself that the nugget was safe and sound. There it was, on display in the locked case. He could only hope it stayed that way.

After admiring it, they made their way back downstairs. Still reluctant to leave, Cade was hit with sudden inspiration. "I'm going down to Bea's to get some coffee. Want some?"

Shelby was already busy behind the counter sorting a stack of ads into the mailboxes. "I'd love some."

He edged a little closer. "I know we've already had dessert, but I'm thinking another dose of sugar might hit the spot."

She smiled back over her shoulder at him. "You're an evil man, Cade Peters. It's bad enough that I haven't hit the gym in several days, but you and Titus keep tempting me with carbs."

"So no to the pastries? Because I'm thinking Bea won't take kindly to learning that you accepted three desserts from Titus, but you don't want any of hers."

She looked totally scandalized by that prospect. "You would tell her that?"

Feigning wide-eyed innocence, he slapped his hand over his heart and staggered back a step. "Would you have me lie to her?"

"Very funny. I'll have whatever you're having, I'll just post a sign blaming it on you when I start wearing my yoga pants to work because none of my jeans fit anymore."

Personally, he thought she'd look just fine in yoga pants. He liked her generous curves. Somehow he doubted that she'd take that as a compliment, so he wisely kept his mouth shut on the subject. "I'll be back in a few minutes. Lock up behind me. I'll knock when I get back."

In a better mood than he'd been for days, he strolled down to Bea's place. But as soon as he entered, he immediately regretted it. He now knew where the mob had gone after he'd kicked them out of the police station. Ignoring the angry stares and muttering, he walked straight to the counter. Bea had been polishing the countertop when he arrived and made no effort to stop.

"I'll have two coffees to go."

Still no response. Fine.

"Never mind. You're obviously too busy to see that Shelby gets coffee and one of your fritters. That's okay. I'll have Titus pack up something for her."

He made it three steps toward the door before Bea caved. "Fine, two coffees and two fritters. I have some that are still warm from the fryer."

No doubt she'd only relented because one of them was for Shelby. That was fine. Thanks to him and her thoughtless friends on the board, she'd been through the wringer over the past couple of days. He paid for the coffee and fritters, adding in a larger than usual tip just because.

He couldn't help but notice the expressions on the faces of his fellow citizens now looked less hostile and more, well, confused. What was up with that? Finally one of the braver members of the group confronted him directly. "Since when do prisoners get fancy coffee and fritters? Not that Shelby doesn't deserve them."

"Actually, I'm dropping these off at the post office, not the jail. When I just left her, Ms. Michaels was busy sorting mail and the library books, which I'm sure is thirsty work. Since I usually stop in here every day, I offered to pick up something for both of us."

His mood much improved, he walked out enjoying the stunned silence he left in his wake. He was still smiling when he returned to the post office.

Shelby was putting fresh batteries in a pair of flashlights when he walked in. After testing to see if they both worked, she set them down to sip her coffee. "I really needed this, but I think I'll save the fritter for later. Right now, we have some exploring to do."

"We do?"

"Yeah, you told the council we would be checking the museum's records for any mention of how we acquired the nugget. The files upstairs only go back a few years. Everything else is down in the basement."

When she offered him one of the flashlights, he asked, "Why do we need these? Doesn't the basement have any overhead lighting?"

"It does." She led him to a door located in the hallway near the restroom. After opening it, she reached in to turn on the light. "But even when the lights are working, they're not bright enough to read by. Watch your step. This staircase would never pass today's building codes."

She wasn't exaggerating, and they both took their time going down. When they reached the basement floor, he looked around. The ceiling was low, and the three bare lightbulbs offered too little light to reach the far corners of the room. There were boxes of various sizes stacked along the far wall on top of wooden pallets.

"Other than Ilse and Oscar, I don't like the docents coming down here for obvious reasons. Right after I took over the museum, I tried to bring some order out of the chaos and arranged the boxes by date left to right. Having said that, there's no guarantees that what's actually in the boxes matches the labels."

She pointed toward some overhead pipes. "The flood was before my time, but from what I've heard, tons of stuff was too badly damaged to save. The staff salvaged what they could, but it's pretty much a disorganized mess."

He walked closer to the boxes and used his flashlight to scan the labels. It didn't take long for him to locate the few left from the turn of the previous century. "It looks like these three might be from the right time period or at least close. Do you want me to carry them upstairs or do you want to look through them down here?"

"Would you mind bringing them upstairs?"

"Not at all, but let's take a quick peek in them first. No use in hauling them up if they're not actually from the right time."

He picked up the first box and started toward the staircase where the light was brighter. Shelby followed right behind him with the second one. Just as he set his down, she screamed bloody murder and dropped her box with a thud. He spun back around to see what was wrong. Her eyes were huge and horrified. "Where is it? Where did it go?"

"Where did what go?"

He got his answer when he spotted a huge wolf spider skittering across the floor to take refuge under the pallets. "It's out of reach."

She shivered and showed no interest in picking up her box. He didn't blame her. If any of the spider's relatives were still inside it, he didn't relish picking it up either. "Are you all right?"

When she shook her head, he said, "Come here."

He gathered her into his arms and held her, gently stroking her back until she gradually relaxed against him. "Sorry, but I really hate spiders. I'll be twitchy for hours just knowing it's here in the building."

Maybe a distraction would help. He used the side of his finger to tip her face up to the right angle. "Maybe you can think about this instead."

He brushed his lips across hers and then hesitated before ramping up the intensity to give her a chance to respond. She leaned back just enough to meet his gaze. "I like the way you think."

He gave it his all for the second time that afternoon, loving the feel of her in his arms, loving the taste of her kiss on his lips, maybe just plain loving her. He'd started this for her benefit, but she wasn't the only one who would be thinking happy thoughts for the rest of the day.

"Shelby, are you down there? Do you need help?"

Well, rats. Unless Cade was mistaken, Ilse Klaus was about to join them. Talk about bad timing. He took some comfort in knowing Shelby looked every bit as disappointed as he was. She stepped back and called out, "Chief Peters is helping me bring up some of the old records to go through. We'll be right up."

"You go ahead," Cade said. "I'll bring up the boxes after I check them for creepy-crawlies."

She kissed him one last time. "I owe you big-time."

Three trips up the steps and two dead spiders later, he set the last box on the table in the workroom. By that point, Shelby had enlisted Ilse's help to sort through them. As much as he hated to leave, it was past time for him to get back to work. Shelby followed him to the door. "I'll let you know if we find anything."

"Okay. And don't forget to call me when you're ready to go home."

"Normally I'd remind you that I'm perfectly capable of walking, but after the past couple of days, I'd really appreciate the ride."

He slipped in one more quick kiss to get them both through the afternoon and headed for his office.

CHAPTER THIRTEEN

"DO YOU WANT me to move out?"

Maxim Volkov held his breath as he waited for Rikki Bruce's answer. For what seemed like an eternity, she continued to stare out the front window at the small group of people who were marching back and forth in front of her bed-and-breakfast while carrying signs protesting his presence in their town. Maybe she was trying to decide if the amount of money she stood to make if he remained in residence was worth the hassles it might cause her here in Dunbar.

"Just say the word, and I'm gone."

She finally turned to face him, her clear gray eyes practically shooting sparks. "Are you unhappy with the service here?"

Not the question he was expecting, and it took him by surprise. "Of course not. I'd give this place a five-star rating every day of the week."

"Have I complained about anything you've said or done while you've been staying here?"

"No."

"Then if you're not unhappy here, and I'm not unhappy with you as a guest, why would I ask you to leave?"

As nice as her assessment of the situation was to hear, she was daft if she didn't think there might be unpleasant consequences if the protesters decided to up the ante. He pointed out the window. "You know that if I win my case about the Trillium Nugget, the fine citizens of Dunbar will be up in arms about it. I don't want you and Carter to get caught in the middle. Eventually I will go back to Portland, but this town is your home."

"You let me worry about us. I won't give in to bullying tactics ever again, and no one else will dictate how I operate my business. I get that they're upset, but that doesn't give them the right to act like fools."

This wasn't the first time Maxim had had this same conversation with Rikki. If he was any kind of gentleman, he wouldn't leave the decision up to her. It wasn't as if he needed to stay in Dunbar while his claim was being evaluated. He'd heard Chief Peters had discussed the matter with the city council, and Max expected to receive an update on the situation. If Cade didn't contact him soon, he'd make another trip to the police station. "I'm going to hang out at the café for a while. Can I pick up anything in town for you while I'm out and about?"

"Thanks for offering, but I can do my own shopping."

He knew she could, but couldn't the stubborn woman let him help out once in a while? Well, two could play at that game. He'd been ordering his dinner to go at the café rather than eating it there. The other patrons didn't usually speak to him directly, but their angry stares and muttered comments took the shine off even Titus's excellent cooking.

"I'll be back by six. This time I'm bringing enough dinner for all three of us. My treat."

She gasped in shock. "No, I can't let you do that, Max."

He grinned at her surprised outrage. Had no one ever done something nice for her just for the heck of it? "Sorry, but you can't stop me."

He retrieved his pack from the coffee table and headed out the front door. He could easily avoid having to face the protesters by slipping out the back door, but he wanted to make sure they knew he was leaving.

Before stepping out onto the porch, he gave Rikki one more hard look. "I admit that I can't force you to eat what I buy, but just for once I'd like to enjoy a meal with someone who doesn't hate my guts."

He closed the door with care. Bracing himself for whatever came next, he started toward the sidewalk. Most days the protesters hung back to follow him at a distance. This time was different, their mood uglier than before. It was hard not to pick up speed as he walked, but he wouldn't give them that much power over him. He would leave town if Rikki asked him to, but he wouldn't be driven away by anyone else living in this wide spot in the road.

When he finally reached the main street, he debated which way to go. His mind was made up for him as soon as he spotted Cade Peters headed in his direction. It was past time for them to talk again, and he wanted the police chief to see what Max dealt with every time he stepped out of the bed-and-breakfast.

Cade didn't look all that happy to see him,

but his expression turned even more grim when he spotted Max's fan club waving their signs. Cade stopped and waited for Max to reach him.

Looking past him toward the protesters, he sighed. "How long has that been going on?"

Max kept his back to them. "For a few days now. I don't care if they want to get their exercise following me around, but I don't appreciate them protesting in front of Rikki's place. It's not fair to her or her kid when none of this is their problem."

"Has she complained about it?"

"She's not happy about it." Max let more of his frustration show. "I left the house hoping they'd follow me and leave her alone for a while."

"Are they staying on the public sidewalk? If so, there's not much I can do about it. But if they set a single foot on her property, I can issue a warning. If that doesn't do the job, I'll see if she wants to press charges."

"She won't." Max knew that for a fact. Then he muttered, "I've never met such a stubborn woman."

Cade's mouth quirked up in a small grin.

"What makes you say that? Not the stubborn part, but why wouldn't she press charges?"

"She said something about her not giving in to bully tactics anymore. Maybe she thinks that pitching a fit would only validate their behavior."

He finally checked to see if his followers had dispersed now that the chief of police was there, but no such luck. Instead, they remained huddled together watching him and Cade. "Seriously, I hate that this could affect her business when I'm the one they have a problem with. When I offered to move out, she got all up in my face over that. Evidently it's nobody's business if she chooses to rent me a room."

Sometimes he wished he'd never decided to dispute the town's ownership of the nugget, not that he'd admit that to Cade. The man would probably do cartwheels down the middle of the street if Max withdrew his claim. That wasn't going to happen. He'd come this far, and he'd see it through.

"So you're staying."

It wasn't a question. That didn't mean Max wasn't going to answer. "I am. Do you have any news for me?"

For the first time, Cade was the one who looked uncomfortable. "I'm actually surprised that you didn't come banging on my door yesterday or first thing this morning."

Why would he think that? Something must have happened regarding the nugget, and whatever it was had left the chief of police looking a bit off-kilter. He didn't know Cade all that well, but he didn't come across as someone who was easy to rattle. "What happened to the nugget? Where is it?"

Because he'd go ballistic if it had conveniently gone missing.

"It's right where it belongs—in its case at the museum. I checked on it myself just a little while ago."

Nice dodge on Cade's part. It might be there now, but Max bet it hadn't been there at some point. He could imagine the furor that would've caused. "I'm heading for the café for some coffee. Why don't you join me? It will be my treat, and you can fill me in on whatever it is you don't really want to tell me."

Looking resigned, Cade nodded. "Just promise you'll remember the nugget is right where it belongs. Also, I'll pay for my own order. I can't have anyone thinking I'm accepting bribes from you."

Yeah, Max got that. The man was walking on a tightrope right now. "I promise to remember the nugget is safe and sound. I also understand the position you're in, so separate checks it is."

That didn't mean he wouldn't be mad about whatever had happened. Maybe it was time to demand that the nugget be entrusted to a third party for safekeeping. And if the town fought him on that, it was time to call in the big guns and let his attorney take over.

"YOU POOR THING, are you okay?"

Shelby closed her eyes and prayed for patience. If one more person asked her that question, she was going to scream. She was no one's "poor thing."

"Thanks for asking, but I'm fine."

She'd already had to suffer through Elizabeth making a huge fuss that included hugs, tears and an offer to use her rolling pin to knock some sense into Cade's head. However, Elizabeth's concern about Shelby was well rooted in their long friendship. If the situation was reversed, Shelby would've been the one to show up at Elizabeth's door with a casserole and hugs.

However, that most certainly wasn't the case with the woman who currently wandered through the room, trailing her fingertips across various surfaces as if checking for dirt. Fortunately, Shelby had dusted the entire room, top to bottom, right before Eileen Southworth had dropped in for a visit.

"You may say that now, but who knows what effects being incarcerated and exposed to hardened criminals will have on your life. I plan to insist the mayor and the town council formally reprimand Cade Peters at our next meeting for his abominable treatment of one of Dunbar's leading citizens."

Again, Shelby didn't want to hear it. Cade had apologized to her multiple times and then bought her a fritter. It was time to move on and forget the entire episode. That process would start by derailing whatever Eileen Southworth was planning. "First, Chief Peters was just doing his job. Second, there weren't any hardened criminals anywhere in sight, and I was not charged with anything. It was all a simple misunderstanding."

Eileen gave a disgusted sniff. "I beg to differ. Not only did he throw an innocent woman into jail, he threatened to do the same to me as well as some other justifiably concerned citizens. We will require your presence at the hearing."

Pasting on a hard-edged smile, Shelby used her superior height to look down her nose at the councilwoman. "I don't know what kind of petty game you're playing, but I won't be part of it."

She came around the counter and opened the door. "Now, if you'll excuse me, one of us has some real work to do."

Eileen stared at her in stunned silence. She looked like a guppy as her mouth opened and closed several times with no sound coming out. Finally, she sashayed out the door with head held high and her nose in the air. "As I said, we will require your presence."

"Require all you want, but I still won't be there. In fact, I'm pretty sure I'll be out of town that day."

"We haven't set the date as yet."

Shelby flashed her another dark look. "What can I say? My plans are flexible. Pick any date you want, but I'll be gone."

If she shut the door hard enough to rattle

the glass, too bad. It had been a long day, and she'd had enough. She locked the door to shut the rest of the world out. In fact, it was definitely past time to be heading home. Catching up on her work and going through the files had taken longer than expected.

She'd promised to call Cade when she was ready to leave. Normally she walked home when the weather was nice, stopping to chat with friends and neighbors along the way. That was the last thing she wanted to do today. If her hand trembled just a little as she made the call, it was to be expected. She was running low on both energy and patience after a day of dealing with well-meaning friends and others like Eileen Southworth, who were more like sharks circling in bloody water.

Cade's phone rang three times and then went to voice mail. Well, that wasn't useful. Should she leave him a message? Yeah, probably. He wouldn't be happy if he came looking for her and found her gone.

"Hey, I'm ready to go home. I realize you might be out on a call or something and can't come. If I don't hear from you in fifteen minutes, I'll just walk. It will be fine."

She hung up and used the time to gather up her purse and retrieve the basket from the refrigerator as well as the casserole Elizabeth had brought her. She might just freeze it, since she still had all the food Titus had sent her. At some point, she'd have to stop and thank him for his generosity.

Hoping to buy a little extra time for Cade to get her message, she made one last trip upstairs to make sure the nugget hadn't once again mysteriously disappeared. There it sat, all bright and shiny. She didn't know they used to polish it, but they'd done a bang-up job. Her heart ached knowing it could soon be gone again, this time forever. There had to be something she could do to prove that the town owned it, not Max Volkov and his family.

For Cade to have taken the Volkovs' claim so seriously, Max must have found some solid information to support it. That meant the town desperately needed to find some proof of ownership to counter it. She and Ilse had quickly gone through the three boxes, but they hadn't found anything useful. Just as she feared, not everything in the files dated from the right time period. The few things they did find were mostly paid receipts for bills and the minutes of city council meetings that shouldn't have been in with the museum's stuff in the first place.

The bottom line, they needed to access some other source of information to prove their case. But where? On her way to the staircase, she passed by a display of books. About halfway down the steps, she came to a screeching halt and then charged right back up to look at the books again. These weren't published histories like the one they sold downstairs in the gift shop. Instead, they were journals written by various citizens who had spent most or all of their lives in Dunbar and its immediate surroundings.

Some weren't all that old, but others dated as far back to when the first settlers arrived in the area. All were handwritten, and the ink in some was so faded and blurred as to render the words nearly illegible. She'd browsed a few since taking over the museum, but she'd never sat down and read any of them from cover to cover. Maybe it was time she did.

Pulling two of the oldest off the shelf, she set them aside long enough to post a notice on the front of the bookcase that she was the one who had borrowed them. After the fiasco with the nugget, she needed to set a good example for everyone else. She also signed them out in the ledger the museum maintained for just that purpose. Considering how dusty it was, she doubted than anyone had made use of it in years. The books were small enough to fit in her purse, so no one would notice her carrying them. As curator of the museum, she had every right to borrow them; she just wasn't in the mood to answer questions about why she was doing so now.

The fifteen-minute warning she'd given Cade had expired twenty minutes ago. His absence was disappointing, but the man had a job to do that didn't include offering taxi service to a former prisoner. It was time to go home. She lived less than a mile from the museum, so it wouldn't take her long to get there. Her energy levels might be running on fumes, but she could make it that far.

She'd gone less than a block when a car pulled to the curb right behind her. Dreading to see who it was, she gave a quick peek over her shoulder and then sighed in relief. Cade was out and heading around to the passenger side of his SUV. "Sorry I'm late. I was with someone and didn't get your message until just a couple of minutes ago."

"That's all right. I knew you might be busy."

He took the picnic basket from her hand and frowned. "This has gotten heavier since you left the station. Did Carli foist the casserole off on you when I wasn't looking or did Titus decide to feed you again?"

Cade didn't exactly look happy about that last prospect. Why would he care if Titus snuck her more food? Regardless, she hastened to explain. "No, that's Elizabeth Glines's doing. She came to see how I was adjusting to life as an ex-con."

To make sure he knew she was kidding, she smiled and patted him on the shoulder. "She brought me a casserole and offered to hit you upside the head with her rolling pin if you ever decide to arrest me again. Don't say you weren't warned."

"Duly noted." He set the basket in the back seat and then opened the passenger door for her. "Did you and Ilse have any luck?"

"Not so far. We even tried looking in a few more boxes, but they were all too new."

"That's too bad. Other than that, how did the rest of your day go?

"Lots of foot traffic. Some folks came in for their mail. A few like Elizabeth genuinely were concerned and wanted to see how I was doing."

He waited until he joined her inside the vehicle before continuing the discussion. "And the others?"

"They were looking for grist for the gossip mill. I referred them to your office if they had questions. I then politely said that I had work to do."

After a brief hesitation, she decided to warn him about what Eileen Southworth had planned. "You should know that Councilwoman Southworth stopped by. At first, she occupied herself by checking to see if the counter and shelves were dusty, but I had just finished cleaning before she came in. So disappointing for her. Then she claimed to be concerned about the long-term effects having been incarcerated with hardened criminals would have on me."

Cade groaned. "That woman. What did you have to say to that?"

"I told her that you were only doing your job, and that I was fine."

Seeing his worried look, she reassured him.

"I wasn't lying, Cade. I'm fine, but I am concerned that she seems intent on causing trouble. She rather nastily announced that she plans to insist the mayor issue you a formal reprimand. Not just for putting me in jail, but also because you threatened to do the same to her."

He remained silent until they turned into her driveway. "I don't know why, but she's made it clear from the beginning that she doesn't like me. It wouldn't surprise me if there's more going on with her beyond the current situation."

The man had good instincts.

"She was just so…so smug, is the best description of how she was acting." Shelby laid her hand on Cade's arm, needing that small connection with him. "I think that woman has every intention of ruining your career."

CHAPTER FOURTEEN

SHELBY LET CADE absorb that much before continuing. "She wants to use me against you, because she proclaimed that my presence will be required at the council meeting."

"And you said?"

"That I would not be attending." She smiled, savoring the sour grapes look that had appeared on Eileen's face at that pronouncement.

"I'm sorry she's trying to drag you into this."

"It's not your fault, Cade." She frowned. "Maybe she's simply upset that you're forcing them to toe the line when it comes to the law, but I think it's something more. You know, like she has some kind of personal stake in the outcome of this whole affair."

At least Cade mulled over her assessment of the situation and didn't reject it out of hand. "I don't know the woman at all well. But now that you've mentioned it, she almost seemed to be performing for an audience both at the council meeting and again at the police station this morning."

"Maybe she plans to run against both Ilse and Otto Klaus for mayor in the next election."

Cade looked horrified by that prospect. "I guess we'll just have to wait and see what happens."

He retrieved the picnic basket from the back seat and followed Shelby into the house. Without waiting to be invited, he took a seat at the kitchen table. "I hope you don't mind me hanging around for a few minutes, but I need to catch you up on a few things."

"That's fine. Why don't I put on some coffee?"

"Sounds good. I could use some."

After setting the coffee to brew, she stashed everything from Titus's basket in the refrigerator except for the cheesecake. That she cut into two servings and carried them over to the table. She sighed as she collapsed into the chair across from Cade's. "I've never eaten this many desserts in one day, but I swear that sugar and caffeine are the only reasons I've been able to function at all."

"I know what you mean. It's been a hard

couple of days, which is why I'm heading straight home from here."

At least she wasn't the only one running on empty right now. "I think we could both use some downtime and a good night's sleep. You mentioned wanting to catch me up on some stuff. What's up?"

He leaned back in his chair and let out a deep breath. "I kept Max Volkov company while he grabbed a late lunch at Titus's place. That's where I was when you tried to call me. Seems our fellow citizens have taken to protesting in front of Rikki Bruce's place whenever they think he's inside."

She didn't feel the least bit sorry for Max, but that wasn't fair to Rikki. "Can you do anything about that?"

"Not much, and for the same reasons I can't make Max leave town. As far as I can tell, the protesters haven't done anything illegal. Max isn't happy about it, but Rikki hasn't actually complained about it to me herself. When Max tried to convince her to call us, she dug in her heels and said she's done giving in to bullies and their tactics."

Shelby got back up to pour each of them some coffee. "Don't you think there's something odd about her response? Like something like this has happened before. Has Rikki had trouble with anyone here in town that I don't know about?"

"Not that I'm aware of, but it could be something happened before I took over as chief of police." He pointed at her with his fork. "Considering your connections here in town I would think you would've heard if something had happened."

She washed down a bite of the cheesecake with a sip of coffee. "Me, too. I haven't actually gotten to know Rikki very well. She mostly keeps to herself, but that's not surprising considering she has a young son and that enormous house to look after."

"Anyway, like I said, there's not much I can do. The only reason I learned about the situation was because I ran into Max in town with his sign-waving entourage following him down the street. Evidently, he went for a walk to draw the protesters away from her house."

"That was surprisingly considerate of him."

"Shelby, Max Volkov isn't a bad guy just because you're on opposite sides on this one issue. If you'd met under different circumstances, you might even like him."

"I doubt it."

Cade looked disappointed in her comment, but he didn't argue. "Anyway, I told Max I was surprised that he hadn't been banging on my door about the nugget going missing. Turns out he never heard about what happened until I brought it up. I guess I shouldn't have been surprised by that since no one in town talks to him unless they have to, and you said Rikki keeps to herself."

"What did he have to say?"

"Since it was all over and done with, there wasn't much he could say other than it had better not happen again." He finished the last bite of his cheesecake before continuing. "Actually, his main concern was about the impact all of this might have on Rikki."

Shelby found the man's concern for the woman confusing. While he didn't want Rikki to suffer because of him, he didn't care how stealing the nugget would affect the entire town. "Why would he care more about Rikki than he does the rest of us?"

"My best guess is because he's gotten to know her and her son, so he sees them as real people. He's also spent time with me and Titus, so I'm betting he now sees us as individuals, too. Before that, Dunbar was a faceless symbol of what his family had lost. It will be interesting to see if his feelings about the nugget change as he gets to know more of us here in town."

She understood what Cade was saying, but Max seemed pretty determined to see his so-called mission through to the end. "Even if he feels bad about what he's doing, I doubt that it will change his mind."

"We can always hope."

Sadly, they both knew hope alone wasn't going to cut it. They had to find some way to counter Max's claims about the nugget. Which reminded her, she hadn't told Cade about the journals. "I'll be right back. I've got something to show you."

It only took a second for her to dig the two books out of her purse. She returned to the kitchen and handed one to Cade. "We can't face off against Max without having something concrete to counter his arguments about the nugget. That's hard to do when I don't even know what kind of evidence he's put together."

"That is a problem. I was waiting for the mayor to meet with an attorney and then ask if I can share the file with you as the curator of the museum." Cade thumbed through the book, his face set in a frown. "You know, it's kind of weird that no one can tell me how the nugget came to be in the museum in the first place, and the display only says it was mined locally. Someone had to have known more at some point."

"That's what I was thinking, which is why I checked these two books out of the museum's library. Over the years, local people have donated journals and diaries to the museum that were written by their family members. Not many date back as far as when Max's great-grandfather was supposed to have been in the area, but we have a few. I have no idea if we'll find anything useful."

He closed the book. "If I can take this home with me, I'm willing to give it a shot. How many books cover the right time period?"

"Maybe four or five. It would help if we could narrow down the time frame, but I don't know how we can do that."

Cade finished his coffee. "These books seem like a good place to start. Maybe one of your board members could reach out to the newspapers in the area to see if they can find any mentions of the nugget in their archives."

"Good idea. It sounds like something that Ilse Klaus would love to sink her teeth into."

His mouth quirked up in a slight grin. "By the way, I think she's already planning her next political campaign. If she could find the right information to save the nugget, winning the job of mayor back would probably be a slam dunk for her."

"You sound like you're rooting for her to win."

His cheeks flushed a little red. "I would prefer to keep a low profile when it comes to local politics. Having said that, Otto lost my vote when he went fishing rather than sticking around to help deal with the missing nugget situation. He's being paid to be a leader, and heading out to drown worms when the town is in crisis mode doesn't exactly inspire confidence in the man."

"I hadn't heard he'd done that. I'm surprised Ilse didn't chain him to his chair to make him stick around."

Cade pushed his empty plate and cup aside. "If she's already planning her campaign, letting him go fishing would give her that much more ammunition to use against him."

Shelby couldn't help but laugh. "You'd think that competing against her own husband might cause problems at home, but it doesn't seem to. They celebrated their fiftieth anniversary last year and are still going strong. That's rare these days."

He waggled his eyebrows. "Who knows, maybe facing off against each other injects a certain extra spice into their relationship."

Not an image Shelby wanted in her head. "Do me a favor. Let's not go there."

She loved the sound of Cade's deep laughter. Thanks to all of the troublesome stuff they'd both been dealing with over the past week, neither of them had had many reasons to laugh. The small bit of humor helped her shed some of the stress, and she hoped it did the same for Cade.

He checked the black cat clock on the kitchen wall, its tail ticking off the seconds and grimaced. "I'm sorry, Shelby. I promised I was only going to stay a few minutes, and I've been here almost an hour."

"No apologies necessary. I feel better now

that we have a plan of attack to counter Max's claim."

Then just to tweak his nose a bit, she added, "Plus, any night I'm not sleeping in a jail cell is worth celebrating. Don't forget that Eileen Southworth is convinced that doing hard time like that has probably damaged my delicate self in all kinds of horrible ways."

Even if she was laughing as she added that last part, Cade apparently didn't find it funny. He immediately got up and carried his dishes over to the sink. She followed after him and reached up to pat him on the cheek. "What's the matter? Too soon?"

He caught her hand and pressed a kiss to her palm. "Yeah, but I'm glad you can find some humor in the situation. I am so sorry."

She edged a little closer, holding his gaze with her own. "I know, and that's the last time you should apologize for what happened, Cade. It wasn't funny at the time, but we backed each other into that corner."

His dark eyes locked on to hers as if he still wasn't convinced. She rested her hand against his cheek. "I mean that, Cade."

Then she kissed him to further convince the man that all was forgiven. She should've known that he would take control of the moment, but considering Cade's talent for turning a simple kiss into something so much more, she wasn't about to complain. Both of them were breathing a little hard when he finally pulled back.

After offering her a small smile, Cade leaned forward to rest his forehead against hers. "I really don't want this whole situation to get in the way of us."

At first glance, she liked the sound of that. She hadn't been part of an "us" since college. Her parents had homeschooled her, and she'd graduated from high school early. Enrolling in a huge state college in Seattle at such a young age had proven to be a major culture shock for her. Too many people, too much going on, life lived at a dead run. She was a small-town girl with no desire to be anything else. When the guy she'd been dating in college declared he had no interest in living in a place like Dunbar, that had been a deal breaker for her. There was no use in pursuing a relationship that was bound to cause heartache in the long run.

Cade pulled back, the happy look in his dark eyes fading as he studied her. "What just changed? You tensed up. Was it something I said?"

She didn't bother trying to deny there was a problem. He deserved her honesty. "I haven't dated anyone seriously in a long time, mainly because I haven't found anyone whose life goals meshed with mine."

"Then what happened that has you looking so sad?"

Wrapping her arms around herself, she leaned against the counter for support. "There was a guy in college who I thought might be the one. He came from another small town, so we had a lot in common. I couldn't wait to finish college and move back home to start our lives together. That dream lasted right up until Kyle came home with me to meet my parents. He took one look at Dunbar and basically laughed at the idea of living here. His future plans had changed at some point, and he suddenly wanted to live in a big city. That wasn't going to work for me, and he knew it. Dunbar is my home."

She blinked several times to hold off the threat of tears. "I'd been clear about that from the beginning, but I guess he never took me seriously. In his mind, it was a wife's role to support her husband's career. If that meant a lifestyle she wasn't suited for, so be it. He thought he was being generous when he offered to give me some time to come to my senses."

"What happened after that?"

"It was scary watching him walk out the door, and I'm not saying his dreams weren't important. Of course they were, but so were mine. I called him an hour later to say I'd had enough time and wished him the best in his future endeavors. You can imagine how well that went over, but I made the right decision for me. Life in the big city was too much for me. I came home as soon as I graduated."

Cade nodded at her assessment of the situation. "You made the right decision. In the long run, it saved both of you a lot of pain. I wish my ex-fiancée and I had gotten that smart a whole lot sooner. She wanted a guy who worked nine to five and came home for dinner every night. I was already in the army and wanted to make a career of it."

Shrugging, he continued, "Anyway, neither of us wanted to be the one to admit we were making a mistake, so we kept moving forward with the wedding plans. We were less than a week away from the big day when she finally had the courage to say I had to make a choice—either I finish out my current enlistment and walk away from my career or she was calling off the wedding."

"How did you take that?"

He laughed just a little. "At the time, not all that well, especially since I was already a soldier when we met. It wasn't something I sprang on her out of the blue. Looking back, I was also relieved." He stepped aside to stare out the window toward the trees in Shelby's backyard. "Eventually, though, I realized how much courage it had taken for her to do that. Last I heard, she's married to a contractor who owns his own business. They've got three kids and are doing well. I'm happy for her."

He finally faced Shelby again. "So what does this unhappy trip down memory lane have to do with us?"

"I like you, Cade. A lot. But we don't really know each other all that well. Other than the day we went hiking, this is probably the longest personal conversation we've had."

"And?"

"You've never said why a man with your

credentials would take a job in a town the size of Dunbar." She frowned, wondering how much she should say. Deciding now wasn't the time to hedge her bets, she did her best to lay it all out for him. "Everyone knows you're overqualified for the job. You've lived all over the world and seen amazing places. Dunbar is just a teensy-weensy dot on the map. Why live here? What happens if you get bored dealing with small-town politics and complaints about parking tickets?"

He didn't look happy about the direction the conversation had taken, but at least he remained calm. "You're right—I have bounced all over the world. As exciting as that might sound, it gets old. At least it did for me. Not to mention that a lot of the excitement came when people were shooting at my unit out on patrol. A few years back, I was stationed at the joint bases over near Tacoma and fell in love with the Pacific Northwest. I've known for a long time that this was where I wanted to live once I left the service."

He brushed his fingers through a lock of her hair. "When I started job hunting, I looked for a place where I could put down roots. Being near the mountains was also at the top of my list. I've had enough of deserts to last a lifetime. Dunbar fit all those criteria."

"You could've taken a job in any number of bigger towns and still been within sight of the Cascades."

"Seeing them in the distance isn't the same as having a spectacular view of Dunbar Mountain right outside your kitchen window. I took the job for the long term, Shelby, not on a whim. I like living here. I'm starting to make friends." He stroked her cheek. "And then there's you. I'm not ready to label what I'm feeling, but you're important to me."

"That's good to hear, Cade."

After all, she'd started this conversation by pointing out how much she liked him. Maybe even more than liked him. It was more than those broad shoulders and to-die-for chocolate brown eyes. There was his obvious intelligence, sense of humor and the patience he showed with some of the town's more interesting citizens.

But then he dowsed her brief surge of hope for their burgeoning relationship with one more bit of honesty. With a whole lot of regret in his voice, he said, "I want to explore whatever this is between us. But all things considered, especially with our rocky pasts when it comes to relationships, maybe we should proceed with some caution. Again, I didn't settle for this job. I turned down others to take it because this is the kind of place I wanted to make my permanent home. Regretfully, I may not have a choice in the matter."

The resignation in his voice made her heart hurt for both of them. "Why not?"

"Because if the nugget goes home with Max, the people around here will want someone to blame. It won't be the mayor or the town council. Most of those people have lived their whole lives here and are part of the fabric of the town. Being a newcomer makes me the most likely candidate for the scapegoat. If they demand my resignation, I'll have to go. I have a contract with the town, but the police department can't function if no one trusts the man in charge."

"So you'd leave?"

"Like I said, I may have no choice."

When she didn't immediately respond, he sighed. "I'll see myself out."

CHAPTER FIFTEEN

CADE LEANED BACK in his office chair and rubbed his eyes. He'd spent Sunday out on patrol so that Moira could have the day to deal with family issues. It had been a quiet day, which meant he'd had plenty of time to stew about everything else. Now his head ached from lack of sleep and good old-fashioned aggravation. Last night he'd been too antsy to relax worrying about the way his time with Shelby on Saturday had ended, so he'd stayed up to all hours reading the journal she'd given him.

He'd always been a history buff, so normally reading a firsthand account of what life was like more than a hundred years ago in and around the Cascade Mountains would've been fascinating. Instead, his frustration had only grown as he'd struggled to read page after page of faded ink without finding anything to help the cause.

He supposed checking one journal off the list of possibilities was progress of a sort, but it didn't feel like it. He hoped Shelby had had more luck with her book. As tired as she had been on Saturday, she might have gone straight to bed. He wouldn't blame her if she had. After everything that had happened, she deserved a decent night's sleep.

Not that it was his problem anymore. At least that's what he kept reminding himself since walking out of her house Saturday. But no matter how many times he replayed their conversation in his head, he still believed she was his to worry about. The thought that they were so close to finding something special together and might fail made him absolutely furious.

His phone pinged announcing a text message. With luck, someone needed him to respond to a crisis of some kind. Nothing major, but at least complicated enough to distract him for a while. Heck, he'd be happy if it was just Titus letting him know that he'd decided to make sweet potato pie again. Not that he and the man were in the habit of exchanging text messages. Still, right now he was the closest to a personal friend that Cade had in Dunbar.

A glance at his phone left him disappointed. Ordinarily, he would've been happy to hear from Shelby. But sadly, the few words on the screen were to the point and totally impersonal. Did you get anything from the journal?

For a few seconds, he considered how to respond. Probably the best option was to keep it simple and just answer the question. A simple no would suffice, but that wasn't going to happen. Yeah, he'd been the one to suggest they should proceed with caution, but that didn't mean two people couldn't meet over lunch to discuss a matter of mutual concern. Shelby might not appreciate his underhanded tactics, but too bad. He needed to know if she had decided to shut him completely out of her life. There was only one way to do that.

Holding the phone in one hand, he started typing. It took him four attempts to get the wording exactly right. Before he could chicken out, he read his message one last time and hit Send.

I'll tell you over lunch. My treat. See you at the café at 1:00.

His phone pinged a few seconds later. He smiled when he saw Shelby's single word response agreeing to come. Feeling better by the minute, he set his cell aside and went back to wading through emails and all the paperwork generated by Dunbar's small police force.

CADE USUALLY ENJOYED strolling down to the café, stopping periodically to chat with people. It was his way of making himself both visible in the town and available if someone had a concern that they thought he should know about. The way he figured it, the willingness to listen was good public relations. Today, he simply nodded and smiled as he passed people by but made no effort to encourage conversation.

He stopped several feet shy of the café entrance to look up and down the street but didn't see Shelby. It was still five minutes before the hour, so he remained where he was with his pulse pounding in his head. He hadn't been this nervous about a date since he was fourteen and mustering up the courage to ask a girl to the freshman dance.

Finally, he stepped through the door only

to run right into her. She'd been hovering just inside with her back to the door. Only quick action on his part kept them vertical instead of sprawled on the floor, which would've been a disaster. He was already taking heat for locking her in that cell; knocking her to the ground would only add fuel to the fire.

Luckily for him, she didn't protest and instead gave him a considering look. "Ordinarily I would ask why you're in such a hurry to get inside. But considering it's Monday, I figure I already know."

It took him a second to connect the dots. Oh, yeah, Monday meant chicken potpie. However, that wasn't what had him all fired up at the moment. Leaning in close to her, he whispered, "As much as I love Titus's cooking, you're the real reason I'm happy to be here."

Before Shelby could respond, the server cleared her throat to remind them to get with the program. "We have a table in the back corner. It's set for four, but it's the only spot available. Is that okay?"

Cade knew what she really meant—on the café's busiest days, no empty seat went unclaimed for long. The last thing he wanted was uninvited company joining them for lunch, but there wasn't much he could do to prevent it. Besides, if they were picky about where they sat, Titus might run out of specials before they got a table.

Shelby smiled at her. "That will be fine."

"If you'll give me your drink orders, I'll circle around and meet you there."

Again, Shelby went out of her way to be nice to the woman. "Thanks, Rita."

After they ordered two coffees, Cade let Shelby lead the way through the crowded café toward their assigned table. Outside on the sidewalk, he wouldn't have cared what he had for lunch as long as Shelby was with him. But now that she'd brought up the subject of the Monday special, he really hoped Titus still had a couple of servings left. If there was only one, he'd play the gallant gentleman and let Shelby have it. Not that he wouldn't envy every bite she ate.

Besides, it would give him something to think about other than Shelby's rather lukewarm welcome.

It took longer than he liked to reach the table. Shelby apparently knew each and every person in the room, and all of them wanted her to stop and talk. More than a few gave him a puzzled look as if wondering why she was there with him. He could have explained that they were there to discuss the nugget issue over lunch, but it wasn't really anyone's business.

As soon as they were finally seated, Rita appeared with their drinks. "I ordered two of the specials for you. We're bound to run out, I didn't want to risk you not getting any."

Then she was off and running before he could properly thank her. At least he could leave her a generous tip for her thoughtfulness. "To be honest, I somehow completely forgot it was Monday, probably because I worked yesterday. I've got to keep better track, because I would've been really mad if we'd missed out on the potpie."

Shelby laughed. "Anyone who can forget about Titus's specials deserves to go without."

Titus walked up to their table just as she spoke. Without waiting for an invitation, he took the chair next to Cade's. "I'll take that as a compliment."

"You should, and I want to thank you for those two picnic baskets you brought to Cade's office on Saturday. It was very kind of you and much appreciated."

Titus didn't look particularly comfortable with her gratitude, but he ducked his head just enough to acknowledge the message was received and understood. "How are you doing?"

Shelby seemed surprised that Titus was that concerned about her. "I'm fine. I was still pretty tired yesterday after everything that happened, but I'm better today."

He offered her one of his rare smiles. "Are you able to get any work done? I heard half the town has dropped by your office for a friendly chat today."

Cade hadn't realized that was still going on, but he probably should have. He frowned, but Shelby just shrugged. It was her way of saying without words that it was simply how life in a small town worked. "I was kind of expecting it, so I came in early to get a head start on sorting the mail. Considering the constant flow of people in and out of the place, it was a good thing I did."

Their conversation was cut short when one of Titus's helpers shouted at him through the pass-through window behind the counter.

"Hey, boss! You're needed back here in the kitchen. Ned's causing problems."

Looking much put upon, Titus stood up. "I swear that dog is more trouble than he's worth. He needs to remember who foots the bill for his food. Enjoy your meals."

As soon as Titus disappeared through the batwing doors that separated the kitchen from the dining room, his deep voice rang out over the ambient noise. "Darn it, Ned, how many times do I have to tell you to leave the staff alone? They have jobs to do that don't include feeding a mooching, flea-bitten mutt."

Cade chuckled. "Bet you a dollar that he's in there bribing the dog with fancy organic doggy treats."

Shelby grinned back at him. "No way I'd take that bet. I wouldn't blame Titus for meeting that dog's demands. Have you seen how huge he is? If it takes treats to keep him happy, then so be it."

"I've done more than just see Ned. I was pretty surprised when he invited me to pet him. From what Titus told me, he's not even sure the dog likes him all that much. I told Ned if he ever needs a place to hang out once in a while, I've got a corner in my office he can use. I thought about picking up a bed for him in case he decides to come by for a visit, but I haven't had a chance to do that yet."

Her eyebrows shot up in mock surprise. "Why, Cade Peters, you're a softy. And here I thought you were a hard-nosed cop with a heart of stone."

"Keep your voice down, woman, or you'll destroy my intimidating reputation. If that happens, we'll have nothing but chaos on the streets of Dunbar."

"Well, we can't have that, can we?"

It felt good to be joking around with her. Maybe that boded well for the two of them getting past this rough patch if everything worked out about the nugget. If it didn't, well, they'd deal with the situation when the time came.

The arrival of their food put a hold on further conversation. The normal lunch rush should have been winding down, but several people were still lined up by the door. Sadly, that meant it would be rude to linger too long just because he wanted to spend more time with Shelby. Besides, there was always the possibility that someone might want join them.

After making some serious inroads into

the generous helping of chicken ambrosia as Shelby had described it, he took a break to bring up the subject of the journal. "In answer to your text, the journal made for interesting reading, but there wasn't anything in it about the Trillium Nugget."

Her disappointment was obvious. "I didn't get very far in mine and haven't run across anything helpful. I'll keep going, though."

"I didn't think to bring it with me, but I'll swing by your office this afternoon and swap it out for another one. I probably won't get as much read tonight, but I can at least get started on it."

"Are you sure? You must have better things to do with your time."

"If it will help get the matter settled one way or another, it's worth making the effort. Did you have a chance to check in with Ilse about talking to the newspapers?"

Shelby laughed. "Yes, when I asked if she would have time to reach out to the newspapers, she leaped at the chance. She's also going to drive to one of the bigger libraries in the area to see what they might have on file."

It was a huge relief to see that bright spark was back in her pretty green eyes. He just wished he was the reason that it had returned. "For the sake of the town, I'll keep my fingers crossed that our efforts pan out."

"Not just for the sake of the town, Cade. You have a lot riding on this turning out the right way." Then her fair skin turned rosy as she added, "We both do."

Before he could think of how to respond, she glanced toward the door. "I suppose we should hustle a bit. Other folks are still waiting to eat."

Those other folks could starve as far as he was concerned right then, but that attitude might not go over all that well with Shelby. He wasn't the only one with a soft heart. Picking up his fork, he went back to eating.

BACK AT THE OFFICE, Shelby quickly ran out of things to do, but she'd missed too much work recently to take off early. It also didn't create a good impression if people noticed her sitting at the counter reading a book. Finally, she'd turned off the lights in the front office and locked the door. In case anyone needed her, she posted the sign that said to knock loudly or call her for assistance. For the past hour, she'd been sitting in the break room while she drank coffee and read the journal she'd started the night before.

Like Cade, she wasn't having much luck. It didn't help that the contents of the journal made for pretty dry reading. The author had moved to the area as a young bride. Most of her entries talked about the weather, how well her garden was doing and how far she'd gotten on the sampler she'd started working on the previous winter.

Yawning for the third time, Shelby skimmed a paragraph about how many eggs the chickens had laid over the past week. When she turned the page, the words were too blurry to read. Either her eyes were so tired they couldn't focus or else the ink had faded beyond legibility. It was time to do something more active.

There were some coupon flyers that were supposed to go out in the mail tomorrow. Maybe she'd get a head start on them. It wasn't until she reached the front of the building that she heard the muffled sound of someone walking around up on the second floor. That was puzzling. Normally, she heard the bell chiming over the front door on the other side even when the door between post office and the museum was closed. Maybe she'd missed hearing it when she was back in the break room.

That didn't explain who was up there or what they were up to. Considering the Trillium Nugget had already disappeared once under questionable circumstances, she needed to find out what was going on. The only question was whether she should notify Cade first. She was pretty sure that was the deal that they'd made. If there was any chance someone was after the nugget again, he'd never forgive her if she didn't call him.

While she waited for him to answer his phone, her curiosity got the better of her. She quietly opened the door a crack and listened for a few seconds. There were two… no, at least three different voices coming from above. All were familiar and belonged to members of the museum board. Were they meeting without her?

"Shelby, what's up?"

Shelby jumped a foot. She'd been so intent on what was going on upstairs that she'd forgotten about calling Cade. She whispered, "Just a sec, Cade."

Retreating to the other side of the building,

she pushed the door almost closed. "Sorry about that. I heard footsteps overhead and got a little spooked. I probably should've investigated first and then made the call."

Her words came out in a rush, leaving her a bit breathless. "Anyway, I'd already dialed your number when I recognized the voices. I don't know why they're here, but it's at least three members of the museum board."

His voice flipped from friendly to cop mode. "Were you expecting them to be there?"

"No, actually I wasn't. The museum is closed on Mondays so we don't schedule any docents to work. Anyway, I'm sorry I bothered you. I'll go see what they're up to."

"No you won't, Shelby. Not until I get there."

"But it's just the board—"

"Who aren't supposed to be there. Do I really need to remind you that these are likely the same people who made off with the nugget once already?"

She hated it when he was right. "No, you don't."

"Then stay put until I get there. I'm already walking out of the station. Make sure the front door of the post office is unlocked."

Surrendering to the inevitable, she undid the deadbolt lock and then went back to stand by the museum door to see what she could hear from upstairs.

"You know Shelby won't like it. Not one bit."

The speaker was Earl Marley, always the most cautious of the board members. The next one not so much. Helen Nagy sniffed in obvious disapproval. "She's not thinking straight these days. Even after how Chief Peters treated her, she met him for lunch today. I wouldn't have believed it if I hadn't seen it with my own eyes."

"I'm still not sure this is a good idea. The chief is just doing his job."

That came from Oscar Lovell. Ooh, that wasn't good. Cade wouldn't be pleased to find one of his officers plotting against him. Far more troubling, the next voice didn't belong to a member of the museum board at all. "I'm pretty sure dating on company time isn't part of their job descriptions. At the very least, on behalf of the museum board, you should ban him from the premises for the foreseeable future. He's completely mishandled this threat to the Trillium Nugget. I also think Shelby's recent behavior shows a definite lack of good judgment. When I insisted her presence will be required at an upcoming council meeting, she claimed she'd be out of town."

Earl spoke up in Shelby's defense. "She almost never takes time off from work. We can hardly complain if she's taking time that is due to her."

Eileen heaved a huge sigh as if praying for patience. "Well, Earl, that might be true. However, in this instance, she's using that as an excuse to avoid testifying to the city council about Chief Peters's abusive behavior."

That did it. Shelby might give the others the benefit of the doubt, but she drew the line when it came to Eileen Southworth. Who was she to judge how Shelby and Cade spent their lunch hour? Had it even occurred to the them that she and Cade might've been conferring over what to do about the nugget? Obviously not. The whole bunch of them should mind their own business, especially Eileen Southworth and Helen Nagy. Shelby's relationship with Cade was no one else's concern. Period. Granted, getting tossed in the slammer hadn't been any fun. But in the grand scheme of things, it was a minor hiccup. The town had a lot more important things to worry about right now.

The front door clicked open. She rushed back over to put her hand on the bell to keep it from chiming. Cade slipped inside, his face set in hard lines. "You didn't go up there, did you?"

"No, I just listened for a few seconds."

She bit her bottom lip, not really wanting to tell him what she'd overheard. If she didn't, though, he'd be mad at her for trying to hide things from him. "As far as I can tell, there are four people up there. Three are members of the board—Helen Nagy, Earl Marley and Oscar Lovell."

Cade had looked all tough cop when he arrived, but the mention of Oscar's name kicked his bad attitude up another notch. If he was that unhappy about Oscar's involvement, she could only imagine what he'd have to say about the councilwoman sticking her nose in museum business.

"Eileen Southworth is up there, too. Near as I can tell, she's trying to browbeat the board into banning you from the museum for the foreseeable future. She and Helen also think I've been showing a distinct lack of judgment because I had lunch with you today. I didn't hear what they had to say after that."

But the more she thought about it, the madder she got. "I can't wait to give them a piece of my mind."

To her surprise, Cade started grinning. "Hold on there, tiger. If we go in with guns blazing, it will only give them more fuel for the fire. I will calmly ask Oscar why he's over here instead of on patrol. I've already made my expectations clear when it comes to his duties as an officer of the law."

"Fine, you handle him while I'll deal with Helen Nagy and Earl Marley."

Cade stared up at the ceiling, listening to footsteps overhead. "That leaves the councilwoman."

An evil thought popped into Shelby's head. "Is the jail cell empty?"

"It is.

"What are the chances that her being here when the museum is closed could be construed as trespassing?"

"While I like the way you're thinking, I'm afraid that would be a pretty big stretch considering she's here with members of the board. Having said that, I'm not a lawyer or a judge."

She rubbed her hands together with greedy glee. "Can we toss her in the cell until you can get a definitive legal opinion?"

"Probably not, but that doesn't mean I don't want to. I wish I knew what has her all fired up and trying to make our lives miserable."

"There's no telling. Meanwhile, I will express my very sincere displeasure that members of the board are discussing matters regarding the museum with an outsider. That is against established policy."

"Which is?"

"If a member of the board has a concern that needs to be addressed, it should be added to the agenda for the next scheduled meeting."

"Fine. Like I said, I'll deal with Oscar as his supervisor. You can weigh in on him and the two board members as the curator of the museum. And before we do any of that, I will suggest that Ms. Southworth leave before you file an official complaint regarding her possible trespassing."

"Can I do that?"

"It probably won't go anywhere, but I don't see why not."

Ordinarily Shelby didn't like confrontations. This time, though, those people upstairs had no idea what was headed their way.

"Shall I lead the charge?"

To her surprise, Cade offered her his arm. "I think it will have more of an impact if we present a united front. Besides, no one will be able to sneak past us on the steps if they decide to make a break for it."

She slipped her hand through the crook of his arm. "Then by all means, let's go have some fun."

They stepped through the door and started up the staircase, making no effort to avoid detection. Far better to let the culprits sweat a little.

CHAPTER SIXTEEN

THE FOUR CONSPIRATORS stood huddled together, looking at the Trillium Nugget display. Once they realized they were no longer alone, their expressions ran the full gamut from defiant to defeated. Oscar positively wilted when Cade made a point of looking him straight in the eye. Earl Marley ignored Cade, but he appeared apologetic when he glanced at Shelby before dropping his gaze down to the floor.

The two women were a whole different ballgame. Helen Nagy's lips were pinched in disapproval while Councilwoman Southworth looked as if her dreams had just come true. Whatever was going on with that woman, she clearly thought that Cade and Shelby had just handed her all the ammunition that she needed.

Cade jumped in to get the conversation rolling. "Oscar, obviously our earlier talk didn't do the job. You are on the clock, which means you should be out on patrol."

The older man flushed red. "I'm entitled to a lunch break."

"You are, but that does require that you notify dispatch when you are taking your lunch so that someone else can take calls until you return. Did you follow procedure?"

Since Cade hadn't known Oscar was involved until Shelby told him, he hadn't had a chance to check with dispatch. However, he wouldn't have to bother. Oscar was already shaking his head.

Shelby looked at Helen, Earl and Oscar. "I will be adding this incident to the agenda for our next meeting. You are well aware that museum business and museum policy are not meant to be discussed with unauthorized people until the entire board has considered the matter and come to an agreement. If this happens again, I will have no choice but to ask for your resignations. We can't have people who won't follow policy acting on behalf of the museum."

When Helen started to speak, Shelby cut her off. "Not now, Helen. As I just said, we do not discuss museum matters with outsiders."

By that point, Eileen was all puffed up and ready to blow. "Listen to me, young woman, you have no right—"

"Stop right there. I mean it. Not another word." When Eileen gasped in outrage, Shelby gave her a superior smile. "In the future, you will address me as Ms. Michaels. As curator of this museum, I will be treated with respect."

She gave the woman a disparaging look. "You, however, are not a member of the board and have no right to be in the museum when it is closed to the public. This is your last chance to leave of your own accord. Continue to argue with me, and I will ask Chief Peters to consider charging you with trespassing."

The councilwoman drew herself up to her full height. "You wouldn't dare. I am a city official."

"You're also sticking your nose in places it doesn't belong, and you really don't want to test me right now. However, I honestly don't think you're worth the negative press that having you arrested might cause, but I will do whatever it takes to protect the museum. Now, I strongly suggest you leave."

When the board members started to bolt

for the staircase, Shelby blocked their departure. "Hold up. I am not quite done with you."

Seeing three senior citizens getting called on the carpet was pretty entertaining. With some effort, Cade managed to keep his game face firmly in place. "Okay if I escort the councilwoman to the exit?"

Before Shelby could answer, the woman in question swept past him, nose in the air and determined to have the last word. "I will see myself out."

She paused at the top of the stairs. "But I'm putting you both on notice. This is far from over. The mayor and the rest of the city council will be informed that you threatened me."

Cade whipped out his handcuffs and dangled them in the air. "It's not a threat, Mrs. Southworth. If Ms. Michaels ever has reason to believe that you've been sneaking around in the museum again without permission, we will revisit this discussion."

They waited in silence until the museum door opened and slammed shut again. Shelby started to say something but then held up her hand signaling that they needed to wait a second. She disappeared down the steps while he waited at the top. From what he could hear, she was searching the lower floor to verify the councilwoman had actually left the building. A minute later, Shelby reappeared.

"Sorry to take so long. I made sure the deadbolts were all in place so we don't get any more unwanted visitors."

"Good idea."

Helen Nagy proved herself to be the bravest of the three remaining culprits. "You can't hold us prisoners here, Shelby. My daughter will worry if I don't get back to her shop soon."

To his surprise, Earl Marley shut her down. "Helen, quit being such a drama queen. Shelby is upset with us, and I don't blame her."

Turning to Shelby, he shook his head. "We've mishandled all of this so badly. We should have brought our concerns directly to you. I don't know how that Southworth woman got involved, but it won't happen again."

"I understand, Earl. Things are pretty messed up right now, and it's causing all of us to act a little strange."

As always, Shelby was quick to forgive, a characteristic of hers that Cade had benefited from himself. That didn't mean she should let these three slide so easily. But this was her bailiwick, not his, so he'd follow her lead.

Unlike Earl, Helen wasn't ready to surrender. "Aren't you going to tell Chief Peters to leave if we're going to discuss museum business? Or does that rule only apply to people you're not dating?"

Oscar spoke up this time. "Whoever Shelby dates is none of our concern, Helen."

"It is when he's doing his best to make sure that Volkov fellow gets to walk away with our nugget. It was safely hidden away, but we… I mean someone had to bring it back to get Shelby released from jail. Now our nugget is sitting right there where anyone can waltz in and take it."

Shelby threw her hands up in the air. "That's enough, Helen. I ended up in that jail cell in the first place because someone took the nugget without permission."

Cade gave Helen a dark look that had her backing up a couple of steps. "Let me make this clear. No matter how good people's intentions happened to be, stealing the Trillium Nugget was a criminal act. You should also know that the monetary value of that lump of gold would qualify as a major theft. Shelby wouldn't tell me the names of the people who she suspected took it, insisting she was responsible for its disappearance. Her loyalty to the people she cares about is the only reason one or more of you isn't sitting in the county jail facing felony charges."

There, now he had their full attention. "Treat her with a great deal more respect, or you'll be dealing with me."

That pronouncement was met with shocked silence. Satisfied he'd made his point, he glanced at Shelby. "You were saying?"

"To answer your question, Helen, Cade is here because he volunteered to help find information that might prove the nugget belongs to the town. Unfortunately, we haven't had any success finding anything in that mess of files in the basement." She pointed to the glass-fronted bookcase against the wall. "We also thought maybe one of the personal journals that date back to the right time period might prove useful. He's already read one, and I've started reading one myself. We met for lunch today to talk about what we'd found so far."

Helen whispered, "We didn't know."

"And that's my fault. I should have sent out

a notice, but the past few days have been kind of hectic. I've also asked Ilse Klaus to contact the local newspapers to see if she can locate any information in their archives. I can't imagine that there weren't some headlines about a nugget of that size being found."

Earl was looking much happier. "That's good thinking, Shelby. Is there something I can do?"

"Are you up to reading one of the journals? It's pretty dry stuff, but we need to find every scrap of useful information we can."

"I've got nothing but time on my hands."

Oscar's gaze bounced between Cade and Shelby before he spoke. "I'd offer, but I'm already late getting back out on patrol. If you think of something I can do, give me a call."

He started for the steps, but Cade blocked his way. "Oscar, I need to know that I can trust my people."

"Yes, sir. I'll do better." He turned back to Shelby. "I wouldn't blame you if you kicked me off the board, but I'll do better there, too."

Once again, she showed her innate kindness. "I know you will, Oscar. This is a tough time for all of us."

That left them with just Earl and Helen to

deal with. Shelby walked over to unlock the bookcase. After studying several of the journals, she settled on two. "Earl, I think you might enjoy reading this one. It's by a former mayor of Dunbar."

He took the book and started paging through it while Shelby held out the remaining book to Helen. "This one is yours."

The older woman didn't immediately take it from Shelby's outstretched hand. "I never said I would read one."

Evidently Shelby had finally run out of patience with the woman. Her green eyes sparked with anger and frustration. "Let me make sure I understand what's going on here, Helen. You're not willing to do something proactive to protect the nugget. However, you are willing to conspire behind my back, spread unfounded rumors about me and also approve of someone making off with the nugget without authorization."

Her voice took on a harder edge. "Oh, let's not forget you wanted to ban Chief Peters from the museum even though it's his job to protect both it and the town. I wouldn't want to leave that out."

There was no forgiveness left in Shelby's

voice as she finished her summation. "Is that everything? Because I want to include all of that when I make my report to the museum board at our next meeting. It's also important that I have all the facts straight when I write my next column about the museum for the newspaper and say that we'll be needing to replace a board member."

Boy, she was good. Cade couldn't help but admire Shelby's show of strength. She looked like a warrior ready to ride into battle, weapons drawn. Earl stared at her as if he'd never seen the real Shelby before. Maybe he hadn't. Cade doubted that she let her temper off its leash very often, but right now Helen Nagy was bearing the full brunt of Shelby's anger.

The older woman sputtered, "I never said I wouldn't read one of the books, only that I hadn't volunteered yet. Of course I want to do whatever I can to help save the nugget."

The woman had raised the white flag. It would be interesting to see if Shelby accepted her surrender gracefully or with the same icy chill she'd used when summing up the situation. He was betting on the former. Two seconds later Shelby proved him right.

She smiled as she once again held out the

book. "I really appreciate this, Helen. I was worried that we'd never wade through the journals in time to make a difference. We've got to work together to save the day."

The older woman trailed her fingertips over the worn leather cover. "I'll read it right away. I need to check in with my daughter first, but then I'll head straight home and get started."

"Sounds like a plan. I'm still wading through the one I brought home, so they're not exactly a quick read. You two can go ahead and leave after you sign the books out in the log."

Earl pulled a pen out of his shirt pocket. "Good idea. We need to keep track when things are removed from the collection."

He might not have meant that as a dig against Helen, but she took it that way. "That's enough of that, Earl. Sign out your book, so we can get out of here."

They squabbled a bit more on their way down the steps. Shelby rolled her eyes and looked exasperated. How often did she have to referee between the members of the board? Probably far too often.

"Are you done for the day?"

She stopped to lock the bookcase. "I was

ready to be done long before I realized they were up here. I'm going to go straight home and stay there. I love this town, but living in each other's hip pockets gets to be a bit much some days. Everybody knows just what buttons to push when they aren't happy."

He couldn't help but grin. "You mean like hinting that you might write something that's less than flattering about Helen in the paper?"

Shelby had started down the stairs, but she stopped to look back up at him. "Yeah, like that. I should probably apologize to her."

He reached down to touch her cheek. "No, you shouldn't. She deserved that and more for what she did today. Maybe she'll think twice about spreading vicious gossip or conspiring behind someone's back just because she doesn't like what's going on."

"Fine, I won't apologize, but I hate that everyone is so upset right now. Squabbling amongst ourselves isn't going to help anything. Don't they understand that I'm doing my best to deal with the situation?"

Cade joined Shelby on the same step and gathered her into his arms. She didn't resist at all. That she cuddled in close to lay her head on his shoulder said a lot about the toll all of this was taking on her. "Maybe now they know better, but they also need to understand that this isn't only your burden to bear. Max's claim has thrown all of us for a loop, which means everyone needs to get a grip and start working toward the common goal instead of pointing fingers and making unfounded accusations."

Then he leaned in closer. "But for the record, getting together for lunch today to discuss the journals was only an excuse. I wanted to spend time with you for very personal reasons."

She seemed wary. "I thought we agreed to take things slow."

He injected a whole lot of heat in his smile. "We can go slow all right, but I suspect we're talking about two very different subjects."

He brushed his lips across hers and then charged down the stairs, leaving her staring at his back. "I've got to get over to the office. I'll pick up the next journal you want me to read at your place after I get off work. I'll bring back the first one, too."

He didn't need to look at her to know she was pretty exasperated with him by that point. "And you couldn't have reminded me to give you the journal while we were upstairs?"

"Yeah, but then I wouldn't have an excuse to see you this evening. I'll bring dinner. See you around six o'clock."

He was pretty sure she muttered "sneaky man" just before he shut the door on his way out. She was right that he was being sneaky, but she also didn't sound all that upset about it. Maybe she was just as happy as he was to have a reason to spend more time together.

He was still grinning when he walked into the police station, and even wading through the stack of reports he'd yet to finish couldn't take the shine off his good mood.

CHAPTER SEVENTEEN

TWO MORE DAYS had passed with no real progress on building a case to counter Max's claims about the nugget. Shelby's eyes ached from reading two and a half journals over the past forty-eight hours. She hadn't finished the last one because the time period it covered was too recent to be of much use.

Earl was nearly done with his book and had promised to finish it that evening. He'd made a few notes along the way, but he wasn't sure they would be of much help. Helen's findings were pretty much the same. It was all so depressing. Telling themselves at least they'd tried wasn't going to be much comfort if things played out as she very much feared they would.

The one suggestion Earl had made was that they should make note of every person mentioned by name in the journals. What use he thought that would be wasn't clear, but she'd passed along the idea to both Cade and Helen. Maybe once they'd compiled the list, inspiration would strike. She could only hope.

The bell over the door chimed, dragging her out of her thoughts. Her already bad mood darkened as soon as she recognized her visitor. What did that jerk Max Volkov want now?

She realized she'd said that last part out loud when the man in question flinched. Ordinarily she would apologize for the rude greeting, but he couldn't possibly be surprised that she was less than happy to see him. That said, she was being paid to provide quality service to her customers whether or not she actually liked them. With that in mind, she calmly closed the journal she'd been reading and set it aside. "Mr. Volkov, how can I help you?"

He hovered near the door, maybe having second thoughts about whatever had brought him into the building. Finally, he held up a padded envelope. "I'd like to mail this. If you'd rather I go elsewhere, I will."

Tempting, but she wouldn't have it said that she didn't do her job. It didn't take her long to weigh the envelope and determine the postage. "The mail has already been picked up today, so it will go out tomorrow. It should arrive three days after that."

He tucked the receipt in his wallet. "That'll be fine. Thank you."

Habit had her answering him the same as she would have any other customer. "You're welcome. Have a nice day."

He seemed hesitant to leave. Finally, he sighed. "You might find it hard to believe, Ms. Michaels, but I am really sorry that we're on opposite sides regarding the nugget."

Seriously? Did he really think anyone would side with him against the best interests of the town? "How did you expect the citizens of Dunbar would react to your claim? You couldn't possibly have thought you would be welcomed with open arms."

"Of course not. I knew not everyone would be happy about it." He glanced out the window at the people walking by. "But I didn't expect that some innocent folks would get sucked into the turmoil. I do regret that."

Was he talking about her or Cade? No, it was far more likely he was referring to Rikki Bruce having to contend with the protests outside of her bread-and-breakfast. Shelby gave the man credit for at least recognizing the impact his presence might have on Rikki's business.

Max seemed to be waiting for some kind of response from her. Finally, she sighed and said, "I'm sure Rikki appreciates your concern. But if you're worried about her, why are you still staying there?"

"Chief Peters asked me the same thing. I'll tell you what I told him. When I offered to leave, it only made Rikki madder at me than she was at the protestors. I'm staying put because it seemed important to her that I do so."

He frowned and shook his head. "You have my word that if things get worse, I'll move out regardless of how that stubborn woman feels about it."

Shelby really didn't want to like a single thing about Max, but her innate sense of fairness insisted she at least give him credit for being concerned about someone other than himself. Maybe Cade was right. When Max had first started on this ridiculous quest, the citizens of Dunbar had been the faceless crowd he held responsible for the theft of his family's treasure. But now that he'd spent some time in town, at least a small portion of the population had become real three-dimensional people to him.

Not that it mattered. It might cause him to have a few regrets, but it obviously wasn't enough to make him stop. Time to hustle him along his way and get back to work. Well, back to reading the journal at any rate.

"If there's nothing else…."

"No, that's all. Thank you, Ms. Michaels."

Unfortunately, before he made it out the door, another unwelcome arrival came sweeping in full of self-importance and bluster. Max stepped out of the way to give Mayor Klaus room enough to make his entrance. Otto gave Max a disdainful glance. That didn't surprise Shelby one bit, but that he gave her the same kind of look did.

"Good morning, Mayor. How can I help you?"

Before responding, he drew himself up to his less than impressive height and puffed his chest out. "You can begin by not consorting with the enemy."

Really? Did the man not have any idea how ridiculous that sounded? She glanced past him to where Max remained watching with a slight smirk on his face.

"Mr. Mayor, I prefer to think of it as just doing my job." She waved her hand in the air to indicate their surroundings. "This serves as the post office for the town. When people bring in something they need to mail, I figure out how much postage to charge and then make sure the package or envelope gets in the bin to be picked up when the mail truck comes through town. I would've thought you knew that."

Then to rub salt in his pompous wound, she actually smiled at Max. "You've left your envelope in good hands, Mr. Volkov."

His eyes twinkled with humor as he nodded his head in a small bow. "Indeed I have, Ms. Michaels. Good day, Mayor Klaus."

Instead of just letting him leave, Otto flushed bright red and threw gas on the fire. "I'll tell you what will be a good day, Volkov. It will be when our spineless chief of police throws you out of town like he should have the moment he met you. His office will be my next stop where I will inform him that you have been here harassing our postmistress and preventing her from doing her job."

Okay, enough was enough. Shelby abandoned her position behind the counter to stand right in front of the mayor. "Otto, talk to Chief Peters if you want to. That's your prerogative, but you will leave my name out of it. For your information, Mr. Volkov has been nothing but respectful since he came in. That is more than I can say about you."

She hoped Otto didn't have a heart condition, because right now she'd bet his blood pressure was on the rise. "Young lady, remember who you're talking to."

"I do remember. And before that, I was talking to a paying customer. Again, that's my job."

Otto wasn't done. "And your other job is curator of the museum. I'm sure you would agree that protecting the Trillium Nugget from thieves and other disreputable sorts is your primary duty." He stopped to give Max a sharp look to make sure he realized that Otto was referring to him before continuing. "As far as I can tell, you are failing to do that."

Shelby had had enough. "Otto, I won't stand here and let you talk to me that way. You have no right to question my integrity or my ability to do my job. I think you need to go. Like right now."

She should've known that would only make

him dig in his heels. "Why? So you can continue to plot with that guy on how best to steal our nugget?"

That was it. Instead of arguing with him, she dialed Cade's number and put the call on speaker phone. "Chief Peters, you wanted to know if anyone causes me any trouble. Well, Mayor Klaus has just accused me of coordinating efforts with Mr. Volkov to steal the nugget. He's also interfering with my ability to serve members of the public who need to buy postage. Will you please remove him from the premises?"

"I'm on my way."

The mayor was looking a bit wild-eyed by that point. She didn't know how he'd envisioned this encounter would go, but it was pretty obvious it hadn't played out like this in his head. "You can't do that."

"I already did." She leaned to the side to look out the front window. "If you hustle, you might make out of here before Chief Peters arrives.

Max spoke up, startling her. "Nope, he's already crossing the street."

With her outrage and attention both focused on Otto, she'd almost forgotten Max was still there. She watched as he stepped closer to Otto. "For the record, Mr. Mayor, I don't take kindly to men bullying women nor do I much appreciate having my good name smeared by you. I am not a thief. My claim on the nugget is valid whether you like it or not."

Otto made no effort to make a hasty retreat as he went right on hurling insults at both her and Max. "I know no such thing. That file of yours is a packet of fabricated lies. Shelby knows that, but she's too busy going on hikes and having lunches and flirting with every man who walks through that door to put a stop to this nonsense."

Shelby's hands itched to heave something at Otto's head, but not even the nugget itself would put a dent in his thick skull. Luckily, Cade arrived just in time to hear the last of Otto's tirade. Cade would never lift a finger to hurt her, but one look at the predatory expression in his dark eyes had her wanting to duck for cover behind the counter. She might even invite Max to join her just in case.

Cade slowly prowled across the floor to stand in front of his intended prey. Staring down at the badly shaken mayor, he growled, "You will apologize to Ms. Michaels or else."

Otto wasn't getting any smarter. Instead of offering her even an insincere "sorry," he blurted, "Or else what, Chief Peters?"

As soon as the words slipped out of the mayor's mouth, Cade growled. Actually growled. Otto must have realized his error because he immediately backpedaled toward the door. Unfortunately for him, Max made a quick move to block the exit, leaning against the door with his arms crossed over his chest.

Trapped between a man he'd just insulted and a very angry chief of police, Otto did the one thing none of them expected. He broke down and cried.

OVER HIS CAREER in law enforcement, Cade had confronted more than one troublemaker who broke down and sobbed. Most of them had been kids right out of basic training who'd gone out on the town for a good time. After a few too many beers, any chance for common sense went right down the toilet. It wasn't until confronted with the consequences of their actions that reality hit, and their worst fears came to light. It was hard not to laugh when they begged him not to tell their mothers or their sergeants, and in that order.

This case was different only because there was no beer involved and it was his wife Otto was afraid of. Cade didn't blame him. Meanwhile, true to form, Shelby was trying to comfort the distraught man even though he'd been hurling insults at both her and Max Volkov only seconds before. Seriously, the woman must really have some serious saint genes somewhere in her family tree.

"Come on back to the break room, Otto."

Before she led him out of the room, she stopped to issue a few orders. "Max, would you lock the door and turn the sign to say I'm closed for the time being?"

Then she stopped. "Sorry, Max, that's not your job. You probably have other things to be doing. Cade can lock the door if you'd like to leave."

"That's probably a good idea." Max grinned at her. "For your sake, and not the mayor's, we'll keep this whole incident between us."

Cade didn't particularly like the guy getting all chatty and friendly with Shelby. She'd given him no reason to be jealous, but that didn't stop him from wanting Max to depart. He went so far as to open the door for him, but Max evidently wasn't done talking. The cheerful expression he'd offered Shelby had been replaced with one that made it clear that he was capable of playing hardball when the occasion called for it.

"Mayor Klaus, I'll give you a pass this time for the accusations you made against both me and Ms. Michaels since you're obviously under some kind of emotional strain right now. But any repeat of this kind of attack against either of us, the next person you hear from will be my lawyer. I had hoped we could settle the matter of the nugget without involving attorneys, lawsuits and law enforcement beyond Chief Peters here. I'm a patient man, but my patience is not unlimited. If you keep delaying, it will only cost your fine town more money and a lot of bad press."

Then he sauntered out the door. Cade figured the man had every right to be disgusted with the situation. He also appreciated the way Max had backed Shelby against the mayor's accusations. However, his threat to escalate the situation was worrisome. Max was right—he'd been incredibly patient with the town's slow-moving response to his claim. But he must be already poised to take further action if his first response to Otto had been to bring up all kinds of scary things like lawyers and legal actions that the town couldn't afford.

He wasn't about to go chasing after Max to beg for more time. It wasn't his job, and he wasn't sure it would accomplish anything. No, confronting a different man might be far more productive right now. And lucky him, there was a good candidate close at hand. Shelby with her soft heart and forgiving nature might be willing to treat the mayor with kid gloves, but not him.

Cade had only caught the tail end of the conversation between Shelby, Otto and Max, but it had been more than enough to light the fuse of his temper. Now that the rest of the town was locked out, he had a few choice words for Otto, ones he'd rather Shelby not hear. Knowing her, she'd tried to calm the waters with one of her warm smiles. Normally, he might even enjoy letting her soothe his anger.

But not this time. No way, no how.

It was Cade's job to protect her and the town. If that entailed giving Otto Klaus a figurative kick to the behind, then that's what he'd do. He marched down the short hall to the small break room located in the back of the building. Just as he expected, Otto was seated at the table with a chilled bottle of water in one hand. Fine. He probably needed it. It was the fact he was also holding Shelby's hand with his other one that had Cade clenching his teeth as he dropped into the chair across from Otto.

He put his elbows on the table and leaned forward. Infusing his voice with a whole lot of grit, he aimed his words at his intended target. "Mr. Mayor, we're going to have us a little talk. Just the two of us. You're not going to like what I have to say, but you will listen. Am I making myself clear?"

Otto about jumped out of his skin while Shelby looked over at Cade with a touch of reproach in her eyes. He shook his head at her, hoping she'd take the hint and leave him alone with Otto. But, no, she sat there holding the old fool's hand. He tried another tack. "I could use a bottle of water myself."

She knew what he was up to and didn't fall for his attempt to get her up and moving. "Help yourself. It's in the fridge there."

That left him no choice but to get one for himself, not that he really wanted it in the first place. Returning to his chair, he set the bottle aside and resumed his scrutiny of the mayor, who was looking slightly better by that point. Maybe he thought Shelby would continue to shield him from the consequences of his boneheaded behavior. Fat chance of that.

"First, I want to add my own comments on the incredible disrespect you showed to Shelby out there a few minutes ago. She has done nothing to deserve such outrageous accusations. She's worked day and night trying to find some way to disprove Mr. Volkov's claims about the nugget."

He put his elbows back on the table, his hands clenched in fists. As he leaned forward, he took some pleasure in Otto jerking back as if he thought Cade was about to pounce. "So before you go criticizing other people for not being able to solve the problem, tell me what you've done so far to deal with the situation. Besides going fishing, I mean. I'm sure wading in the water and casting your fly rod was really helpful."

Otto glared at him. "I'm entitled to go fishing on my own time."

Shelby tossed a little snark into the conversation. "Just like Chief Peters and I were entitled to go on a hike the other day. Isn't that right, Mr. Mayor?"

Otto flushed red and nodded.

"Then I'm sure you want to apologize for all those despicable things you said to me. You marched all the way down here from city hall to attack me for no good reason, and I won't stand for it."

Okay, maybe she wasn't as sympathetic with the mayor's issues as Cade had thought. The other man muttered, "Sorry, Shelby."

Good for her. It was almost unsportsmanlike to double-team Otto, but the man had brought it on himself. Back to the matter at hand. Cade gave the man his best tough cop stare. "So, have you talked to an attorney about the situation?"

It was no surprise when Otto shook his head. "Haven't had time."

That shocked Cade even though it probably shouldn't have. "Any reason for that?"

"Not all of the council was convinced it was necessary. We all know Volkov is just grasping at straws hoping to make a quick buck. Eventually he'll give up and go away."

Shelby was staring at Otto like he had lost his mind, She dropped the mayor's hand and scooted her chair farther from his. "Did you hear what Max said out there? You know, when he threw out words like *attorneys* and *lawsuits*? That didn't sound like a man who will simply disappear because we don't like what he has to say."

Cade needed some clarification. "I was at the council meeting where this was discussed. When the meeting adjourned, the plan was to pay an outside attorney to review the file and advise the council on what can be done. When did that change?"

Otto's gaze dropped down to the tabletop, a clear signal his answer wasn't going to make Cade happy. "Councilwoman Southworth and I continued the discussion. We decided there was no reason to waste the town's limited resources on a high-priced attorney when Volkov's claim is unfounded."

That brought Cade to his feet as he roared, "Did you even bother to read the file?"

"Not completely, but there was no need. Everyone knows the Trillium Nugget belongs to the city of Dunbar."

If it weren't undignified, Cade would've banged his head on the wall. "We'd all like that to be true, Otto, but we may have to offer actual proof in a court of law. I can assure you that judges aren't in the habit of just taking your word for such things, especially if the other party comes in armed with little things called *facts*."

Shelby added her support to the point he was trying to make. "Proof which, despite our best efforts, we don't yet have, Otto."

He still wasn't getting it. "What about possession is nine tenths of the law or whatever that saying is?"

It was like talking to a toddler who'd taken someone else's ball at the playground. "Yes, Otto, we have it. We'd also like to keep it, which means we have to be proactive about this whole situation."

Cade pointed toward Shelby. "Take Shelby. She's organized volunteers to read the journals in the museum's book collection that cover the right time period. We're still working on that, so it remains to be seen what we'll learn. She also asked your wife to help with some research."

Otto was staring back at Cade in bewilderment. "That's what Ilse's been doing?"

"She didn't tell you?"

"No, all I knew was that she was spending

a lot of time on the phone and online doing a bunch of searches." His eyes went kind of shifty. "She always deletes her search history. She thinks I snoop."

Shelby rolled her eyes. "Sounds like she has cause to think that, but what did you think she was doing?"

If anything, Otto looked even more dejected. "Figuring out how to have me removed from office. I know she was a better mayor than I am, but she doesn't need to rub it in."

At least Shelby had saved Cade from having to ask whether Otto actually did spy on his wife. He doubted anyone would ever understand the dynamics inside the Klaus marriage.

"Maybe you should do something to impress the lady, Otto. Until the voters say otherwise, you are our mayor. Why not take charge and show everyone that you're working hard to save the Trillium Nugget? If you pull that off, then not even Ilse will stand a chance of beating you next election."

Otto blinked as if that idea had never crossed his mind. "You mean something better than preventing the town's van from being painted like our old VW?"

Shelby beamed at him. "Even better than that."

"That would be great. I'll do it."

Cade already knew where this was headed, so he just leaned back in his chair to enjoy the show. It took less than thirty seconds for Otto to realize the one problem with the plan. As soon as he did, he wilted.

"I want to be a strong leader. I really do." Then he heaved a huge sigh as a single tear trickled down his cheek. "But I have no idea how."

CHAPTER EIGHTEEN

In the end, Shelby had patted Otto on the hand and sent him on his way after promising she would give some serious thought to what he could do to help. Before letting him escape, Cade had offered the mayor one suggestion. Well, it was more like he'd handed the older man his marching orders.

"Call the attorney, Otto. None of us are qualified to determine how Max Volkov's file will stand up in court. Not me, not Shelby, not you and certainly not the other members of the city council."

Still looking defeated, Otto nodded. "I'll call someone even if I have to foot the bill myself."

Shelby watched as Cade took a step closer to the older man, using his proximity to underscore the seriousness of his next question. "When?"

Maybe it was unfair to pile on Otto when

he was already down, but Cade was right. If they didn't make a concerted effort to counter Max's file, their case was lost before it even got started.

Otto hesitated and then said, "Tomorrow?"

Sadly, rather than an assertion of fact, his answer was more of a question laced with a subtle hint of a whine. Cade was clearly gearing up for a major explosion which wouldn't shore up Otto's confidence. To prevent that from happening, Shelby stepped between them. On impulse, she did her best to imitate the look her friend Elizabeth gave her kids when they had made bad choices—a cross between exasperation and expectations. "Not good enough, Otto."

He practically scuffed his shoe like a five-year-old kid who'd forgotten to pick up his toys. "Fine, I'll go back to my office and make a few calls."

Still following her friend's example, Shelby beamed at him for getting the answer right on the first try. "That's great, Otto. I look forward to hearing what you've learned. I'll expect your call first thing in the morning."

After shepherding him out of the building, she turned the lock and then slumped back against the door in exhaustion. She smiled at Cade. "I don't know about you, but I've had enough drama for one day."

"Think he'll actually make the call?"

"We didn't leave him a lot of wiggle room on the matter. Besides, now he knows his archrival-slash-wife is already working on the nugget defense." She paused for a second. "Do you think we should come up with an official name for the few of us who are doing the hard work of trying to counter Max's claims? You know, like the Trillium Defense Team?"

His mouth immediately quirked up in a small grin. "That's one possibility."

He did his best to look serious, but the twinkle in his eyes betrayed him. "Okay, Cade, out with it. What's your suggestion?"

"I'm thinking the Max Maulers or, better yet, the Defenders of the Mighty Nugget."

As worried as she was, injecting a little humor into the situation wasn't a bad idea. "That last one has a certain cachet. We could do matching T-shirts."

Then she cocked her head to one side and studied the man standing a little too far away from where she wanted him to be. Cade gave her a puzzled look. "What's going on in that brain of yours?"

"I could say that I'm trying to think of another logo we could use on the T-shirts, but that would be a lie."

Sometimes it seemed as if Cade could read her mind, but right now his radar was definitely offline. If it had been working, he'd already have her wrapped in his arms. Instead, he lingered just out of reach as he asked, "So what's the truth?"

"That I could really use a hug."

There were many things she liked about Cade Peters, and the list was getting longer every day. At the moment, it was the fact he was a man of action when given a clear mission. Two seconds after she spoke, she was surrounded by his gentle strength. She closed her eyes as she breathed in his scent, an appealing mix of soap, a hint of sweat and something mysterious that was unique to Cade. It soothed her on so many levels.

His fingers threaded their way through her hair to cradle the nape of her neck and then tucked her head against his chest. She smiled and listened to the steady thump of his heart. "Thanks, I needed this."

"Anytime."

They both had other stuff they should be doing. She wanted to get back to reading that journal. He had a police department to run. That didn't mean she was going to feel guilty for stealing a few minutes of peace after the day they'd both had. The quiet settled around them, gradually smoothing off the rough edges left from dealing with the mayor's meltdown.

A few seconds later, she heard an unwelcome buzzing coming from Cade's shirt pocket. When she started to step back so he could answer the call, he tightened his hold on her with one arm while he fished the phone out of his pocket. "Chief Peters here."

He listened for a few seconds. "I'll be there in five minutes."

Before disconnecting the call, he stared down at her mouth for the longest time and then amended his answer. "No, better make that six, maybe seven minutes."

Then he kissed Shelby, gently and with such amazing care. As if that moment mattered more than duty, more than the need to breathe. It didn't last long, but the memory of its simple perfection could last a lifetime.

She wanted to protest when he broke it off to stare down into her eyes.

"I'm guessing it might be dereliction of duty if I called my office back to tell them that I need another few minutes…or maybe the rest of the day."

She fiddled with a button on his uniform shirt. "Probably, especially after we both just browbeat the mayor into doing his job. What kind of example would we be setting?"

"Otto is old enough to be my father. I shouldn't be the one having to set the example."

Shuddering just a little, she pretended a horror she really didn't feel. "If he was your father, Ilse would be your mother. Just imagine being driven to school and basketball practices in a flower-covered van by a woman who still thinks tied-dyed clothes are the height of fashion."

"That's a heck of an image." He pressed yet another small kiss to her cheek. "But you're right. I need to go see what's going on over at the station."

"I hope it's nothing serious."

"Me, too. We've both already been through

enough for one day. Besides, I'm pretty sure if it was, Moira would've said so."

"That's good. Tell her hi for me." She stepped away from the door so she could unlock it for him. "I'll let you know what Otto has to say about how his phone calls went. I'll give him until midmorning tomorrow to contact me before I hunt him down."

"Let me know if you need backup. The timer is running down on the whole situation. Max wasn't bluffing about getting the courts involved if that's what it takes. I don't want to think about what will happen when he wins."

When he wins? She drew a sharp breath. Did Cade really believe a victory for Max was a forgone conclusion? Cade must have realized how that had sounded and tried again. "Sorry, I meant to say *if* he wins."

Regardless of his correction, Shelby could tell Cade had serious concerns that the town's best efforts were doomed to fail. She didn't want to even consider that a possibility. They both knew if a court ordered the museum to surrender the nugget to Max Volkov, it would likely have side effects that tumbled like dominos throughout the town.

Although Cade hadn't mentioned it lately, he must still worry that failure to save the nugget could cost him his job. If he left town, where would that leave the two of them? She hadn't been lying when she'd told him that Dunbar was the only place she'd ever wanted to live. But how could she stand by and watch him walk away if the town forced him to resign? It would devastate her. Was living in Dunbar more important to her than being with Cade?

That was the real question.

Worrying about what-ifs would accomplish nothing. All she could do was continue reading the journals and hope for a miracle. Trying to keep things light, she gave Cade a small shove to get him moving in the right direction. "I've got some more reading to do, and I'm pretty sure your six, maybe seven minutes are all used up."

He accepted her dismissal with good grace. "Okay, I'll go. But to be very clear about this, Ms. Michaels, I'd rather stay right here."

Something about his tone made her wonder if that special radar of his had picked up on her thoughts somehow. That he was talking about spending more time not just in her office, but the town. "I'd like that, too. Better yet, I wish we were both down at the café enjoying a late lunch and a piece of coconut cream pie. Well, that's what I'd be having. You'd probably prefer the sweet potato pie. Unfortunately, we both have work to do."

He gave her along look as if he wanted to say something more but wasn't sure he should. Finally, he settled for, "I'm glad you called me."

Then he was gone. After closing the door, she watched from the edge of the window as Cade crossed the street. Boy, she loved the way that man moved, all strength and confidence. From the way a few other feminine heads turned in his direction, she wasn't the only one who thought that way. The casserole brigade had ceased operations, but Carli showing up with dinner for Cade made it clear its members stood ready to leap back into action if he was ever back on the market. That wouldn't happen, not if it was up to her.

It wasn't until he disappeared through the front door of the police station that she realized she was stroking her lips with a fingertip, reliving that kiss, and hoping it wouldn't be the last one they shared.

CADE LEANED BACK in his chair and put his feet up on the porch railing. He'd been later than usual getting back to his house thanks to the microcrisis that Moira had needed him to handle. He knew her pride had taken a hit having to call him in to deal with two of the old-timers in town, but they'd refused to believe that a woman cop could handle their problem.

He'd invited them into his office and then proceeded to explain in no uncertain terms that they didn't get to pick and choose which officer was assigned to any particular case. He'd also pointed out Officer Fraser was a highly qualified officer, one a town the size of Dunbar was lucky to have. If she wasn't good enough to handle their problem, then they could just handle it themselves. At least the old coots had had the good grace to apologize to her on their way out.

Next, he'd checked in with Moira to make sure she was okay. She wasn't, not that she would admit it. He figured she was both angry and embarrassed. He settled on simply reminding her that she was darn good at her job and to tell him if anything similar happened in the future.

But that was a problem for another day. Right now, he just wanted to enjoy the quiet for a while. The deer made their usual appearance, grazing their way across the clearing. He'd just settled in when a familiar truck pulled into the driveway. Titus stopping by on his way home after the café closed was getting to be a habit. This was the first time, though, that he brought an extra guest. Ned hopped out of the truck and trotted over to the porch to plop down beside Cade's feet.

The deer froze right where they were, lifting their heads to do a threat assessment. Cade was surprised that the sight of the huge dog didn't send them bolting back into the trees. Instead, they gradually relaxed and returned to their evening meal.

Cade slowly reached his hand out toward Ned and waited to see how he reacted. Ned kept his eyes on the deer, but he finally bumped Cade's hand with his head, granting him scratching privileges. By that point, Titus had joined them. As usual, he hadn't come empty-handed. He set three smaller paper bags on the porch and opened a fourth that was considerably larger. "I brought Ned's dinner with me."

He pulled two disposable aluminum foil pans out of the bag. After setting one on the arm of the closest Adirondack chair, he filled the second one with water at the spigot next to the garage door. After putting it down in front of Ned, he unwrapped the other container to reveal a heaping pile of kibble with what looked like bits of steak scattered across the top. The dog followed his every move, maybe to make sure that neither human got between him and his dinner.

As soon as Titus set the food down next to the water, Ned made a lunge for it. His owner wasn't having it. "Did I say you could eat?"

The dog sat back down and grudgingly waited for Titus to get situated. When he was comfortable, he finally granted Ned permission to chow down. "Okay, boy, have at it."

After giving Titus a pretty disgusted look, Ned sniffed his bowl and then dug right in. Titus shook his head and glanced at Cade. "We've been working on his manners. It's an uphill battle, but we're making progress."

"So you've decided to keep him?"

"It's more like he's decided to put up with a few rules if it means getting fed on a regular basis."

"Smart dog."

With his roommate taken care of, Titus peeked into the next bag and held it out to

Cade. "This one is yours, but we should wait for your other guest to arrive."

Cade studied the bag's contents and smiled before rolling the top closed. A huge sandwich and a piece of pie would definitely hit the spot. "Did we have a dinner date that I forgot about? Not that I'm complaining, mind you."

Titus checked the next bag and set it aside. "I heard rumblings that both you and Shelby had a tough day and thought you both might appreciate not having to cook. I offered to pick her up on the way, but she wasn't at home. Something about getting some kind of journal back from Earl Marley. She'll come here from there."

The quiet settled around them again. Well, other than the sound of Ned crunching away on his kibble. It was the first moment of real peace Cade had enjoyed since duty had dragged him away from holding Shelby in his arms. That had definitely been the high point of his entire day. Although knowing she would be pulling into his driveway any second now also ranked right up there.

"I'd ask who has been gossiping about me

and Shelby, but it pretty much has to be Max Volkov."

Titus didn't bother to deny it. "He was all wound up when he came storming into the café this afternoon. He clearly doesn't care much for Mayor Klaus. After swearing me to secrecy, he said it was one thing if the man wanted to insult Max, but it is unacceptable for him to cast aspersions on Shelby's honor. Something about the woman having been nothing but professional, and at least she's doing her job. And how can the mayor fault her for selling Max postage? There was more, but you get the drift."

He'd been watching the deer, but he turned to give Cade a considering look. "I had to wonder if he'd gotten his facts right considering I saw Otto walk by a little later. He still had all his teeth and wasn't bruised up and bleeding."

Cade answered the question Titus hadn't actually asked. "Max wasn't lying or confused. Otto marched into the post office and pretty much accused Shelby of conspiring with the enemy. He made her mad enough that she called me to toss him out when he wouldn't leave on his own. Max hung around until I got there, and I managed to catch the tail end of Otto's diatribe."

Even now, hours later, he wanted to do some serious bodily harm to the guy for upsetting Shelby so much. "Max left not long after that."

"And how did Otto fare? Because despite his age, I would've had a tough time not decking him for disrespecting Shelby, and she's not even my woman."

Was Titus saying Shelby belonged to Cade? He decided not to ask, but then he had some serious thoughts along that line himself. "It was a close call. Unfortunately, it's against my code of ethics to punch someone who is already crying."

Titus looked incredulous, but Cade nodded to confirm the truth. "Yep, but don't share that with anyone. We all need him to look like he's in control of the situation. Having everyone in town laughing behind his back wouldn't help things."

"What happened after that?"

"Shelby gave him his marching orders. Otto has to do his part in figuring out how to defend the nugget from Max. For now, that means he needs to find a qualified attorney to give the town some direction in how to handle the matter if it ends up going to court. Otto is supposed to report in to her tomorrow morning on what he's accomplished. Failing that, she'll hunt him down."

"Tough lady."

Who was just pulling into the driveway. "She can be, but sometimes she's a little too forgiving with people."

That assessment brought a hint of a smile to Titus's face. "You mean like the guy who let her think she'd been asked out on a date. Then she finds out the truth of the situation when he dumps a huge mess in her lap half-way up the side of a mountain."

Give the man credit for going for the kill shot. "Yeah, just like that."

At least Titus dropped the subject as Shelby joined them on the porch. Cade stood up because it seemed like the polite thing to do. Besides, it gave him the chance to give her a proper greeting, which meant a quick hug and even quicker kiss. When her back was turned, Titus smirked at Cade for using caveman tactics to stake his claim on Shelby.

Meanwhile, Cade offered her the chair next

to his, putting himself between Shelby and Titus. "Have a seat."

"I hope you don't mind me showing up uninvited, but Titus promised me pie. That trumps good manners any day."

Titus held out the third bag to pass along to Shelby. "You were invited—by me. Cade here never complains when I show up without calling as long as I feed him."

She leaned forward so she could see Titus. "Good to know. I'll keep that in mind. Thanks for feeding me, too."

"Like I told him, I heard you two had a hard day."

That had her giving both Cade and Titus a puzzled look. Maybe she thought Titus just hung out with Cade so he could fill him in on all the local gossip. He set her straight before Titus had a chance. "Evidently after Max left your office, he ended up at the café where he swore Titus to secrecy before venting about the mayor."

Once again, she looked past Cade toward Titus. "I've heard Max hangs out at your place when he's not holed up in his room at the bed-and-breakfast."

"Yeah, lucky me. Even Ned here hasn't

managed to run him off." He glanced down at his four-legged companion. "Worthless dog."

Even as he complained, he stroked the dog's fur. Shelby laughed. "Yeah, it's easy to tell you don't like Ned very much."

Cade chimed in. "He didn't make Ned wait until you got here to feed him. And he put bits of steak on top of the kibble."

Titus wasn't appreciating the turn the conversation had taken. "I'll remember all of this verbal abuse the next time I get the urge to do something nice for you two."

Cade tightened his grip on the bag holding his dinner when Titus added, "I don't have to always make sweet potato pie or even coconut cream, you know."

"If you want me to apologize, it's not happening."

Shelby looked at Cade like he'd lost his mind. "Well, I will. Maybe you can survive without that vegetable side dish you call dessert, but I'd never put my access to coconut cream pie at risk."

Then in a singsong voice, she said, "Sorry, Titus, if we hurt your feelings."

Cade burst out laughing at the sour lemon look on Titus's face. The man in question pointed toward the bag he still had clutched in his hand. "Eat before I give it to Ned. He loves pie."

The dog momentarily lifted his head to see what the three humans were doing. Two seconds later, Ned was already back to sleep and snoring softly. He didn't even twitch when they unwrapped their sandwiches and started to eat. Cade was hungry enough to have eaten cardboard, but Titus had outdone himself this time. The huge kaiser roll was piled high with thinly sliced roast beef, Havarti cheese, sliced tomatoes and leaf lettuce. The spicy-hot mustard added just the right burst of flavor with every bite.

The man sure didn't cut corners when he wanted to feed someone. Someday Cade was going to get around to asking Titus where he'd learned to cook. For now, they all made quick work of their meals. Cade took their trash into the house and brought back tall glasses of iced tea. "I should have offered drinks before this."

Evidently tired of sitting, Titus was now standing up and leaning against the porch railing. "Much appreciated."

Shelby smiled up at Cade as he handed her a glass. "Thanks."

Cade topped off Ned's water bowl before sitting back down himself. "This is nice. Good food and good company."

Shelby set her glass down. "I stopped at Earl Marley's house on my way here."

"Titus told me. Did he or Helen manage to come up with anything that might help the cause?"

He didn't really expect to hear that anything had come from their efforts. Earl might have made a real attempt to help, but Cade wondered if Helen put in anything but a minimal effort.

To his surprise, Shelby was looking pretty excited. "I told you Earl was making a list of everyone who was mentioned by name in his journal. I did the same after he told me what he was doing. So did Helen. When we compared the lists, we realized how many of those people still have relatives living in the area."

He wasn't sure where she was going with this. "Do you need me to go back through the books I've read and do the same?"

"It wouldn't hurt, but we already have quite a few names. Maybe someone on the list knows something about the provenance of the nugget, but it's hard to decide where to start. It also doesn't help that we don't know how long it will be before someone else makes Max mad enough to start court proceedings."

She was right. If Otto or Eileen Southworth did something to set the man off again, the town could end up in deep trouble. "I guess all we can do is start at the top of the list and work our way down. You can give me some names to contact. Maybe some of the museum board members could be trusted to help."

She only looked more discouraged. "What should we ask? Maybe some of them might have more journals we could read, but we're running out of time."

Titus spoke up for the first time. "Ask for the names of the oldest family members and start with them. They wouldn't have been around when the nugget was found, but they would be the most likely ones to have heard tales about it growing up. I'm betting they'd love to know someone is interested in listening to their old stories."

Now, why hadn't Cade thought of that himself? Before he could say a thing, Shelby was up out of her chair and headed straight for Titus. She threw her arms around him and squeezed him tight. "You, sir, are a genius. Thank you, thank you, thank you."

Cade might have objected to her hugging another man if Titus hadn't looked so uncomfortable with the whole situation. He gently extricated himself from Shelby's tight grip while giving Cade an apologetic look.

"It's nothing. You would have figured it out yourself."

"Maybe, but possibly not in time."

She was almost vibrating with excitement. "If I leave right now, I can start making calls before it gets too late."

Darn, Cade had been really hoping Titus would leave first so he and Shelby could have a little alone time, but he understood what this meant to her. "Let me know what I can do to help."

She gave him a quick kiss on his cheek, Ned a pat on the head and Titus another bright smile. Then she was off and running. All the three males could do was watch as she backed out of the driveway and tore off down the road.

Titus finally returned to his chair. "Think talking to the old folks might actually work?"

Cade had no idea, but at least it gave Shelby another line of inquiry to pursue. "I hope so. Regardless, it was nice to see her look genuinely happy and hopeful for once. But if it doesn't pan out..."

When he didn't finish his thought, Titus did it for him. "You're worried she'll crash and burn."

Considering everything both of them had riding on the outcome of the situation, he'd be hitting bottom hard himself. He wasn't quite at the point where he'd start polishing up his résumé quite yet, but it still might come to that.

"Let's just hope some of the old-timers have some real interesting stories to tell."

Titus stroked Ned's head and watched the deer start making their way back into the trees. "Fingers crossed."

Cade held up his own two fingers twisted together. "Amen to that."

CHAPTER NINETEEN

THE FRONT DOOR of the museum opened just as the old grandfather clock in the corner chimed nine times. As usual, Cade was right on time. Not to wish ill on anyone in town, Shelby had been almost hoping something had come up at the police station to delay their planned outing. It wasn't as if she didn't relish the chance to spend more time with him. She was seriously down with that idea.

It was the reason he was there to pick her up this morning that had her all tied up in knots. The loud ticking of the clock had stretched her nerves to the breaking point. It was a depressing reminder that time was running out on their chances to find a credible defense against Max Volkov's claim on the Trillium Nugget.

The attorney that Otto had talked to hadn't been all that encouraging about their chances if the case went to court. Meanwhile, she and

Cade had spent the past two days talking to the eldest members of the Dunbar population that they could locate. They'd learned a lot about the history of the town, but nothing that pertained to the nugget itself. They had two more names left on the list, and Cade was taking her to meet with them, starting with an elderly lady with deep roots in Dunbar. Their final stop would be to talk to a gentleman who now lived about thirty miles from town. They were supposed to meet with him early in the afternoon.

"Shelby?"

She walked over to the top of the staircase to answer his summons. "I'm up here."

When Cade started up the steps, she returned to her vigil in front of the case that housed the Trillium Nugget. A small voice in the back of her mind whispered that a lump of gold, regardless of its size, shouldn't be the one thing that defined the town of Dunbar. The fact was that most folks went about their daily lives without giving the nugget much thought.

Cade joined her in front of the case. When he slipped his arm around her waist, she leaned into the comfort of his touch. "You're looking pretty sad there, Shelby."

"I'm indulging in some rather traitorous thoughts."

"Like for instance?"

She pointed at the nugget. "I'm angry that a piece of shiny metal has somehow become more important than the people who live here. Maybe that's not true, but right now it feels that way. Seriously, if it disappeared right this instant, what would really change? Yeah, it's the museum's pride and joy. But the truth is most tourists come through here because we're close to hiking trails, rivers, ski slopes and campgrounds. Even if the museum had to close its doors, the town's economy wouldn't take much of a hit."

"All of that's true, Shelby."

She wasn't done yet. "Yeah, it's worth a lot of money. But again, as long as it just sits there, the value doesn't really matter. We can't use it to pay for fixing potholes in the streets or to educate our kids or anything else that would improve the quality of life for the people who live here."

"You'll get no arguments from me." He leaned in closer to the cabinet. "I bet that less than a handful of people in town have ever been lucky enough to hold it in their hands. It could be a hologram for all they know."

That made her laugh, at least a little. "Want to be one of the lucky ones?"

Before he could answer, she headed over to the control panel and turned off the alarm. Then she let the security company know that she was the one who'd disabled the alarm, and that she'd be turning it back on within five minutes.

Cade looked pretty excited about the prospect of holding the nugget. Still he asked, "Are you sure we should be doing this?"

"No, but this might be our last chance ever."

She opened the cabinet and reached in to remove the nugget. After holding it up to the light to admire all of its nooks and crannies, she handed it over to Cade. The nugget looked huge even in Cade's big hands. "Wow, this thing is heavier than it looks."

"That's always my first thought."

He continued to study the nugget, turning it over and running his fingers over its surface. "And what's your second?"

It was the same thing she'd wondered the

very first time she'd ever seen the nugget back when her fourth grade class had toured the museum. Should she tell him? After all, he was the chief of police. "That it's way too big to slip into my pocket without anyone noticing."

He cracked up at that. "Now that I know that you're given to having larcenous thoughts, I should start frisking you on a regular basis. You know, all in the line of duty."

She liked the sound of that. "Hold that thought."

After returning the nugget to its stand and locking the case, she reengaged the security alarm. With that done, she parked herself back in front of Cade and held her arms up in the air. "You probably should make sure that I actually put the Trillium Nugget back in the case. After all, it could be that hologram you mentioned."

His dark eyes gleamed with anticipation. "I'll need to be pretty thorough."

"Bring it on, lawman. Never let it be said that our chief of police didn't do his job."

As soon as the words were out of her mouth, the mischievous light in Cade's eyes died. Rather than making good on his threat…or promise, depending on how she looked at it… he gently tugged her arms back down and wrapped them around his waist.

Holding her close, he remained silent. Finally, she couldn't stand it any longer. "What did I say wrong, Cade?"

"Nothing."

She caught his face between her hands and forced him to look directly at her. "Tell me."

"We both know things aren't looking good for the nugget staying in Dunbar. I'm not saying we should give up, but we also can't ignore the possibility that Max Volkov's claim will prove stronger than the town's."

"And? Like I was just saying, losing the nugget won't destroy the town. We won't let it."

He smiled at her, but that sadness still lingered in his eyes. "Stubborn woman. I'm beginning to think that you should give both Otto and Ilse a run for their money when it comes to the next election. Or you could run for the city council. I'm betting you'd crush Eileen Southworth."

She didn't even want to consider the possibility. "It's hard enough wrangling the board

I already head up, and all we have to do is balance the budget for the museum."

"You'd be good at it and good for the town because you always see the big picture rather than focusing on what would benefit you. At the very least everyone would sleep better at night knowing they're in no danger of waking up to find all of the local official vehicles have been decked out with hippie artwork."

That had her laughing. "There is that."

He still hadn't answered her question. Maybe she shouldn't press him on the matter if it was painful for him, but she suspected it was something she needed to know or at least he needed her to hear. "Tell me what I said that hurt you."

"You didn't say anything wrong, Shelby." Cade sighed and turned to study the Trillium Nugget again. "None of us knows how all of this is going to play out. Win or lose, there are a few key players in town who have decided to hold me responsible for the fact that Max's claim is being taken seriously at all."

With obvious reluctance, he pulled a folded envelope out of his uniform pocket and held it out to her. "This was delivered this morning."

A wave of icy dread washed through

Shelby making her reluctant to take it. Cade's own reaction to the envelope and whatever it contained was enough to warn her there was nothing good inside.

But hiding her head in the sand wasn't going to help either of them. The letter was short and to the point. Three of the city council members had decided to issue an edict, one that questioned Cade's every action regarding what they described as a blatant and fraudulent attempt on the part of one Maxim Volkov to rob the town of its most valued prize. They were putting Cade on official notice that his employment would be terminated in thirty days. Period. No discussion. It didn't matter if his efforts resolved the problem in favor of the town. It was no surprise that Eileen Southworth's signature was at the top of the list.

Shelby wanted to run the letter through the shredder or, better yet, burn it. But it wasn't her letter, and Cade might need it if he decided to pursue legal action to retain his position with the city. After folding the letter with care and returning it to the envelope, she gave it back to him. "This is ridiculous, Cade. They can't do that. It's no more your fault than anyone else's. They may as well blame me for letting him into the museum in the first place or Titus for letting him eat at the café. And then there's Rikki Bruce who has been offering him safe harbor in her home."

Why wasn't he screaming bloody murder about the unfairness of it all? But maybe he'd been expecting this to happen. He'd already told her he'd make an easy scapegoat if the people wanted someone to blame for the loss of the nugget. Then there was the issue that some members of the council had been against hiring him in the first place. Cade might be resigned to his fate, but she wasn't.

"You were hired to enforce the laws. And that means all of them. You can't pick and choose, and neither can they. If Max hasn't done anything wrong, you can't run him out of town. You were also the one who insisted on the mayor getting legal counsel on how best to deal with the situation. These people can't be allowed to fire you for simply doing your duty."

He didn't dispute anything she'd just said as he carefully returned the envelope to his pocket. "Maybe not, but being a cop is a hard job on a good day. I can't serve the town if the people here don't want me here."

His assessment of the situation hit her so hard that her breath caught in her chest. "You would find it that easy to leave Dunbar?"

Not to mention her. Didn't he know how much he meant to her? Not that she'd put it into words, but Cade had to have some idea. And maybe it was now too late for her to admit that she had some pretty powerful feelings for him, the kind that went way beyond simple friendship.

Still staring at the lump of gold inside the case, he finally answered. "Never think for a minute that it would be easy, Shelby. Packing up and moving on would be one of the hardest things I've ever done. Dunbar is my home now. For the first time since I joined the service, I've put down some roots and made some real connections with people here. I respect the other officers I work with, and I really like knowing that most of the folks I see every day will be around for the long term."

He hesitated before continuing. "Don't get me wrong. I don't regret the life I had in the army. I made a lot of friends over the years, but we never had any control about how much time we'd actually be stationed together. Some of us try to stay in touch, but it's hard when we're scattered all over the planet."

"I can't even imagine..."

"I know, Shelby, and that's the problem." He straightened his shoulders as if bracing himself for an unexpected blow. "This is your home, and you've made it clear that it's where you plan to spend the rest of your life. I want that for you because it's what makes you happy."

She dreaded hearing the rest of what he was about to say, but she owed it to him to listen. It took several tugs on his arm to get him to face her while he talked. "Tell me the rest."

"I'm proud of the time I've spent here, and I'll walk away knowing I did the best I could. But if I have to leave Dunbar, it will mean leaving you, too."

He lifted his hand as if touch her face, but then let it drop back down to his side. "And losing you will be the one thing I'll regret."

"You haven't lost me, Cade."

"Are you saying you'd consider going with me?"

The lump in her throat made it impossible for her to respond. He did stroke her cheek this time. "That's what I thought."

"Don't give up, Cade. Don't let them win."

"It's not that simple, Shelby. I can't do the job with people here second-guessing my every decision."

Her heart hurt. "But I've only just found you, Cade. What we have is special. We can't let that darn nugget and a few shortsighted fools take it away from us."

"And you shouldn't have to choose between the life you love and me. I can't and I won't ask that of you."

But maybe she could ask it of herself. Cade was so different from Kyle, the man she'd once thought loved her. Maybe he did, but he hadn't understood her. He'd also made the assumption that her own dreams and needs weren't important, especially if they ran counter to his. At the time, living in a big city surrounded by strangers had been overwhelming, but she no longer was that naive young woman. And she'd never be alone, not with Cade in her life.

It was tempting to share that amazing epiphany with Cade. The clock chimed the half hour, jarring her out of the past and into the moment at hand. "We're going to be late if we don't leave right now."

"Do you still want me to come with you?"

Distancing herself from Cade might be the smart move at this point to give herself time to think, but she wanted every possible minute with him. "Yes, of course. That letter doesn't change anything, especially when it comes to our investigation. Once we disprove Max's claim, we can deal with the council."

"Okay, let's hit the road."

Shelby picked up her purse and the notebook she'd been using to take notes as they'd asked their battery of questions. Beyond the usual basics of name, address, age and family information, she and Cade had devised a series of questions that were designed to gain some perspective on the subject's history in the town of Dunbar. Sadly, none of the people they'd met so far had offered anything particularly helpful when it came to the nugget.

Once they were on the road, Cade asked, "So the woman we're going to visit this time is a great-aunt of your friend Elizabeth."

"Yes, she is. I think Elizabeth said Rowena just celebrated her ninety-second birthday. She lives in a mother-in-law house on the back of her son's property."

Cade let out a low whistle. "Wow, can you

imagine all the changes she's seen over her lifetime?"

"I've only met her a couple of times over the years. I do remember Aunt Rowena being a chatty one, so she'll probably love telling a handsome man like you all about her life."

She loved that Cade grinned at that comment. "So you think I'm handsome?"

"I'm sure you have a mirror at home, Cade. You don't need me to tell you how good-looking you are. There's a reason you've had all of the little old ladies we've been interviewing hanging on your every word. I'm only there to take notes."

That had his cheeks turning red. "You're exaggerating the situation."

"So the casserole brigade was only bringing you more food than you could possibly eat just because they felt sorry for you?"

By that point, they'd reached their destination, saving Cade from having to answer. That didn't keep her from laughing at how fast he bolted out of the SUV and headed up the sidewalk toward the house.

CHAPTER TWENTY

Cade didn't think of himself as either shy or cowardly, but he might have to rethink that after spending the past two hours with Great-aunt Rowena. The woman was a definite flirt and all too happy to have the undivided attention of a man roughly a third her age who wasn't a blood relative.

While she was polite to Shelby, it was Cade she'd insisted on sitting next to her on the very small loveseat in her living room, which left less than a handful of inches between them. If that weren't bad enough, she scooted closer when she'd broken out her family photo albums to share with him, her arm brushing his as she turned the pages or held the album up for closer inspection.

Admittedly she was a charmer, her blue eyes twinkling with good humor as she regaled them with stories about her family members, sharing amusing tales about their foibles and adventures. Unfortunately, none of it had anything to do with the nugget. But even he hadn't had the heart to cut and run when she so obviously enjoyed talking about people who were only kept alive in her memories.

Shelby finally managed to extract him from Rowena's clutches, saying they had another appointment to get to. He would've bolted out the door if it hadn't been undignified for a chief of police. It didn't help that Shelby laughed all the way back to his SUV. Once safely inside the vehicle with the doors locked, he glared at his companion. "It's not funny."

"Yes, it is. I'm guessing you've faced down armed insurgents that didn't spook you as much as Aunt Rowena did."

He backed out of the driveway and tore off down the street. "Go ahead, laugh. You're not the one who had to promise to come back for another visit. Evidently she has another dozen or so photo albums we didn't get to."

"Didn't she describe it as a date? Something about she hadn't been on one in decades and wasn't it wonderful that women can do the asking now."

"Again, not funny."

"Oh, come on, Cade. Admit it. You liked her."

There was no use in denying it. "Yeah, I did. I hope I'm that sharp when I'm that age."

"Take her flowers and candy when you go back. It would make her day."

He was slightly horrified by that idea. "What if that makes her think I'm seriously courting her?"

Shelby pretended to give that some thought. "Well, in that case, I'd suggest you reserve a date at the church as soon as possible. Not because of her advanced age, but there are only so many slots available for weddings and the schedule fills up pretty quickly."

"You are such a brat."

"Yeah, but you like me anyway."

There was an understatement if he'd ever heard one. Time to change the subject. "Want to grab some lunch before we meet with Mr. Bolin?"

"I'd love to. There's a restaurant not too far from here that has the best barbecue in the area. It has outdoor seating, which would be nice today."

"Barbecue would hit the spot. I'd like to make one suggestion, though."

"Which is?"

"We talk about anything other than my job or the nugget. Let's relax and just hang out like we're on a date rather than a mission. Agreed?"

She smiled. "It's a deal. Besides, I don't want anything to detract from the smoky goodness of pulled pork with all the fixings."

"A woman after my own heart."

IT WAS A beautiful day to sit at a picnic table and enjoy a good meal. The Cascade Mountains provided panoramic scenery that only added to the experience. The snowcapped peaks were postcard perfect, one of the many things he loved about living in the Pacific Northwest. Making good on their promise, he and Shelby limited the topics of conversation to their worst moments in high school, first cars and favorite movies. It wasn't until they'd finished the last bite on their plates that they finally got down to business.

"So what can you tell me about Mr. Bolin and his family?"

Shelby brought out her notebook and flipped through the pages until she found his name. "His first name is Nils. The Bolin family immigrated to the States in the late 1800s, ending up in the Dakota Territories. Some stayed there to farm, but a few moved out here to find work as loggers. In fact, that's what Mr. Bolin did for a living."

"So at least some of his family could have been in this area around the same time as Max's great-grandfather."

"Yes, it looks that way."

She closed the notebook and returned it to her purse. "I only found out about him by happenstance. Earl Marley was on duty at the museum when I was working on our list of possibilities. He was studying one of the pictures we have on the wall in the logging section of the museum. Out of curiosity, he took it down and turned it over to see if any of the men in the picture were identified. There were a couple of Bolins listed, and one of them was Nils. Earl tracked down Nils's nephew to get his contact information."

"Well, maybe that bit of luck will be the break we've been looking for."

"We can only hope." Shelby stared past him toward the mountains. "You know, I almost don't want to talk to him. What if it's just another dead end?"

He forced a smile, hoping it looked more

genuine than it felt. "We keep trying. I'm not going to give up now. We—meaning you and me—have too much riding on this."

"Yeah, we do if for no other reason maybe it would give you ammunition to convince the council to let you keep your job." She smiled right back at him, even if it was a little bit sad. "So let's go find out what Nils has to say."

To lighten the mood, Cade grinned. "Who knows, maybe we can make it a double date, me and Rowena, you and Nils."

Her laughter rang out, drawing the attention of several other diners. "We could go for the Early Bird Dinner Special at Titus's café."

Cade hadn't heard about that. "Is that even a thing at his place?"

"No, but I bet your good buddy Titus would make an exception for us."

They were still chuckling about that as they approached Nils's apartment, but had themselves back under control when the door finally opened. Cade let Shelby take the lead since she seemed to have a knack for putting people at ease. "Mr. Bolin, thank you for seeing us today. I'm Shelby Michaels, and this is Cade Peters. He's the chief of police in Dunbar."

The elderly man shook hands with each of them and then carefully maneuvered his walker back a few steps to give them room to enter. “Please come in and have a seat. My nephew said that you were on a mission to talk to a bunch of us oldies who grew up in Dunbar. Can’t imagine why you’d find my old family stories interesting, but I’ll tell you what I can.”

Cade followed along behind Nils. “We really appreciate it, Mr. Bolin.”

“Let’s sit in the kitchen. I have some photos to show you and that will be easier at the table. I also made coffee and put out some cookies if you’d like some.”

Cade helped Nils get settled at the table while Shelby poured the coffee. It was hard not to groan when he spotted the huge pile of photo albums stacked on a TV tray next the old man’s chair. They’d spent way too many hours flipping through pictures of total strangers in a futile attempt to learn anything about the Trillium Nugget. He wasn’t optimistic that this time would be any more productive. Evidently he wasn’t all that successful at hiding his dismay when their host chuckled.

"Don't worry, Chief Peters. I'm not going to torture you with my entire life history. I spent the last couple of days going through the family albums. From what I can tell, only a couple have pictures from around the right time period."

Shelby joined them, setting their mugs of coffee within easy reach. "That was nice of you, Mr. Bolin. Has anyone told you what's been going on in Dunbar?"

"My nephew mentioned something about the Trillium Nugget, but he didn't know any details. He's never lived in Dunbar himself, but he knew I grew up there."

Cade gave him a brief summary of the recent events that had led him and Shelby to Mr. Bolin's door. "So, we're trying to find out how that nugget came to be in the town's possession."

To their surprise, their host looked delighted rather than doubtful. He pointed at the stack of albums. "Chief Peters, can you hand me those top two?"

"Sure thing."

"You folks go ahead and enjoy your coffee. This might take me a minute to find the right page."

He started turning the pages, taking his time to study each of the faded photos. Cade sipped the coffee and then stopped to add some more sugar and cream. Mr. Bolin definitely liked his coffee strong. Cade studied Shelby over the rim of his mug, hating the discouragement she was trying so hard to hide. If Mr. Bolin couldn't help them, they were running dangerously low on chances to disprove Max's claim. They were still waiting to hear back from Ilse about what she'd learned from the newspapers, and the reference librarian she'd contacted.

"Here it is." Mr. Bolin sounded triumphant as he tapped his finger on a page of photos. "I wasn't even born when these pictures of my grandparents were taken. Their names were Frieda and Emil Bolin."

He passed Cade the album so he and Shelby could look at it. She stared at it in wonder with a huge smile on her face. Her hand trembled as she pointed at the picture. Cade knew just how she felt. It wasn't who was in the picture, but what. There was no mistaking that Emil Bolin was holding the Trillium Nugget in his hands.

"Turn the page. There's more."

Sure enough there were at least another half a dozen photos of people holding the huge piece of gold in their hands. And unless Cade was mistaken, Lev Volkov was also in a couple of the photos. But what did it all mean?

"Did you ever hear any stories about the nugget?"

Nils smiled and nodded. "Sure did. My grandpa told me about what happened."

After sharing the story, Nils tapped a finger on one of the pictures. "I'm pretty sure the man on the left is the Volkov fella you mentioned. If you turn the page, there's a newspaper article about him."

Cade turned the page and rotated he album so both he and Shelby could see it. The paper had become brown with age, but the text was still legible. First, they both skimmed the article and then went back and read through it again more carefully.

Shelby's eyes shined bright with tears. "This is exactly the information we've been hunting for."

"Now we just have to show it to Max Volkov."

Cade fought the urge to snatch up the photo album and bolt for the door. Instead, he turned back to their host. "Mr. Bolin, I cannot tell you how happy we are to have found you. Would it be possible for us to borrow your photo album? We need it to show Mr. Volkov's great-grandson how the Trillium Nugget came to belong to Dunbar instead of his family. I promise I will personally see that the album is returned to you."

"Take it, Chief Peters. Bring it back when you get things settled. I'll be interested in hearing how it all turns out."

Cade stood and held out his hand. "You have no idea what a difference this is going to make in people's lives, Mr. Bolin. When I come back, I'd love to hear more of your family stories. I'll even bring dinner."

That promise clearly pleased the old man. His eyes twinkled with a hint of mischief when he said, "As much as I'd enjoy talking with you, tell me you'll also bring Miss Michaels here. I don't get to spend much time with such a lovely lady very often anymore."

Shelby laughed. "I'll be here."

"You two should get going. You have more important things to do than hang out here with the likes of me." Mr. Bolin stood and started toward the door to escort them out. "I'll look forward to seeing you again soon."

On their way to Cade's car, Shelby did a little dance. "We did it, Cade. We've saved the nugget."

He was hopeful, but it wouldn't pay to get too cocky. It also didn't resolve the issue about his job. Still, he wouldn't rain on her happy parade. "At least we have something concrete to take to Max Volkov."

Looking a little more somber, Shelby nodded and crossed her fingers. "I hope he decides to be reasonable."

"Me, too."

Because if he didn't, Cade didn't have a clue what it would take to salvage the situation.

CHAPTER TWENTY-ONE

MAX CARRIED HIS duffel to the front door. "I'll be back."

He addressed his words to Carter, but he was very much aware that Rikki hovered nearby. The small boy studied Max for several seconds. "Are you leaving because of those bad people out on the sidewalk? Because if you are, I'll make them go away."

Max hated that Carter sounded so worried. He also wondered what he'd done to earn such a staunch supporter. "No, not because of them. I have some business I have to take care of back in Portland where I live. It shouldn't take more than two days. I've already paid ahead for another week here. You can ask your mom. It would be silly of me to do that if I wasn't planning on returning."

Finally Carter nodded. "Okay. We'll see you when you get back."

"You will. I promise."

After a brief hesitation, Max decided that he needed to clarify something for his small ally. "Carter, they're not bad people. They just don't agree with something I'm doing. They think if they can make me leave that the problem will go away. They're wrong about that, but it's okay if they don't agree with me. But like I said, I'll be back."

Although Carter's mother might not approve, Max gave in to the urge to give his little friend a big hug. As he did, he whispered, "I might even bring back some surprises. Any suggestions for your mom?"

Carter gave it some thought. "She likes stuff that smells good. You know like air freshener, but for people."

It was hard not to laugh, but Max wouldn't insult the boy's earnest attempt to help him choose the right gift. "Thanks for the heads-up, kiddo."

His mother finally joined the conversation. "Carter, Mr. Volkov has a long way to drive, so we shouldn't delay his departure any longer. Besides, I think there's a cookie on the counter with your name on it. You earned it by picking up your dirty clothes without having to be told."

The boy was off like a shot, yelling "Bye, Mr. Max!" over his shoulder.

Rikki smiled as he disappeared down the hall, but her expression turned serious when she turned back to Max. "Do you mind if I give your room a good cleaning while you're gone?"

He'd prefer to do it himself when he got back, but he knew it bothered Rikki that he wouldn't let do her job. "Knock yourself out, Rikki."

There was one more thing she needed to know. "I'll tell my fan club out there that I'll be gone for two days. Hopefully they'll find something better to do with their time for the duration."

She looked exasperated. "You don't have to do that. I've told you before that I don't care that they're out there."

Maybe she didn't, but Max did. He might as well confess the rest of his plan. "I'm also going to stop at the café to buy a meal to go and then at the coffee shop for a couple of pastries and a latte. The way that gossip flies through town, everyone will know that I'm gone within the hour."

She finally laughed and shook her head. "Have a safe trip."

"See you soon."

He remained conscious of her watching him as he approached the small gathering of protesters. Did she think they would actually go on the attack? He couldn't remember the last time anyone had worried about his well-being. It felt good and bad at the same time. Good because she cared about him, and bad because he knew that her feelings would start to fade as soon as he checked out of her B and B.

For now, he'd make sure everyone knew he was gone, so Rikki and Carter could walk out their front door without having a bunch of busybodies waving signs and demanding she kick Max to the curb.

He was in no hurry to leave her hospitality behind, but maybe it was time to call the town's bluff and make good on his threat to turn his claim on the nugget over to his attorney to handle. Once that happened, he'd have no reason to remain in Dunbar. And for some reason he couldn't quite fathom, he'd really hate walking away for good.

ONCE AGAIN, Cade found himself out on his porch with his feet up on the railing. Earlier in the day, he'd stopped by Rikki's bed-and-breakfast to touch base with Max Volkov. He wanted to make sure the man knew that the town was making progress in formulating their response to his claims about the Trillium Nugget. It should've been disappointing to learn Max had left town for a couple days, but it felt more like a reprieve. Now he had some time to think about what came next for him.

After all, the information they had uncovered was no guarantee that Max would drop his claim on the nugget. Who knew how much weight one faded newspaper article and an old man's memories would carry in court if it came to that.

He'd had one thought about his professional future and still wasn't sure how he felt about it. Shelby was insisting he fight to keep his job, but he wasn't sure how that would play out. However, if he did end up resigning as the chief of police, maybe he could work for the county sheriff's office instead. He'd be back out on patrol, but it would be a good place to start rebuilding his career. The one real positive would be that he could still live in Dunbar. A few people in town might not like it, but their opinions didn't count. How Shelby would feel about it was the only thing that mattered to him.

But Cade didn't have to make any decisions until they presented their findings to Max. Rather than worry about the future, he decided to kick back and relax. If these were to be his last few days in Dunbar, he was going to enjoy them. Not that he had any plans. Shelby had something going on with her friend Elizabeth's kids, so she was otherwise occupied.

He probably should've stayed late at the office to catch up on reports. Rather than do that, Cade had made a list of things to enjoy while he could. Tonight, he'd started with an easy one—watching his personal herd of deer. For now, he would savor a cold drink and watch them graze their way across the meadow.

No sooner had he gotten comfortable when the peaceful silence was interrupted by the sound of someone pulling into his driveway. It wasn't Titus, because the man had turned down his invitation to join him for an evening of beer and pizza. Cade had been disappointed, but Titus evidently had something else going on.

So who else would show up without calling first? He really, really hoped it wasn't the mayor or, worse yet, Eileen Southworth. He was off duty and deserved an evening of peace and quiet. Barring a legitimate emergency, he didn't want to be bothered.

He stood up as soon as he recognized Shelby's car. As happy as he was to see her, he had to wonder why she was there when she was supposed to be having a pizza and movie night with Elizabeth's kids.

Shelby turned the engine off but didn't immediately get out of the car. She leaned her head forward onto the steering wheel, looking as if she didn't feel well or she was bracing herself to deliver bad news. He'd been waiting for her to come to him, but now he charged around the back of her car and yanked open the driver's door.

"Shelby, what's happened?"

She slowly lifted her head and looked at him with red and swollen eyes as if she'd been crying her heart out about something. He repeated the question she still hadn't answered. "What happened?"

At the same time, he offered her a hand, gently tugging her out of the car into his arms where she belonged. The waterworks started up again which left him no choice but to let her cry it out. Finally, she settled against his chest and held him in a death grip.

When her breathing settled into a quiet rhythm, he risked another question. "Why aren't you eating peperoni pizza and watching a movie with the kids?"

"Elizabeth took one look at me and canceled. She told the kids that they would do a family movie night instead." She swiped at her face with her hands. "Sorry, but I can't stop crying."

He could tell that. What he didn't know was why. "Honey, I can't help if I don't know what's wrong."

She sniffled a few times and drew a ragged breath. "You shouldn't lose your job. Not because of some chunk of metal or that awful woman."

"It's not up to me, especially if Max Volkov doesn't accept what we've learned about the nugget."

She snuggled into his chest, her arms holding on tightly. "Your happiness…my happiness...our happiness can't depend on what someone else does or doesn't do. It has to be our choice, not theirs. Once I finally came to a decision, I had to come tell you."

When she didn't immediately continue, he gave her a verbal nudge. "Which is?"

Shelby smiled up at him through the sheen of her tears. "I've decided that no matter what happens, I choose you, Cade Peters. Whether we live here or in the biggest city in the country. I choose you."

His knees went weak. It was time for both of them to sit down and talk this out. "Hold that thought."

He swung her up in his arms and carried her over to the porch where he settled her on his lap in his favorite chair. When they were both comfortable he held her tight and brushed a kiss across her lips. "I love that sentiment, Shelby, but I won't ask you to leave your home."

She cupped his cheek with her hand. "I know, but that doesn't mean I can't ask you to take me with you."

He could barely hear her words over the pounding of his heart. "You love living here."

"I do, but Dunbar won't be the same without you in it. I don't want to spend the rest of my life knowing I found the right man and just let him walk away."

When he started to speak, she stopped him with a finger across his lips. "Yes, I know that I've always said that this was the only place I wanted to live. But now I know what real love is. If I'd felt that way about Kyle, it wouldn't have mattered where we lived. To make matters worse, most of our friends sided with him which meant I lost them, too. I didn't have the coping skills to deal with being away from home and so alone. It's no surprise I couldn't wait to get back to Dunbar."

She captured his face with her hands and leaned in close. But, I'm not that same young girl anymore. I know what my heart is telling me."

Cade tightened his hold on her and asked the only question that really mattered. "And what is it saying?"

"That I love you, Cade Peters. So, so much. Where I live doesn't matter as long as I'm living there with you." Her smile was a little shaky as she asked a question of her own. "So I guess it all comes down to this. What does your heart tell you?"

If Shelby could take a leap of faith and trust him with her heart, he could do no less. “That I love you. That I want to build a life with you. With luck, it will be here in Dunbar, but the where doesn’t matter as long as we’re together.”

Then he kissed her and found the home he’d been looking for right there in her arms.

EPILOGUE

Three days later

ONCE ALL THE major players were in place in city hall, Shelby sent Cade a text to tell him it was time. A few seconds later, he escorted Max Volkov into the conference room. They'd left a chair for him at the end of the long table and then took the seats on either side of him. She didn't blame the man for acting a little skittish. There was a lot of pent-up anxiety and downright hostility in the room.

When everyone was seated, she gave Mayor Klaus an encouraging nod. It had taken a lot of coaching to get him ready for this presentation, but Shelby had high hopes that the man could pull this off. After clearing his throat, Otto started speaking. "Mr. Volkov, we are here today to present our response to your claim."

Max nodded. "I'm listening."

Otto launched into his prepared statement. "First, I want to thank Ms. Michaels, the museum board of directors and our chief of police for their efforts."

Eileen Southworth immediately interrupted him. "Before we do any thanking, let's find out if they've done their jobs and protected the nugget from that man."

For once, Otto refused to be cowed. "Ms. Southworth, either hold your tongue, or Chief Peters will escort you from the room."

She shot a venomous look in Cade's direction. "You wouldn't dare. And I still plan to demand your resignation after this fiasco is over."

Evidently Otto had had enough. "That won't happen, no matter how this goes. I'm very much hoping Chief Peters will accept the council's apology for how you have treated him and stay. But even if he were to leave, I will never hire your nephew as the chief of police. Five years as a mall cop doesn't qualify him for the position. Now, be quiet. You're only embarrassing yourself and the town."

Shelby exchanged glances with Cade. So that's why the woman had been determined to force Cade out of office. The councilwoman looked ready to blow. But when she opened her mouth, Ilse Klaus spoke up. "Eileen, that's enough or I'll be leading the charge to have a recall vote to remove you from office. You might want to save yourself the humiliation and resign after the meeting."

Having put the other woman in her place, Ilse smiled at her husband. "Mr. Mayor, you were saying?"

"So, Mr. Volkov, your file was impressive. We actually learned a lot from the information you provided. You might consider writing up your findings for the museum to display, but that's a discussion for another day. For now, we have someone with a tale to tell, one that was new to all of us. I would ask everyone to listen to what our special guest, Mr. Nils Bolin, has to say."

The elderly man looked a bit uncomfortable with everyone staring at him. To deflect some of that attention, Shelby started the video presentation. Nils's confidence strengthened as he pointed at the screen. "That first picture is my grandfather, Emil Bolin, holding the Trillium Nugget. The other pictures are of people who lived here in Dunbar back in the day."

He glanced in Max's direction. "I'm sure

you recognize the man on the right as your great-grandfather, Lev Volkov. My family knew Lev real well even though Grandpa Emil was a lumberjack, not a miner. From what I was told, when Lev first found the nugget, he kept it secret and hidden in his mine. But like anytime someone works hard and strikes it lucky, there's always someone else who wants to get rich the easy way. Two strangers beat Lev until he gave them the other gold he'd mined, and then they left him for dead. It was sheer luck that my grandfather and another man happened by and found him."

Shelby watched Max, who looked riveted by the photos and narration.

Nils paused for a drink. "They fetched a wagon and brought Lev to Grandpa Emil's cabin. Lev was in pretty poor shape by that point, you see. My grandmother and the other ladies in town did what they could, but no one expected him to pull through. It was touch-and-go for a long time, but come the next spring he turned the corner."

Max finally looked at Nils. "Why didn't anyone in my family know this?"

"I can't say, Mr. Volkov. After this much

time, it's not surprising that the details are somewhat sketchy. Anyway, I was told Lev led my grandfather back out to his mine once he was strong enough to ride. He went back into the tunnel and brought out the nugget. He said he wanted nothing more to do with it. He'd almost died because of gold, but he'd lived because of what the folks in Dunbar had done for him. He gave the nugget to the town to do with what they thought best."

Cade then handed Nils's photo album to Max, already opened to the yellowed news article that announced the Trillium Nugget would be the centerpiece of the newly established Dunbar Historical Museum.

It didn't take Max long to read the article and study the pictures. Finally, he nodded and closed the book. "Thank you, Mr. Bolin, for sharing this with me. I would love to sit down with you sometime and talk about all of this in further detail."

The old man smiled at him. "Anytime, Mr. Volkov."

Then he winked at Shelby. "Especially if you bring Ms. Michaels with you. Like I told Chief Peters, I might be old, but I still like spending time with a pretty lady."

Cade nudged Nils with his shoulder. "Just remember, she's spoken for."

That set Nils to cackling. "What's the matter, Chief Peters? Afraid of a little competition?"

Mayor Klaus cleared his throat. "Can we get back to the business at hand?"

A heavy silence settled over the room as everyone stared down the table toward Max. He gave the pictures on the screen one last look before finally speaking. "So the town isn't disputing that the Trillium Nugget was found by my great-grandfather?"

Otto looked to Shelby and then Cade for confirmation. When they both nodded, he sat tall and stared down the table to meet Max's gaze. "We agree he was the one who found the nugget. But we also believe that he donated the nugget to the citizens of Dunbar for saving his life. Therefore, we respectfully decline to relinquish it to you and your family."

Max went quiet again. Finally, he said, "Actually, I am the last of Lev's direct descendants. As such, it's my duty to protect his legacy."

Everybody in the room held their breath as they waited to see what he'd say next. He slowly stood and picked up his file. He made eye contact with Nils, Cade and then Shelby. "To honor my great-grandfather, I ask that you add a description of how the Trillium Nugget came to be in the museum, along with a display of Mr. Bolin's pictures. Agree to that, and I'll be satisfied."

His announcement was met with cheers followed by an immediate stampede toward the refreshment table. Instead of letting Nils risk life and limb in the scrum, Shelby had already put together plates for him and his nephew, who had brought him to the meeting. After delivering them, she joined Cade, who was talking to Max.

The three of them walked out of city hall together.

"So what's next, Max?" Cade asked.

The other man looked up and down the street. Then he smiled, just a little. "I'll be heading back to Portland in the morning. I've got some articles under contract that need my attention. After that, who knows? Maybe I'll try my hand at writing a book about Lev's life."

Cade patted Max on the shoulder. "Good luck with that."

"Thanks." Max left then, heading in the direction of Rikki's bed-and-breakfast. Meanwhile, Cade took Shelby's hand in his as they started down the street toward the museum and the police station.

"So, Ms. Michaels, I guess we'll both be staying in Dunbar. That okay with you?"

It was important that she reaffirm her decision. "Yes, but I still would've gone with you."

He gave her hand a squeeze. "And I would've tried to get hired by the county so I could stay here in Dunbar."

"Really?"

"Really." He wrapped his arm around her shoulders and pulled her in close. "I do have a couple of questions for you."

"Which are?"

"Didn't you mention that the wedding calendar at the church fills up pretty quickly?"

Her pulse fluttered. Where was he going with this? "Yeah, it does."

"Before we both go back to our respective offices, what do you say we swing by there and see what dates are available? I'm thinking the sooner the better."

He'd been smiling, but now his expression

turned deadly serious. "I realize I'm dancing around the subject, but what I'm really asking is this… Will you marry me?"

Her knees gave out, but Cade caught her before she hit the ground. She blinked her eyes free of tears and smiled up at the man who had turned her whole life upside down. "Yes, Cade, I will marry you."

A round of applause broke out as he kissed her, startling both of them. Somehow they'd ended up right in front of Bea's bakery, meaning they had an audience. Cade gave her a wry smile. "Should we take a bow?"

"Might as well. Bea's already on the phone spreading the news."

Several people snapped pictures as the two of them bowed with a flourish. Happier than she could imagine, she kissed Cade again, garnering more applause. After waving goodbye to the crowd, they headed toward the church to plan their future together.

* * * * *

Be sure to look for the next book in the Heroes of Dunbar Mountain series by Alexis Morgan, available in August 2023!

Get 4 FREE REWARDS!
We'll send you 2 FREE Books plus 2 FREE Mystery Gifts.
FREE
Value Over
$20
Both the Love Inspired® and Love Inspired® Suspense series feature compelling novels filled with inspirational romance, faith, forgiveness and hope.
YES! Please send me 2 FREE novels from the Love Inspired or Love Inspired Suspense series and my 2 FREE gifts (gifts are worth about $10 retail). After receiving them, if I don't wish to receive any more books, I can return the shipping statement marked "cancel." If I don't cancel, I will receive 6 brand-new Love Inspired Larger-Print books or Love Inspired Suspense Larger-Print books every month and be billed just $6.49 each in the U.S. or $6.74 each in Canada. That is a savings of at least 16% off the cover price. It's quite a bargain! Shipping and handling is just 50¢ per book in the U.S. and $1.25 per book in Canada.* I understand that accepting the 2 free books and gifts places me under no obligation to buy anything. I can always return a shipment and cancel at any time by calling the number below. The free books and gifts are mine to keep no matter what I decide.
Choose one: ☐ Love Inspired Larger-Print (122/322 IDN GRHK)
☐ Love Inspired Suspense Larger-Print (107/307 IDN GRHK)
Name (please print)
Address
Apt. #
City
State/Province
Zip/Postal Code
Email: Please check this box ☐ if you would like to receive newsletters and promotional emails from Harlequin Enterprises ULC and its affiliates. You can unsubscribe anytime.
Mail to the Harlequin Reader Service:
IN U.S.A.: P.O. Box 1341, Buffalo, NY 14240-8531
IN CANADA: P.O. Box 603, Fort Erie, Ontario L2A 5X3
Want to try 2 free books from another series? Call 1-800-873-8635 or visit www.ReaderService.com.
*Terms and prices subject to change without notice. Prices do not include sales taxes, which will be charged (if applicable) based on your state or country of residence. Canadian residents will be charged applicable taxes. Offer not valid in Quebec. This offer is limited to one order per household. Books received may not be as shown. Not valid for current subscribers to the Love Inspired or Love Inspired Suspense series. All orders subject to approval. Credit or debit balances in a customer's account(s) may be offset by any other outstanding balance owed by or to the customer. Please allow 4 to 6 weeks for delivery. Offer available while quantities last.
Your Privacy—Your information is being collected by Harlequin Enterprises ULC, operating as Harlequin Reader Service. For a complete summary of the information we collect, how we use this information and to whom it is disclosed, please visit our privacy notice located at corporate.harlequin.com/privacy-notice. From time to time we may also exchange your personal information with reputable third parties. If you wish to opt out of this sharing of your personal information, please visit readerservice.com/consumerschoice or call 1-800-873-8635. Notice to California Residents—Under California law, you have specific rights to control and access your data. For more information on these rights and how to exercise them, visit corporate.harlequin.com/california-privacy.
LIRLIS22R3

Get 4 FREE REWARDS!
We'll send you 2 FREE Books plus 2 FREE Mystery Gifts.
Secret under the Stars
ELIZABETH BEVARLY
The Maverick's Marriage Pact
STELLA BAGWELL
The Cowboy's Ranch Rescue
Lisa Childs
His Partnership Proposal
FREE
Value Over
$20
Both the Harlequin® Special Edition and Harlequin® Heartwarming™ series feature compelling novels filled with stories of love and strength where the bonds of friendship, family and community unite.
YES! Please send me 2 FREE novels from the Harlequin Special Edition or Harlequin Heartwarming series and my 2 FREE gifts (gifts are worth about $10 retail). After receiving them, if I don't wish to receive any more books, I can return the shipping statement marked "cancel." If I don't cancel, I will receive 6 brand-new Harlequin Special Edition books every month and be billed just $5.49 each in the U.S. or $6.24 each in Canada, a savings of at least 12% off the cover price, or 4 brand-new Harlequin Heartwarming Larger-Print books every month and be billed just $6.24 each in the U.S. or $6.74 each in Canada, a savings of at least 19% off the cover price. It's quite a bargain! Shipping and handling is just 50¢ per book in the U.S. and $1.25 per book in Canada.* I understand that accepting the 2 free books and gifts places me under no obligation to buy anything. I can always return a shipment and cancel at any time by calling the number below. The free books and gifts are mine to keep no matter what I decide.
Choose one: ☐ Harlequin Special Edition (235/335 HDN GRJV) ☐ Harlequin Heartwarming Larger-Print (161/361 HDN GRJV)
Name (please print)
Address
Apt. #
City
State/Province
Zip/Postal Code
Email: Please check this box ☐ if you would like to receive newsletters and promotional emails from Harlequin Enterprises ULC and its affiliates. You can unsubscribe anytime.
Mail to the Harlequin Reader Service:
IN U.S.A.: P.O. Box 1341, Buffalo, NY 14240-8531
IN CANADA: P.O. Box 603, Fort Erie, Ontario L2A 5X3
Want to try 2 free books from another series? Call 1-800-873-8635 or visit www.ReaderService.com.
*Terms and prices subject to change without notice. Prices do not include sales taxes, which will be charged (if applicable) based on your state or country of residence. Canadian residents will be charged applicable taxes. Offer not valid in Quebec. This offer is limited to one order per household. Books received may not be as shown. Not valid for current subscribers to the Harlequin Special Edition or Harlequin Heartwarming series. All orders subject to approval. Credit or debit balances in a customer's account(s) may be offset by any other outstanding balance owed by or to the customer. Please allow 4 to 6 weeks for delivery. Offer available while quantities last.
Your Privacy—Your information is being collected by Harlequin Enterprises ULC, operating as Harlequin Reader Service. For a complete summary of the information we collect, how we use this information and to whom it is disclosed, please visit our privacy notice located at corporate.harlequin.com/privacy-notice. From time to time we may also exchange your personal information with reputable third parties. If you wish to opt out of this sharing of your personal information, please visit readerservice.com/consumerschoice or call 1-800-873-8635. Notice to California Residents—Under California law, you have specific rights to control and access your data. For more information on these rights and how to exercise them, visit corporate.harlequin.com/california-privacy.
HSEHW22R3

COMING NEXT MONTH FROM

HARLEQUIN
HEARTWARMING

#475 A COWBOY SUMMER

Flaming Sky Ranch • by Mary Anne Wilson

Rodeo star Cooper Donovan can handle bucking broncs, but not die-hard fans. His family's ranch is the perfect hideout—until he finds pediatrician McKenna Walker already there. Sharing the ranch for a week is one thing—falling for her is another!

#476 A SINGLE DAD IN AMISH COUNTRY

The Butternut Amish B&B • by Patricia Johns

Hazel Dobbs has been waiting years for her dream job of being a pilot. But when she's with groundskeeper Joe Carter and his adorable daughter, it's her heart that's soaring...right over Amish country!

#477 FALLING FOR THE COWBOY DOC

Three Springs, Texas • by Cari Lynn Webb

Surgeon Grant Sloan doesn't plan on staying in Three Springs, Texas—he's working there only temporarily. Even though his time in town is limited, he just can't stay away from rodeo cowgirl Maggie Orr.

#478 THE FIREFIGHTER'S FAMILY SECRET

Bachelor Cowboys • by Lisa Childs

After breaking off her engagement, Doctor Livvy Lemmon is permanently anti-romance. Then she meets firefighter Colton Cassidy—he's handsome and kind, and it's impossible not to fall for him. But after losing herself so completely before, can she trust her heart again?